DEAD MEN NEED NO RESERVATIONS

Terry Ambrose

DEAD MEN NEED NO RESERVATIONS

A Seaside Cove Bed & Breakfast Mystery

Terry Ambrose

COPYRIGHT

BOOKS BY TERRY AMBROSE

Seaside Cove Bed & Breakfast Mysteries
A Treasure to Die For
Clues in the Sand
The Killer Christmas Sweater Club
Secrets of the Treasure King
Treasure Most Deadly
Lies, Spies, and the Baker's Surprise

McKenna Mysteries
Photo Finish
Kauai Temptations
Big Island Blues
Mystery of the Lei Palaoa
Honolulu Hottie
North Shore Nanny
A Damsel for Santa
Maui Magic
The Scent of Waikiki
On the Take in Waikiki
Mystery of the Eight Islands

Beachtown Detective Agency
The Case of the Amorous Assailant

License to Lie Thrillers
License to Lie
Con Game
Shadows from the Past

Anthologies with Stories

Paradise, Passion, Murder: 10 Tales of Mystery from Hawai'i
Happy Homicides 3: Summertime Crimes
Happy Homicides 4: Fall into Crime
Happy Homicides 5: The Purr-fect Crime

ABOUT THE AUTHOR

Once upon a time, in a life he'd rather forget, Terry Ambrose tracked down deadbeats for a living. He also hired big guys with tow trucks to steal cars—but only when negotiations failed. Those years of chasing deadbeats taught him many valuable life lessons such as—always keep your car in the garage.

Terry is a mystery and thriller writer. Several of his books have been award finalists. His thriller, "Con Game," won the San Diego Book Awards for Best Action-Thriller in 2014. His series include the Trouble in Paradise McKenna Mysteries, the Seaside Cove Bed & Breakfast Mysteries, the Beachtown Detective Agency Mysteries, and the License to Lie thriller series.

You can learn more about Terry and his writing at terryambrose.com.

1

ALEX

Hey Journal,

Wow, I still get goosebumps every time I get to call Marquetta my mom. She's awesome, Journal. Best. Mom. Ever! I got a cool photo of her today that I'll add to the scrapbook I've been working on. I snuck in on her while she was taking a nap in my dad's office. She had her eyes closed and her feet up. Since my dad taught me how to get candid photos of people, I've gotten super good at taking shots when nobody's looking. Mom and Dad will be totally surprised when I give them the scrapbook after the baby's born.

We also went to Scoops & Scones this afternoon to celebrate Mom and Dad's ten-month wedding anniversary. My dad says there won't be time for a real anniversary celebration after the baby comes. He's probably right 'cause Operation Baby Brother is almost complete! There's only about a month to go before Mom's due date, and I'll take any excuse to go for ice cream!

While we were at Scoops & Scones, the mayor was bragging about how she's 'guided the town out of the darkness' with her strong leadership. Seriously? She was mayor while all the murders were happening, and she didn't stop them! It's totally lame that she wants to take credit for finding all those killers.

I didn't say anything 'cause Mom gave me a wink like she was telling me to let Mayor Carter go on. I guess that's okay. The mayor owns the ice cream shop, so I guess I gotta be nice to her. And we haven't had a murder in a long time now. So it doesn't hurt to let her brag—even if she didn't do anything but kinda get in the way. It's, like, so typical for her. I do kinda wish she'd give Chief Cunningham credit. And my dad. And me, of course, since they wouldn't have cracked those cases without my help.

When I said something about the murders on our walk back to the B&B, my dad reminded me that I promised him I wouldn't investigate anymore. I'm only supposed to report on crime. I think he's kinda proud that I'm following in his footsteps of being a reporter. I'm not sure I wanna give up on crime solving, Journal. Oh well, I can't help it if I just happen to solve a murder while I'm writing a story for the CoveTalkers Newsletter. Right?

I'm getting super excited about the big trip my class is taking to the Silver Gulch Mine on Friday. Eighth grade is fun! We've gotten to take some awesome field trips. This one's gonna be the best! Our teacher told us there's a treasure hunt. Me and Sasha and Robbie decided we wanna be a team, so we'll all get to work on finding the treasure together. We know it's not like real treasure. That doesn't matter. It would still be awesome for our team to have bragging rights! Kinda like the mayor, except that we'll really do it!

Xoxo,

Alex

2

RICK

"You're sure everything is in place, Traci?" Rick Atwood raised his eyebrows and gave Marquetta's best friend what he hoped was a pleading expression. For all he knew, he looked more like a wounded cat than a man trying to surprise his pregnant wife with a girl's brunch.

The pout Traci gave him when she stuck out her lower lip would make a seven-year-old proud. Then, in a flash, her smile returned. She playfully poked his shoulder. "Stop worrying, silly. I've got this. All the girls think brunch is a great idea."

"Even Sally?"

With a dismissive flip of her hand, Traci said, "Sally Costas has known Marquetta almost since the day she was born. She was delighted to open up the Rusty Nail for this. Everybody in town loves Marquetta and would do anything for her. My end's covered. Have you taken care of yours?"

"Lydia and I will handle the B&B. Alex sees this as a chance to practice her culinary skills without Marquetta watching over her."

Traci blew out a breath and laughed. "Thanks to what Marquetta's taught her, your daughter already cooks better than most adults. She could get a job as a sous chef tomorrow if she wanted."

"You forget one little detail. She's thirteen."

"Going on thirty," Traci shot back.

"I know. Just between you and me, I wish she'd give up her fascination with crime for something to do with food."

"She's still finding herself, Rick. Don't worry about it. Alex will get there. She's smart as a whip." Traci glanced past Rick to the front door. "Oh, here comes Adam."

The high-pitched tinkling of Traci's entry bell pierced the air. It reminded Rick he'd been away from the B&B longer than he'd planned. For some reason, it felt like the brunch had a lot of moving parts, and because the event was a surprise for Marquetta, all those parts had to be managed secretly.

Rick turned and watched Adam Cunningham wend his way through the maze of tables displaying a variety of candles. "Chief Cunningham, I presume."

"Just the man I wanted to see," Adam said, then flashed Traci a boyish smile.

At just over thirty years old with green eyes beneath thick eyebrows, Adam was the exact opposite of his predecessor. Not only was he less than half the man's age, but Adam's management style was different. Where the previous chief kept a vice-like grip on the town, Adam maintained order by asking people to do things, not coercing them. To be truthful, with his youthful ideas and good looks, Adam didn't look the role of a police chief. It proved that looks were deceiving. Crime— especially murder, didn't go unpunished in Seaside Cove. What worried Rick was that Adam wanted to see him. He could only hope this was nothing more than a social visit.

"Uh oh. Sounds serious," Rick said. "Please don't tell me you've got a case and need my help."

Adam raised his hand and held his thumb and index finger about an inch apart. "No to the first part. Yes, to the second. It's just a teensy little favor." He smiled at Rick, then looked past him at Traci. "How's my girl?"

"Waiting breathlessly for my man to show up," Traci drawled.

It was a passable Scarlet O'Hara imitation, up to the point where Traci burst into laughter. Based on how quickly Adam had changed the subject, Rick suspected Adam was trying to slowly rope him into something. Well, two could play that game. Rick nodded firmly at Adam and crossed his arms. "Take that, Mr. Chief of Police. This young lady's tired of waiting for you to tie the knot." Rick paused, then added, "So when are you two going to do the deed?"

"August 18th, smarty pants. We set the date last night." With a smile, Adam added, "So there. Seaside Cove's youngest police chief ever is getting married. Oh, by the way, you're my best man. Whether you want to be or not."

Rick hoped that was the favor Adam had mentioned. "Are you kidding? I'm honored. Man-hug." He pulled Adam closer, and the two embraced for a few seconds. When he stepped back, he held his arms open and hugged Traci. This time, the hug was more tender, and there were no firm backslaps.

"I can't believe we're finally doing it," Traci said. "I want Marquetta to be my matron of honor." She stopped, rolled her eyes, and added, "Oh, gawd. That sounds so old-fashioned."

In the two years since he and Alex had moved to Seaside Cove, Rick had come to love the town and the people in it. It was so different from New York, where he'd never felt a close connection to anyone.

"What's the matter, buddy?" Adam cocked his head to the side and eyed Rick.

"I was thinking about how lonely life was in the city. In all the years I worked at the paper, I never got close to my coworkers. Alex's mom was always off chasing her career. It was really just Alex and me."

Adam moved closer to Traci and slipped his hand to her back. "Huh. Hard for me to imagine a life like that. The thought of spending most of my waking hours working or commuting holds no appeal for me. I'd much rather be able to spend more time with the ones I love."

Traci leaned away from Adam, gave him a mock look of shock, then kissed his cheek. "And here I thought you were just a big lug with no feelings."

"You two are quite a pair. You're perfect for each other. I guess you're right, Adam. There were so many times when I wondered what it would have been like to have friends at work. I never found out because that would have come at the expense of my time with Alex. She's the one who kept me going all those years. Letting her sit on my knee while I worked on a story late into the evening was sometimes the highlight of my day."

Adam nodded eagerly, and Rick had a sinking feeling he'd just walked into the trap.

"Now you get to see her when she's awake," Adam said cheerily. "Which brings me to that little favor I need."

"I was hoping that being your best man was the favor."

"That's more like a best friend's obligation. The favor has to do with the eighth-grade outing to Silver Gulch. About twenty kids are going out to the mine for a field trip. Unfortunately, they're short a chaperone. I was hoping you'd volunteer. Think of how much time you'll get to spend with the munchkin."

"And a whole bunch of her friends. She'll want nothing to do with me."

"Don't underestimate yourself. You're kind of a celebrity in this town. Owner of one of the town's biggest businesses. Special consultant on crime to the police chief. Plus, you've been an award-winning reporter for one of the biggest papers in the country."

Rick stared at Adam for several seconds, trying to decide on a response. Being a chaperone wasn't what he'd expected. A few hours spent ferrying kids around on a field trip really didn't fit into his Friday plans. Rick cleared his throat. "I run a B&B, not a conglomerate. I don't get paid to work with you on cases. And these kids are in eighth grade, so I don't think they care one bit about any awards I've won. I'll give you kudos for trying anyway. Tell you what. I'll talk to Marquetta. If she's okay with me being away, I'll give it some thought. I'm trying to take the load off of her, though. She needs time to rest."

"Fair enough. Let me know right away. If you're not going to do it, I need to find someone else. Fast." Adam gave Traci a quick kiss, then started toward the door. "See you tonight?"

Traci planted the back of her hand on her forehead and gazed at the ceiling. "I'll be counting the moments one by one."

Rick shook his head and sighed. "What did you two do? Watch *Gone with the Wind* last night? No. Don't tell me. I need to get back to the B&B. See you both later."

He picked up the bag of groceries he'd placed on the countertop when he started talking to Traci and got out of the store before she could lob another Scarlet response at him. All the way home, he kept wondering if her good mood was because they'd finally set a date for the wedding or if it had something to do with the excitement of planning the brunch. Either way, it was nice to have friends he and Marquetta could rely on.

Rick's musings about Traci's mood stopped abruptly when he walked through the front door and found Marquetta frantically trying to quiet an argument between a half dozen guests.

3

RICK

CHAOS. IT WAS THE ONLY word Rick could think of to describe the situation. A rush of heat surged through his veins. These people must be their six new guests. They all stood in the lobby, trying to talk or yell over the others. Not one paid any attention to Marquetta's pleas for them to settle down. On the walk home, he'd briefly wondered how difficult it would be to keep the peace with a group of excited eighth-graders on the Silver Gulch field trip. That would be easy compared to this. Without a doubt, those kids would be better behaved than these supposed adults.

Marquetta shot him an exasperated glance, shook her head, and grimaced. She muttered something to herself, probably about enough being enough. Rick stepped forward to take charge, determined to get these clowns under control before they involved other guests.

An earsplitting whistle silenced all of them before Rick could utter a word. His jaw dropped as Marquetta removed two fingers from her mouth. The rowdy guests, now stunned into silence, were all doing the same thing as Rick—staring at Marquetta.

"Knock it off! I've had it with all of you." Marquetta planted her hands on her hips and took a step forward. "You will all go sit quietly in the lobby on the couches and wait for me to call your names. I'll call the two couples first, then the two singles. Any questions?"

Six heads shook. Make that seven, thought Rick. Even he felt intimidated. Although he'd seen his wife be firm before, he'd never seen her this forceful. He suppressed a chuckle. This was drill-sergeant level.

"Then why are you still standing there?" Marquetta demanded. "Go sit down! And no more arguing."

While the six guests shuffled quietly into the living room, Rick approached Marquetta with a sheepish grin on his face. "I had no idea you could do that."

"What? Whistle?" She smiled at him, rubbing her swollen belly as she did so. Leaning into him, she gave him a quick kiss and winked. "It's one of my superpowers. Just don't tell anybody."

"Your secret's safe with me, Wonder Woman. And here I was, worried about you."

"I keep telling you, Rick. I'm fine. I get a little tired late in the day. That's about it."

Rick eyed her. Indeed. Pregnancy did seem to agree with Marquetta. Other than a few hormonal hiccups and a very healthy appetite, she'd been going strong with almost no change in her routine. Her cheeks had a rosy glow, she was a little fuller in the face, and her gray eyes sparkled the same as they had when they'd first met.

"Do you want me to take some of them? You mentioned couples first."

"That would be a big help." Marquetta stretched her back. Her lips parted into a smile, and she lowered her voice to a whisper. "The sooner we get them out of the lobby, the less likely it is that they'll start in again. I can't believe they're all friends. They're constantly fighting like cats and dogs."

Rick snuck a peek at the band of six troublemakers sitting glumly in the living room, all studiously ignoring the others. Marquetta was right. The minutes were ticking away, and it wouldn't be long before trouble erupted again. "Who do you want me to take first?"

"Barnaby Pauley and his wife, Liz. She uses her maiden name, Ravel. So don't make that mistake. I'll take the other couple, Brid Ochoa and Guy Silvan. Welles has been flirting shamelessly with Liz Ravel, so I think that with the two couples out of the way, the other two men will just sit quietly."

"Aye, aye, Captain. Let me put these in the kitchen first."

As he strode past the living room, Rick glanced at the six newcomers. Even now, there was trouble brewing. One of the men was leaning shoulder-to-shoulder with the woman next to him. When the man on the other side of her barked at the flirter to stay away from his wife, Rick quickly matched the names on their registrations with the guests.

Marquetta had only mentioned one married couple in the group, Barnaby and Liz. The other couple, Brid Ochoa and Guy Silvan, sat on the other couch. Based on what Marquetta had told him, the flirter had to be S.A. Welles. That meant the final member of their group, Carson Coulson, was sitting on the end of the couch closest to the fireplace. Coulson had his hands cupped over his mouth and was alternately breathing warm air onto his fingers and rubbing them together.

By the time Rick returned from the kitchen, Marquetta had already called the other couple back to the front desk. Welles still sat uncomfortably close to Liz Ravel, something she didn't seem to mind. Rick could see how Welles's flirting could have caused the argument in the entryway. Those two were just a little too obvious. Just what the B&B needed, a marriage on the rocks with a suitor in the wings.

"Mr. Pauley, Ms. Ravel? Would you come with me?" Rick waited while they stood.

He guessed both of them were in their early thirties. She had light brown skin and parted her tightly curled hair down the middle. Slender with an erect posture, she looked down on the man who'd flirted with her with intense brown eyes. "You're a toad, Snappy."

She turned, gave Rick a friendly smile, and held out her hand. "I'm Liz Ravel. You must be Mr. Atwood?"

"I am." Rick noticed immediately that she had a very firm handshake. No clamminess. No clinginess. Just solid and assured. Suddenly, the relationship between her and Welles seemed even more complex. "Nice to meet you, Ms. Ravel. Please, call me Rick. And you're Mr. Pauley?"

Rick noticed an immediate contrast with the man's wife. Where her handshake was firm and assured, his was soft and pliable. On the other hand, her voice was more melodic, and his, tinged with gravel when he said, "Call me Barnaby."

"Nice to meet you both. I'll show you to your room." Rick led the way back to the front lobby just as Marquetta was taking her couple up to their room and explaining the breakfast service hours.

"Hey, Brid," Liz called out.

The woman who'd been following Marquetta turned and broke into a smile. "Thanks for sticking up for me, girlfriend."

Liz Ravel gave her a thumbs-up and returned the smile. "What are friends for? Right? Don't let him get to you, okay?"

Rick's gaze darted between the two women. So there was more to the story about the first argument. He'd have to ask Marquetta about it later.

"You two want to meet us for dinner tomorrow night?" Brid Ochoa asked.

Brid's husband shook his head. "That's not gonna work. We're locked into the thing with Snappy."

Rick exchanged a look with Marquetta. She frowned and cocked her head to one side. As hard as it was to not ask why these friends had to have dinner with someone they didn't like, he felt like that was getting too personal.

"We'll let you all work out your dinner plans after we get everyone checked in," Marquetta said firmly. "Please, follow me so we can get you all taken care of."

"Mr. Pauley, Ms. Ravel, I've got your room key right over here." Rick walked toward the front desk. As if they'd been trained at the best obedience school, they both followed while Marquetta shepherded her couple upstairs. There had to be a lot more to the story for Marquetta to be rushing guests. Rick's curiosity got the better of him as he grabbed the key. While he led them upstairs, he asked, "So, did the six of you all plan this trip together?"

"No. This whole thing was Snappy's idea," Barnaby Pauley grumbled. "Personally, I think it's a mistake."

"Stop being so negative, Barnaby. You didn't have to come. Besides, once we've done the Silver Gulch tour and dinner, we'll be on our own. We can forget about Snappy Welles and all of his stupid shenanigans."

"You mean his trying to bed every woman he meets." The man fixed Rick with a blue-eyed stare and added, "Your wife should be safe. Snappy wants nothing to do with pregnant women."

The hairs on the back of Rick's neck prickled at the man's tone. Tact was obviously not his strong suit. As irritating as the whole situation was, Rick was not about to let himself be pulled down into the muck of an argument. It was best just to let it go. He pointed to his left. "Your room's down here. A group from my daughter's eighth-grade class is taking the Silver Gulch tour tomorrow. She's quite excited."

"Eighth grade." Liz Ravel winced and sucked in a breath. "That can be a difficult age."

"She's managing pretty well. She has a good head on her shoulders, and we keep telling her to be true to herself. Living here in Seaside Cove, she can actually do that."

Liz's jaw tightened. She took a short, tense breath, then muttered, "She's lucky. Not all of us had that luxury." She stopped, forced a smile, and added, "I hear that tour's supposed to be a lot of fun. We're going in the afternoon."

"It's new, so I don't know anything about it. I may be chaperoning my daughter's group. Even if I don't go, I'm sure she'll give me a full report." Rick stopped in front of the door to the Mainsail Room. "Here you are. It's next door to the room your friends are in."

"Which friends?" Barnaby stroked the dark, three-day stubble on his chin. "Not Welles, I hope."

"No. You're next to the other couple. That's Mr. Silvan and Ms. Ochoa, I believe."

Liz's eyes lit up. "Is there an adjoining door?"

"I'm afraid not. We've only got two of those, and they were already taken when you booked."

"You and Brid will just have to tough it out." Barnaby smirked, then glanced at Rick. "You'd think those two were joined at the hip or something."

Rick again ignored the man's snideness and slipped the key into the lock. He explained the breakfast service as he opened the door. Barnaby Pauley was one of those people he'd want Alex to avoid. So far, the man had been negative about almost everything, and since there were times when Alex's mouth had no filter, he could see trouble brewing.

"I think it's nice that you have a friend you can talk to, Liz. I felt very isolated prior to moving to Seaside Cove."

Liz lightly punched her husband's shoulder as she contemplated him. "Barnaby's jealous because he spends most of his time working and doesn't have time for friends. Me and Brid haven't known each other that long, but I can't imagine getting through a day without talking to her."

Pauley bristled at his wife's comment. Rick fully expected the man to protest that he had a lot of friends. Not wanting to let the man throw even a minor tantrum, Rick cut Pauley off with question and a smile. "What about the other guys on the tour, Barnaby? Aren't you friends with any of them?"

"No," the man said flatly. "We have nothing in common. Other than the occasional desire to kill Snappy Welles."

4

ALEX

Hey Journal,

It's the big day for our class field trip. My dad decided to be a chaperone after all. That's awesome since I don't get to spend that much time with him when school's in session. He didn't want to do it at first 'cause he didn't want to leave Mom. She finally convinced him it was gonna be okay since both Lydia and her husband Matteo could work today.

I think it's good he's getting out for a day because he's been kinda weird lately. He wants me to stay away from the new guests that came in yesterday. I've kept my distance even though it's kinda lame. It's super obvious Mr. Welles is a troublemaker. I get it. We've got a couple of those in my class. My dad's just doing his usual thing and being overprotective. I'm not worried. LOL! Lydia told me how Mom made them all stop arguing when they got here. Oh man, I wish I could've seen that! Most of them are leaving on Monday, so maybe my dad will get back to normal then. I hope he has fun today.

For sure, me and Sasha and Robbie are gonna have a blast. We decided to call ourselves Team Cool Kids! My dad says this kind of stuff is called orienteering. He did a lot of it when he was growing up. He also told me he heard from Chief Cunningham that we're gonna be timed, and the team that completes the course with the best time is gonna win a prize. That sounds kinda like work, but Team Cool Kids is still gonna rock it!

Gotta run,
Alex

5

RICK

"My name is Roy Andrew Boyd."

At six-foot-two and wearing a wide-brimmed Stetson, the lanky man with a stern voice strode purposefully in front of twenty-four kids from Alex's school. His movements, slow and deliberate, accentuated his imposing image. He spoke with purpose, punctuating each word with a small pause before and after.

He stopped, spun around, and leaned into the crowd. "You, however...you can call me Mr. Boyd."

Nervous laughter rippled through the group. Rick leaned closer to Adam Cunningham and whispered, "The kids seem to like the theatrics. Even Alex. She seems completely enamored with this guy. She's taking photos like crazy."

"You should've seen her earlier," Adam whispered back. "She hasn't missed a thing."

From the Stetson down to his faded checkered shirt, jeans, and scuffed boots, Roy Andrew Boyd came across as the quintessential cowboy. Or, at least, the stereotype of one. If Boyd hadn't been putting on such a show for the kids, Rick might not have doubted his authenticity.

On the other hand, Rick had no doubts about the authenticity of the tools Boyd had assembled on the ten-foot handmade table behind him. The collection included rusted antique lanterns, a pickaxe, a shovel, a hammer, and a chisel. Even the adults seemed fascinated by the display as they waited for the official start time. Most ignored the signs of modern life to the right of the tools—the megaphone, first aid kit, and a list of ten short rules that everyone was required to read. Behind it all was a different sign of modern life, a small travel trailer.

Adam chuckled quietly and cocked his head in Rick's direction. "If nothing else, this guy's a good showman. He's even got the gun."

"Is it real?"

"Starter pistol. Doesn't matter. The kids will love it."

"Mr. Atwood! Chief Cunningham! Do you have something you'd like to share?"

Roy Andrew Boyd's intense brown eyes bore down on Rick and Adam. Rick got the distinct impression that he and Adam had broken one of the ten rules he'd barely skimmed. Wishing he'd read the rules more closely, Rick replied, "Uh, no, Mr. Boyd."

Another round of laughter rolled through the kids and the other chaperones.

Boyd grunted a short acknowledgment, then returned his attention to the kids. "Well, children, as you can see, the rules apply to everyone on this tour. The rules are here for your own safety. We'll go over them in a minute—after I tell you about a treasure that's been lost for over one hundred years. The treasure is a precious artifact known as Levi's Folly. What's that, you ask? I'll tell you. It's a pocket watch that's worth more than a hundred thousand dollars."

The kids all gasped, as did a few of the adults. Even Rick, who'd run across his share of conmen and charlatans while he was reporting in New York, was taken aback. He glanced sideways at Adam, mentally telegraphed a question of 'Is this for real?' and got a shrug in return.

Rick had to give Roy Andrew Boyd one thing; the man knew how to grab a crowd's attention. Especially when the crowd was composed of impressionable children. Miss Redmond, the teacher who had organized this trip, raised her hand.

"We have a question from the crowd. I think I know what it is. Yes, ma'am?" Boyd strode slowly toward the young woman as she asked how he knew about this watch.

"Because it's not just any watch, ma'am. It's an 1865 Patek Phillippe that a man named Levi Clark received on his twenty-first birthday. The watch was stolen by a road agent named Gentleman George in 1871. Do any of you kids know what a road agent was?"

All the heads swiveled from side to side in unison. That seemed to please Boyd, who then turned his fiery showmanship on the adults. "What about you, Chief Cunningham? You should know."

"Stagecoach robbers," Adam replied cooly.

"That's right, children! A road agent was a bandit. There were plenty of them!" Boyd crouched over as he paced in front of the group.

"Show off," Rick muttered.

"Me? Or him?" Adam whispered back.

"You. I haven't heard that term in a long time."

Boyd continued to expound on the activities of Gentleman George. He'd robbed twenty-four stagecoaches between 1867 and 1871. In all of his holdups, he never hurt anyone until his last job. "This is where the watch gets its name, children. It's called Levi's Folly because Levi Clark went to his death trying to protect the watch he'd received as a birthday present. When Gentleman George demanded Levi turn over the watch, the young man refused. George tried to take it by force. Levi, defiant to the end, resisted. In the scuffle, Levi was shot in the stomach. What happens when you shoot a man in the gut, Chief?"

Adam grimaced as all eyes turned to him. Obviously, he wasn't enjoying being put on the spot by Boyd. "Without medical attention, you'd probably bleed to death."

"That's right, children! Levi Clark was murdered by a common bandit. George knew Levi wasn't long for this world, so he took the watch and the gold bullion from the stage and fled. As Levi lay dying in his pregnant wife's arms, he put a curse on the watch and all those who might own it in the future."

Miss Redmond again raised her hand. "What happened to Gentleman George, Mr. Boyd?"

"He was so bothered by having killed Levi that he never robbed again." Without missing a beat, Boyd turned his gaze back on the kids. "We'll be looking for strongboxes filled with silver and gold today, children. Of course, the silver and gold aren't real, but there is an exciting prize for the first-place team."

"That ought to keep their interest," Rick muttered.

"It's got mine," Adam whispered back.

Rick was surprised that he and Adam weren't called out again for talking, but Boyd was off onto the subject of the actual hunt. He explained that in order to open their box of treasure, the kids would need to find three different locations. Locations were marked on the maps the kids would receive. In addition to the map, each team would also receive a compass. The actual strongbox was at one location; the two keys needed to open it were at the other locations. Each team would be looking for its own strongbox, so the teams were all independent.

The kids were forbidden from using their cell phones unless they needed to call for help. One chaperone was assigned to shadow each team, and it was the chaperone's responsibility to make sure the kids were safe and that they lived up to the spirit of the game.

"This is orienteering," Boyd concluded. "It's a competition, and the team who can open their strongbox first wins the prize! So pick your teammates wisely."

While the kids were choosing who they wanted to work with, Rick approached Boyd. "Was that story all true? Or were you just playing it up for the kids?"

Boyd lifted his hat, finger-combed his hair, then put the Stetson back on his head. "Well, Mr. Atwood, I've heard about how you've helped solve a few murders. I heard you also have a daughter who was always in the act."

Rick pointed out Alex, who was off to one side with her best friends Robbie Sachetti and Sasha Bell. "Unfortunately, Alex loves sticking her nose where it doesn't belong. So, what about that story? Truth? Or fiction?"

"All truth, sir. Well, mostly. The fact is there are enough crazy stories that come out of these hills without having to embellish one little bit."

"So what happened to him?"

"Who?" Boyd craned his neck forward, his brow furrowed.

"Gentleman George," Rick said.

"Levi Clark's family was well-connected to the powers-that-be. After his death, Levi's wife prevailed upon her father-in-law, who got the governor to authorize a $5,000 reward for the capture of Gentleman George. George fled and lived alone in the hills between here and San Ladron."

Rick did a double take and looked at the mountains surrounding them. "That would have been a rough life."

"Yessir, it would. Every now and then, George had to come into town for supplies. He couldn't go unnoticed because he'd probably robbed nearly half the people in these parts. One of them reported seeing him. The sheriff sent out posses to find him. They scoured the hills. As hard as they looked, nobody ever found his hideout. His luck didn't last long. Eventually, he was cornered on one of his trips into San Ladron."

"What happened to him?" Rick asked.

"George surrendered willingly and went to trial. The judge sentenced him to hang for the death of Levi Clark. The funny thing is, even on his way to the hangman's noose, he refused to give up the location of his stash. They strung him up on April 15, 1872."

"And the watch was never found? It's lost out here in these hills?"

"Oh, sir, that's not exactly true. Before the governor put a price on his head, Gentleman George traveled to San Francisco and sold the watch. It became a collector's item and disappeared. I doubt if it ever will be found." Boyd cleared his throat. He seemed to sense that the kids were getting restless, gave Rick a curt nod, and stepped back. "I need to get this show on the road before these kids get bored."

6

ALEX

ME AND SASHA AND ROBBIE were sitting together when Mr. Boyd split our class into big groups. Team Cool Kids made it through without getting split up, so we're a team of three against two teams of four. I'm super happy that the three of us are still getting to work alone.

Mr. Boyd's gonna do a show-and-tell with the other big group while we find our strongbox and the keys. Then the two big groups change places. There are a couple of kids left that aren't on teams. One of them is Billy Thornton. I hate him 'cause he's such a bully. None of the other kids like him either. Maybe he won't get on a team at all. And if he tries, I wanna make sure it's not ours.

"If Billy Thornton asks to be with us, we all say no. Right?"

Robbie and Sasha both agree. Then, Robbie's eyes get wide. "Uh, Alex?"

I turn around and see Mr. Boyd coming toward me. Uh oh. Billy Thornton is with him. No. No way. This is not happening.

"This young man is going to be on your team," Mr. Boyd says.

I shake my head. "Mr. Boyd, we don't need anybody else."

Mr. Boyd scowls at me and pushes Billy toward us. "It wasn't a question." When he turns to walk away, Billy smirks at me.

I totally know what Billy did. He deliberately waited until he saw which team I was on, and then he told Mr. Boyd he wanted to be with us. We're kinda stuck 'cause we've only got three. I glare at Billy. I'm not taking any BS from him today. "Robbie's in charge of the map. I'm the team leader, and you'll do what I say."

Billy shakes his head. "I don't take orders from you. Pretty soon, nobody will 'cause once your mom has that baby, you're gonna be all on your own. Nobody's gonna want you or care what happens to you."

I so wanna slam my fist into his face. He wouldn't be so smug then! I would if Mom hadn't told me it's best not to show fear or anger with bullies. She says that makes them even madder. Mr. Boyd's coming again. He's got our map and a compass.

"You're stupid, Billy." When I turn away from him, he grabs my shoulder and shoves me.

"Hey!" Mr. Boyd yells. "There's no fighting on my tours. What happened here?"

"She called me stupid." Billy spits out the last word and jabs a finger toward me.

Mr. Boyd looks super angry. He gives me an evil look that sends a chill down my spine. "Is that right?"

"I told him that because he said that after my baby brother is born, nobody's gonna want me."

"That's right," Sasha says.

Robbie adds, "We heard him."

After he takes a long slow breath, Mr. Boyd motions for Chief Cunningham to join us. He talks to him off to the side for a minute, then returns.

"Young man, it appears that you have quite a reputation. And I don't mean a good one. You may get away with tormenting others in school, but on my property, you abide by the rules. One of those rules is that you treat others the way you'd like to be treated."

Billy's face gets all red, and he points at me again. "She tried to give me orders!"

Mr. Boyd doesn't look happy at all. "Well?"

I try to keep my voice level because I can hear Mom's voice in my ear telling me that shows the other person you're in control. Besides, I've solved multiple murders. I'm way more confident than Billy Thornton will ever be. "I'm the team leader."

"Very well. You're benched, young man. My place, my rules. Now, I can either lock you in the jail over there...." He points at the wagon we all passed on the way in. It has bars on the sides like maybe it was used to transport prisoners in the old days. "It's either that or you sit on the chair outside my trailer. Your choice."

"But...but..."

"The law in this town has decided, young man. Which will it be? If you make me choose...."

Mr. Boyd gazes at the wagon for a few seconds. That would be awesome! Billy Thornton in jail! I'd totally want a picture of that.

"I hate you!" Billy mutters, then storms off toward the trailer.

"Not many people did like a lawman." Mr. Boyd winks at me, then points his finger. "Don't make me regret my decision, young lady, or you'll wind up sitting with him."

"No, sir." My voice sounds super confident even though my knees are shaking as Mr. Boyd nods and walks away. I'm gonna have to watch my back now. Billy Thornton is totally gonna want revenge.

Mr. Boyd walks back to the table with the old mining tools and picks up a megaphone. His voice is really loud when he says, "Are you ready, teams?"

We all yell back that we are, but he uses the megaphone to tell us he can't hear us. This time, we yell louder. He nods, then pulls out a gun from the holster on his side and shoots it in the air.

"Go!"

All the teams start running while Mr. Boyd windmills his arm. The chaperones follow. They're not supposed to do anything other than keep their teams in sight. We had a few minutes to decide which location we wanted to find first. Me and Sasha and Robbie decided to start with the key that's farthest away.

Robbie's awesome with a compass and a map. He's totally into all kinds of boats, and he learned how to sail last summer when he went to a sailing camp. They taught him why the compass spins around like it does. He tried to explain it once. It was totally boring. That's why me and Sasha put him in charge of telling us which way we're supposed to turn. We don't care why a compass does what it does. We only care that Robbie knows how to get us to our first location.

"We turn west here," Robbie says.

Sasha rolls her eyes as she looks at Robbie. "Is that like right or left?"

Robbie points to the right and makes a face. "We gotta go up there."

Whoa. That's a big hill. At least there's a trail that crosses back and forth, so it looks like that'll make it easier. I look around us. My dad is hanging behind. He's keeping his distance and gives me a thumbs-up along with a big smile.

The other teams are going for the closer locations. It's awesome that we're all on our own. At least, I hope it is. Everything depends on Robbie being right. "You're totally sure? We gotta go up the hill?"

"Totally," Robbie says.

I start up the trail first. When we get about halfway to the top, the trail splits. Me and Sasha both look at Robbie. He studies the map for a second, then points at a trail that goes right. It leads us around the hill and down. It looks like the trail is taking us around the hill and back to the bottom. I turn to Robbie.

"Seriously? We're going back down?"

"Well, yeah. We couldn't go through there."

He turns the map around so me and Sasha can see it. It looks like we went up the hill so we wouldn't have to go through Dead Man's Gulch. When I look back to the direction we came from, I can see why. Dead Man's Gulch is filled with huge rocks and lots of brush. All perfect hiding places for a rattlesnake. I can also see how it would have been a perfect place for someone like Gentleman George to use as a hideout.

7

RICK

WITHOUT A MAP OR A compass, it was difficult for Rick to know whether the kids were on track to find the first location or if they were hopelessly lost. They certainly looked lost. Alex was pointing in one direction and Sasha in the other. Robbie stood between them, turning the compass and cocking his head from side to side.

Rick wished he could coach Alex's team. In his younger days, he'd been good at orienteering. Back then, he could navigate anywhere with a compass—or even just a view of the North Star. It would be a lot more fun to teach the kids those skills than to stand on the sidelines watching them flounder. Nevertheless, he'd obey the rules. He'd gotten in trouble with Roy Andrew Boyd once and didn't wish to do it again, especially after the way the man had come down on Billy Thornton.

Looking back through the valley, Rick spotted Adam's team holding up a small box. Apparently, they'd found at least one of their locations. The third team had taken the fork on their trail that branched off through a canyon and was no longer visible.

Adam waved to Rick and raised his arm high, displaying a triumphant thumbs-up. Rick returned the gesture, even though he could hear Alex's team bicker. Apparently, Robbie's role as chief navigator had ended, and they couldn't decide which way to go. Rick pulled in a deep sigh. Thank goodness Roy Andrew Boyd had put a time limit on the exercise.

It was almost another hour by the time all of the teams had assembled back at the starting point for the awards ceremony. Alex, Sasha, and Robbie wouldn't be receiving a medal. They'd finished in the middle of the pack. After getting mired in self-doubts, they'd only found two of their locations.

Roy Andrew Boyd strutted before the kids, looking them over as though he were performing a military inspection. "You all did a fine job today. But only one team excelled. It's my pleasure to announce that first place goes to Chief Adam Cunningham's team. They had the fastest time by ten minutes and found their strongbox and two keys."

"Not fair," Alex muttered. "They're all a year older than us."

Rick put a gentle hand on her shoulder and squeezed. "Hey, kiddo. You had the chance to pick your team. You guys did the best you could." He also suspected that Adam might have fudged on the rules and coached his team just a bit.

Alex scrunched up her face as she looked at the ground for a few seconds, then nodded to herself. When she looked at Robbie and Sasha, she smiled. "My dad's right. We did good."

They exchanged a high-five when Boyd announced that they finished in third place.

By the time Rick dropped off Alex, Robbie, and Sasha at school, it was nearly noon. He was anxious to get back to the B&B and see how Marquetta was doing. Entering through the front door, he half expected to find another scene of chaos. The Band of Six, as he and Marquetta had started calling them, had only gotten into one other snit. That was little consolation. It was amazing how fast things could go wrong with that group.

He found Marquetta sitting at the kitchen island with Lydia and her husband, Matteo. Lydia's dark eyes flicked in Rick's direction when he pushed through the butler door. A heavyset Hispanic woman with full cheeks and a smile to match, Lydia looked like a young version of the type of grandmother he'd wished he'd had when he was growing up.

"Here he is," Lydia said and reached out to squeeze Marquetta's arm. "I told you he'd be home for lunch."

Both Lydia and Marquetta laughed. The worry that had dogged Rick while he'd been out of the house vanished when his gaze connected with Marquetta's. Truthfully, he'd fallen hard for her the first time he'd looked into those eyes. Now, he found himself loving her more every day they were together.

"How'd they do?" Marquetta asked, then immediately started and looked down. "Oh my, Mr. Atwood, I think we're going to have a soccer player in the family."

Rick approached. He kissed Marquetta, then reached down and placed his hand on her stomach. Indeed, the baby was kicking up a storm. "They finished third. Hey, maybe this little guy's going to be a football player."

"Or a professional dancer," Matteo added.

"My middle child was like that," Lydia said. "Dios mio! I was convinced he was going to kick his way out! He surprised us all and has turned into quite the bookworm."

Rick sat on the barstool next to Marquetta. He ran his fingers over the cool surface of the white granite countertop. This was Marquetta's domain. Almost everything in this room had been done to her specifications. From the pale green paint to the white cabinets and countertops, this was her dream kitchen. "I do love this room."

Marquetta nudged Rick. "So do I. Each time I walk in, I wonder why Captain Jack let me have complete control."

That was easy. Marquetta's father and mother had been good friends with Captain Jack, and Marquetta had practically grown up here. Later, when Marquetta was grown, Rick's grandfather gave her control for one simple reason. "Maybe because he didn't know how to boil water, and he didn't want to lose you."

"Oh, that's not true. Captain Jack was a passable cook. He just didn't like doing it. He told everyone he couldn't cook so he wouldn't have to."

"I stand corrected. So, all is quiet here?"

"Even the Band of Six has been playing nice together. They're going for that Silver Gulch tour this afternoon. I think they all went to the Rusty Nail for lunch. After that, they'll head out to the mine."

Rick snickered. "Terrific. A couple of drinks at lunch, and they'll all forget about being nice. Let's hope they don't kill each other on the way. They are one angry group. I can't help but wonder why they even came here."

"It was all because of Mr. Welles. You heard their nickname for him—Snappy. I haven't heard the story behind that...yet. It's probably not for any good reasons."

"Those people don't have a good reason for anything they do!" Lydia shook her head. "They're something else." The corners of her eyes crinkled as she chuckled.

Rick recalled how reserved Lydia had been when she first started. She'd been friendly, although distant, until Alex recruited her to help with the wedding plans. And by the time he and Marquetta returned from their honeymoon, she'd become part of the family. Both Lydia and Matteo now blended in. They cared about the B&B almost as much as Rick, Marquetta, and Alex.

"What is it, Rick?" Marquetta asked.

"Just thinking about what you might call the attachment pecking order around here."

Lydia and Marquetta exchanged a quizzical look.

"You were raised in this house. Captain Jack was like a grandfather to you. You knew him far better than any of us. I might have inherited the place and have a financial interest, but I'd wager this is where your heart is."

Marquetta let out a long breath. "If I, I mean, we, ever had to move, I might be heartbroken. It wouldn't matter though because I'd rather be with my family."

Lydia rested her elbows on the white granite. "That's what matters most—family."

"Don't worry. I'll do everything I can to make sure we never lose this house." Rick reached out and took Marquetta's hand. "I promise."

"You never know what might happen, Rick. Besides, if something tragic did happen, I'd choose you and Alex over this house any day. Now, dish. I want to know about this Silver Gulch tour. What did the kids have to do?"

Rick relayed the events of the morning. When he was done, he added, "I might as well tell you this because I know Alex will bring it up the moment you ask about her day. Adam and I were called out for talking while Roy Andrew Boyd was putting on his show."

"Oh my word," Marquetta laughed. "You are not going to live this down. You and Adam? Basically, called to the principal's office for talking? You're right. Alex will be reminding you about this day for a very long time."

"We weren't the only two who got in trouble. Billy Thornton got benched because he started a fight with Alex." He went on to explain the comment Billy had made and how Alex had responded. "Would you talk to her about it?"

"Of course."

Marquetta looked toward the hutch at the end of the kitchen. Collectible china plates lined the shelves, souvenirs of Captain Jack's voyages around the world. Rick wondered why Marquetta seemed suddenly distracted by the hutch and asked.

"One of the things about your grandfather, Rick, was that even though he was a hard man and never really talked about his feelings, I always knew he loved me as much as my mom and dad. I want Alex to feel that same love. I hope she never has reason to wonder if she's being displaced."

"Are you saying that I'm the one who should talk to her, then?"

"No. You tell her that all the time. I just realized that Alex and I haven't really talked about the changes we'll be going through. We've all been so focused on this baby that she and I haven't had a heart-to-heart in a long time. I'll tuck her in tonight so we can talk like we used to."

Lydia's eyes widened. "You still do that? She's getting a little old for that, isn't she?"

"She'll never be too old for me to want to mother her," Marquetta said with a smile. "And I want her to understand that."

8

RICK

RICK LOOKED ACROSS THE TABLE at Marquetta. She'd dressed
casually for this dinner out and still had her coat draped over
her shoulders. After their talk about needing to reassure Alex of
her place in the family, they'd jointly decided they could all use a
little time away without any possibility of interruptions. The
Crooked Mast seemed like the perfect place for that. Here, they
were the guests. There was no clean-up. No cooking. Nothing
but a little time to focus on themselves.

It was also an opportunity to enjoy the views offered by the
California coast. Blue, gray, and scarlet ribbons streamed across
the sky. Almost black clouds clung to the horizon like a string of
distant mountains. On his first trip here, Rick had marveled at
the view and found himself comparing it to the one from their
back patio. The two were different—and equally spectacular. He
felt sure he'd never tire of either.

Though they sat in a small sea of tables filled with guests,
Rick felt as though they were alone. All around them, the other
diners were engrossed in their own little worlds. They talked,
laughed, and savored the food while they cast glances out the
floor-to-ceiling windows.

"I'm glad we decided to do this." Rick lifted his glass and
raised it. The three of them were all drinking 'white wine,' which

was really sparkling water. "To a wonderful evening with just our little family."

Next to him, Alex beamed. Perhaps this dinner was just what she needed. It was a chance to be reminded that she would never be replaced by another sibling.

"Yay!" Alex took a sip from her glass. "Daddy, this was a great idea."

"I agree," Marquetta said. "It's so nice to have a night off from cooking and doing dishes. I'll take as many of these as you can afford."

"We should be able to squeeze in one more dinner before the baby arrives. Who knows? Maybe two."

Loud voices behind Rick caught his attention. When started to turn, Marquetta grabbed his hand. "Don't. It's the Band of Six. I assume you didn't know they were here. You didn't. Did you?"

"I had no idea. In fact, I didn't even notice them when we walked in."

"You were so busy pointing out the great sunset to Alex that you missed it all. When we walked in, Brid Ochoa was fawning over Mr. Welles. Now, he's brushed her off, and he's getting cozy with Barnaby Pauley's wife again. That man is like a bull moose with his harem at mating season." Marquetta rolled her eyes as she nodded in the direction of the loud voices. "Apparently, she doesn't mind his attention."

"I noticed that at the B&B when they checked in. They were sitting a little too close for comfort. No wonder her husband gets so upset. What I don't get is why she called Welles a toad when she got up. It's almost like she's playing the two men against each other."

Alex turned sideways in her seat and stared. "Daddy! They're gonna get themselves kicked out. Here comes Mr. Grayson."

"Alex!" Rick hissed, "Turn around."

"I wanna see what happens when Mr. Grayson has to deal with them. He looks super mad."

Rick knew that Ken Grayson didn't tolerate anyone disturbing his other guests at the Crooked Mast. He was a stickler for letting guests enjoy themselves as long as they didn't become overly rowdy. It appeared the Band of Six was about to discover they'd once again crossed a line of propriety. Every single pair of eyes seemed to be trained on the spectacle, so Rick succumbed to temptation and turned to watch.

When Ken spoke, he used a commanding voice that would quell any resistance under normal circumstances. "Folks, you are disturbing the other guests. You'll need to quiet down."

"And what if we don't?" Snappy Welles shot back.

"Then I'll ask you to leave."

"That's a good idea." Barnaby Pauley's voice boomed with the abandon of a man who'd had too much to drink. "He's been getting too friendly with my wife."

"Barnaby, knock it off. You're making a scene. It was nothing."

"Nothing? You think I'm blind, Liz? I can see exactly what's going on."

"You can be such a stick-in-the-mud, Barnaby. Let me handle him. You're embarrassing me to no end."

Rick turned back to face Marquetta. She had her phone to her ear and was talking. When there was a pause in the conversation, she looked at Rick and said, "I'm calling Adam."

"Good idea," Rick said as the argument taking center stage escalated. "Looks like Ken might need the help."

When Guy Silvan pushed back his chair and leaned over the table in front of Welles, Rick knew exactly what was coming. "Tell him to hurry," Rick said, then stood.

"Rick! Sit down! Let Ken handle this." Marquetta glared at him and quickly returned her attention to her phone. "Adam, those guests of ours? The Band of Six? They're about to start a fight at the Crooked Mast. Ken needs help."

Rick slowly lowered himself into his seat. "You're probably right. These people defy all social norms."

Some of the other guests were trying to ignore the argument. Most appeared on edge as they waited for some sort of escalation.

"You need to leave," Ken commanded. "All of you."

Liz Ravel stood. She grabbed her husband's arm. "Come on! Look what you've done."

"Me? You're the one who's been cozying up to Snappy since we got here!"

"You don't know what you're talking about. Let's go!"

"I know what I saw!"

"Shut up, Barnaby. I've had it with you and your jealousy. Let's get out of here. We're leaving in the morning."

Brid Ochoa also stood. "I agree with Liz. This getaway has been a disaster. You, Snappy, should be ashamed of yourself even though you've probably never felt a drop of remorse in your life. So why should it start now? Guy, we're leaving."

Guy Silvan glared at Welles, his fists clenching and releasing several times. He was obviously itching for a fight.

Brid snapped, "Guy? Are you coming? Or are you going to find yourself a different room? Because if I walk out that door alone, you can sleep in the car for all I care."

Though he was still seething, Silvan inched to the side.

"Yeah, go ahead and do what the little woman tells you to do," Welles said smugly. His smile fell when he saw Adam and his deputy weaving through the tables and coming toward them. "Looks like the game is over."

Welles stood, pulled several bills from his wallet, and tossed them on the table. He started to walk away quietly. Before he had gone more than a few steps, Adam blocked his path.

"You want me to arrest him, Ken?"

Ken took a look at the bills on the table and seemed to do some sort of mental calculation. "No, Adam. He's leaving and has paid his bill in full. Let him go."

"I'm going peacefully." Welles raised his hands over his head, sidestepped Adam, and walked toward the front door.

"The rest of you, dinner's over," Adam said. "I think the other guests here have had enough excitement for one night."

The remainder of the group filed out, looking sullen and defeated. Even Guy Silvan didn't resist when Brid grabbed his hand and led him away. Adam and his deputy followed the group all the way out the door.

The silence that had fallen over the restaurant during the entire incident gradually gave way to voices as the other guests began talking. Judging by the excited tones, Rick was sure the main topic was the Band of Six.

"Thank goodness that's over," Marquetta said.

"I thought they were gonna get into a fight for sure." Alex shifted in her seat, picked up her fork, and huffed.

Marquetta leaned forward and pursed her lips. The little crow's feet around the corners of her eyes crinkled, and her lips curled up. "You look disappointed, Sweetie."

Rick put an arm around Alex's shoulders and gave her a squeeze. "Seaside Cove getting a little too tame for you, kiddo?"

Alex shrugged. "I thought maybe I'd get a story for the *Cove Talkers*. How can I be a reporter if nothing ever happens? All I get to write about is boring stuff."

Recalling the last time there'd been big news in town, Rick felt an involuntary chill. Though Alex seemed to have a fascination with crime, he was just glad the town had been quiet for all these months. If they never had another murder in Seaside Cove, he'd be perfectly happy.

Rick raised his glass again. "Well, I, for one, am delighted that this little town has become quite boring."

Marquetta picked up her glass and held it up to Rick's. "Here, here. To quiet times."

When Rick looked over at Alex, she picked up her glass and raised it. Even as she clinked hers to his, Rick saw the disappointment. Feeling a certain amount of trepidation, he said, "Don't worry, kiddo. I'm sure something exciting will happen. Eventually."

What he really wanted, though, was for the Band of Six to leave town before that 'something exciting' happened.

9

ALEX

Hey Journal,

It's been a super long day. The trip to Silver Gulch mine was pretty cool. I also have to tell you about something that happened there. Billy Thornton said I'm not gonna be important anymore once Mom has her baby. I never thought about it before, but he might be right. Me and Mom used to talk all the time. We don't do that very much these days. And when we do, it's always about the baby.

I know I'm kinda to blame for that since I'm the one who wanted a baby brother so much. It seems silly now. I always thought it would be awesome to have somebody I could teach all my investigating skills to. Now that he's almost here, I dunno. Maybe...do you think...Am I gonna be forgotten?

What worries me most, Journal, is how much that could be like it was when me and Daddy lived in New York. My real mom was always chasing her career on the stage and never had time for me. Now, Mom might be spending all her time with my baby brother, and I might be forgotten all over again. Oh, man, this sucks. I know if I say something to Mom, she'll tell me I'm being silly...but...am I?

Uh oh, I think she just knocked. Gotta go!
Alex

* * *

I close my journal and slip it into the top desk drawer. It makes me a little sad to think I might be hiding my thoughts from Mom. She's the one who got me my first journal. If it wasn't for her, so many things would be different. Maybe even unbearable.

Despite the lump in my throat, I force it down and call out, "Come in."

The door slips open a crack. Mom pokes her head in like she always used to do when she came in. She's getting super big, and that's just another reminder that she might not be doing this much longer. She closes the door behind her and smiles at me. "I've missed doing this."

The lump is back. It's harder to force it down. I wanna be strong. I just don't know if I can. I've missed our time together, too. I give her a weak smile. "You've been so busy with the B&B and the baby."

"Can we talk?"

"Sure." I shrug.

She sits on the edge of the bed and pats the space next to her. My jaw gets tight. That was what she used to do. Put her arm around me. Tell me everything was gonna be okay even when it seemed like it wasn't.

"Please?" Mom asks.

My eyes burn. Why is this so hard? I get up slowly and sit next to her. Then she leans against me.

"This is nice, Sweetie."

"Yeah." My shoulders are super tight, and my breath feels like it's caught in my chest. The room gets all blurry. Me and Mom never felt awkward around each other before.

"Your dad told me what Billy Thornton said today. It's bothering you, isn't it?"

I swipe at my cheek and look down. "It's okay," I say to the floor even though it's not. Now the stupid floor's too blurry to see. I just wanna crawl under the covers. Maybe there I'll feel better.

She slips her arm around my shoulders. Pulls me close. Just like she used to. "No, Sweetie, it's not okay. Let me tell you what his comment is doing to you. It's making you doubt everything you've wanted. You're now thinking that this brother you've wanted for so long is going to pull your dad and me away from you. You're going to feel abandoned, just like you did with your biological mother."

Stupid room. Now I can't see anything. And it's so hot. I can't hardly breathe 'cause my nose is all stuffy and it feels like if I try to breathe it's gonna come out all raggedy. Then it does even when I try not to let it happen. Mom's arm circles my shoulder. She's pulling me closer. Her touch is tender and warm, and her other hand is stroking my hair and letting me cry into her shirt.

"I'm sorry," I croak.

She just says, "Shhh." And holds me close.

Just when I think I can breathe again, she eases me away. She's got tears running down her cheeks, too. And that just makes me hate Billy Thornton even more.

"It's okay, Sweetie. It's okay."

She pulls me back into her chest. After a long while, I push myself back so I can see her face. "Mom?" I sniffle.

Her eyes are all teary, and she sniffles, too. "You know, I love it when you call me that."

"I love you," I whisper.

"And I love you, Sweetie, with all my heart. And I love your father with all my heart, too, just as I will this baby. That's the wonderful thing about love, Alex. There's always more to go around."

"Stupid Billy Thornton. Tomorrow I'm gonna punch him in the nose."

10

RICK

IT WASN'T UNTIL BREAKFAST THE following morning that Rick even thought about the Band of Six again. Liz Ravel and Barnaby Pauley were the first of the group to show up for breakfast. They arrived at 7:30, and it was the first moment of the morning when Rick's professional guardedness returned. He felt most of the guests could be treated like friends and family. Not these people. When they appeared, he was happy that Alex was helping Marquetta in the kitchen. At least he wouldn't have to worry about her becoming a target of Snappy Welles's hostility.

"Good morning, folks. I've got a table for the six of you already set up over here. I can seat you if you'd like."

Liz Ravel stiffened. The muscles in her jaw clenched for a moment, then she said, "We'd like a table for four, Rick. We'll be eating with Brid and Guy."

"Oh." Rick shot an involuntary glance over his shoulder at the table in the center of the room. "What about the others? They won't want to join you?"

The comment earned Rick a cold-as-ice return. "We don't want to join them. We'll be sitting with our friends."

"Liz." Her husband grunted some sort of apology, then glared at her. "It's not his fault."

She nodded, then took a deep breath. "Barnaby's right. I'm sorry. It isn't your fault this has turned into such a trying weekend. Everything about the B&B has been lovely. Snappy's the one who's made it impossible. I apologize for being rude."

"It's no problem, Ms. Ravel," Rick said, allowing a hint of formality to creep into his response. "I understand completely."

"No, you don't," she said with a slight laugh. "And believe me when I tell you, you don't want to."

"Hey, Liz."

Brid Ochoa approached and put her arms around her friend. The two women hugged while their partners watched in uncomfortable silence. It seemed like an odd friendship. For the women, it was genuine. Not so, for the men. For them, it felt like forced compliance.

As they hugged, Brid asked, "How are you holding up after last night?"

"Good. Snappy's such a jerk." Liz Ravel pulled back slightly and held her friend's hands. "What about you? That whole dinner was over-the-top tense."

Two more guests had appeared behind the couples. "Ladies, how about if I seat you over there? We have a nice table for four. I have more guests showing up."

"Good idea," Barnaby Pauley grumbled. "Me and Guy have a few things to catch up on."

By the time Rick had the two couples seated, there were four more waiting at the entrance. Lydia came out of the kitchen. Her eyes widened, and she rushed forward. "I'm sorry, Rick. Things were so quiet that I went back to help Marquetta with some cleanup. What do you need me to do?"

"Don't worry about it, Lydia. Let's start with the table for six. We won't need it, so break it down. I'll seat the other guests."

Within minutes, he and Lydia had everyone seated and the tables rearranged. By his count, the only ones who hadn't come down for breakfast were Carson Coulson and Snappy Welles.

Rick returned to the table for the two couples, hoping that with Welles out of the picture, the atmosphere would be more relaxed. He was not disappointed when he approached the table and asked what he could get them for breakfast.

Brid Ochoa handed her menu to Rick. "More quiet time like this?" She forced a laugh, then added, "I'll try today's special. The quiche."

"Good choice. I'm hoping there'll be some left over for me later." He went around the table, got the rest of the orders, then returned with the coffee pot to refill mugs. As he was pouring, he overheard the two women talking about someone that he assumed was Welles.

"I haven't seen him, either. Fine by me," Liz said. "If I never see that man again, I'll be happy."

Barnaby Pauley, who had a scruffy three-day beard, stroked his chin. "I don't think you will. And if he does show up, he'll be one sorry puppy."

Rick returned to the kitchen to turn in the orders. He handed them to Marquetta, sat on one of the barstools, and said, "Even when Welles isn't around, he's still the topic of conversation. I'm just hoping he doesn't show up after we close down and start demanding that we feed him."

"I know." Marquetta planted her hands on her lower back and stretched. "If he does, you may have to restrain a crazed pregnant woman from giving him a tongue-lashing."

They both laughed, but Rick knew he'd never let things go that far. He'd do the same thing Marquetta had done the night before at the Crooked Mast, call Adam. The time had come to stop letting Welles get away with his antics.

Rick stood and kissed Marquetta. "I'd better get back out there. You are going to need a break soon. I can see how tired you're getting."

"It's been a long morning. When Lydia's free, she'll help."

"I'll let her know. And since Welles may not be showing up for breakfast, things should stay pretty quiet in the dining room."

Alex, who had been washing dishes, took off her gloves and stood next to Marquetta. "Mom, how about if I cook so you can sit for a few minutes?"

"Oh, Sweetie, I don't know. I'm still doing okay."

"Nonsense. Alex is right. She can take your place. Then Lydia can come back here to help. Take a little time to put your feet up."

"Well, it would be nice to have a few minutes...."

"Awesome." Alex gently edged Marquetta to one side.

Marquetta tugged on Alex's ponytail, then went to sit on one of the barstools. "Far be it from me to interfere with a plan."

Rick returned to the dining room expecting a problem from the four members of the Band of Six that he'd seated earlier. He was relieved to find things going better than he'd expected. Even without Welles, their mood wasn't buoyant, but at least they weren't arguing. The two women talked across the table while their significant others ignored the world around them and focused on their plates. It wasn't a happy table. This time, however, the group didn't seem to be headed toward the state of chaos that constantly brewed around them when they were all together.

Just a few minutes before 8:30, Adam showed up at the dining room entrance. His uniform, rather than having its usual crisp and clean appearance, was rumpled and practically looked like he'd slept in it. The last of the guests who had come down earlier were gone, so they were down to just a few tables.

"Hey, buddy, would you like some breakfast? And what on earth happened to you? You look like you've been up all night."

"That's pretty close. Most of it, anyway. We need to talk in your office for a few minutes."

"Sure. Let me get Lydia or Alex to take over for me" After getting Alex to help, Rick led the way through the living room and up the stairs. At the top, they turned right. As he eased the door to his office closed, he asked, "So what's going on?"

"One of your guests, Mr. Welles, died last night. It appeared he was hit by a car. Deputy Kama got the call. She responded, then called me. We called in the sheriff and the Medical Examiner. Just a few minutes ago, I got a call from the ME. Her initial assessment is that Mr. Welles died from asphyxiation."

It took Rick a few seconds to process the news. When he did, he had a feeling there was more to the story. "If he was hit by a car, how did he die of asphyxiation? Oh no, don't tell me that's why you're here. You want my help on this, don't you?"

Adam sat on the couch, leaning forward with his elbows on his knees. He took a long, slow breath. "There were no external signs of a struggle. Both Deputy Kama and I checked."

"What aren't you saying, Adam?" Rick demanded. The silence in the room suddenly felt oppressive. This couldn't be happening. Not now. "So it was murder?"

"He certainly didn't do this to himself. The ME still has to do the autopsy to be certain, but I think you've hit the nail on the head. And since all the people who knew him are from out of town, I didn't want to wait. I hate to ask this, buddy, but can you slip back into the role of consultant?"

"There's no way, Adam. Marquetta's due soon. I can't be putting that extra load on her."

"Markie's tough, Rick. You know she could handle this place with one hand tied behind her back."

"Right now, she's got two extra hands to worry about." Rick stopped at the sound of someone knocking on the door. He got up, opened it, and was surprised to see Marquetta standing there.

She peered into the room. "I heard you were here, Adam."

"You know why, too. Don't you?"

"There's only one reason you'd show up here and not be sitting in my dining room. Come on. I'll make you two breakfast while you talk this over."

Adam stood. His stomach growled, and he looked sheepishly at Rick. "Sounds good to me. Let's go, buddy. The boss has spoken."

Rick groaned. He knew exactly where this was headed.

11

ALEX

I'M AT THE TABLE FOR Mr. and Mrs. Dixon when Chief Cunningham walks into the dining room. He's probably here to have breakfast with my dad. They do that sometimes.

"Who's that, dear?" Mrs. Dixon asks. She's a super-nice old lady with blue hair that totally works for her.

"That's Chief Cunningham. He runs the police department. He's awesome." I'd love to go talk to him and ask what's going on, but the Dixons have been so nice this morning that I can't just walk away. Not like I could with the Band of Six.

"Would you like more coffee, Mrs. Dixon?"

"You're such a love. Yes, please. I'm still catching up from our flight yesterday." She smiles at me while I pour, and her bright blue eyes watch me over her wire-rimmed glasses. She's super-thin and eats like a bird, and her husband always likes to help her clean her plate. They're fun to watch. They've been together for like fifty years.

My eyes get wide when Chief Cunningham motions for my dad to follow him, and they leave the dining room. Rats! What's going on? I smile at Mr. Dixon. "Where'd you guys come from?"

"Seattle," Mr. Dixon says as he eyes a piece of bacon his wife left on the plate. "You going to eat that, dear?"

"You know I'm not." She holds out her plate and lets her husband take it from her. "It's cold and wet there right now. This looks like it's going to be a beautiful day."

Mr. Dixon scrapes the bacon and the other half of the muffin onto his plate and glances at the door again. "Why was the Chief of Police taking your dad away? He looks like he had a rough night."

"Oh, stop it, Thomas. This is a small town. Maybe the standards are more relaxed."

"You're right, Mr. Dixon. The chief is super concerned about how he looks. He must've been working all night."

Mr. Dixon clears his throat and sits a little straighter. "That could explain it. So why is he talking to your father?"

I explain to him how me and my dad helped solve a bunch of murders. Just about the time I finish, Mom comes to the dining room and looks around. "Alex? Where's your dad?"

"He's with Chief Cunningham."

She nods, says thanks, and leaves without another word.

I look back at Mrs. Dixon, who's watching me with raised eyebrows. What the heck? Right? Why not tell her? "If they're talking in my dad's office, something big must have happened."

"Why do you say that, dear?" Mrs. Dixon tries to turn in her seat so she can see me better, but there must be something wrong with her neck 'cause she can only turn partway, and her face scrunches up like she's in a lot of pain.

"Just then? When I told Mom that my dad was with the chief? She totally got a suspicious look on her face." Oh, man. This sucks. There's no way for me to snoop, either. I totally wanna know what's going on.

I wonder if it's got something to do with the Band of Six? That nasty Mr. Welles didn't show up for breakfast, and Mr. Coulson's not here.... Something could have happened to them.

What if they got into another fight? Even bigger than last night's.

I glance over at the table for the two couples from the Band of Six. Their mugs are getting a little low. Perfect! When the girls see me coming, they stop talking. "Do you guys want more coffee?" I ask.

"Thank you, Alex." Ms. Ochoa looks up at me. She parts her lips. She's got a pretty smile. And kinda cool hair. It's dark with some highlights and has a little bit of curl. Mine is super straight and reddish. My dad says I look a lot like my mom. I guess he's right 'cause I've got her dark-blue eyes, too.

While I'm pouring coffee, I tell her I like her hair. She reaches up and twirls a few of the ends. Then she looks down at the table and blushes a little. "Sorry, I didn't mean to embarrass you," I say.

"Brid, don't be so modest," Ms. Ravel says. "You're beautiful. Isn't she, Guy?"

He looks over at his girlfriend, shrugs, then nods his head. "Yeah. Pretty."

Wow. If my boyfriend treated me like that, I'd wanna smack him. Actually, I guess I don't have a boyfriend yet. Robbie still doesn't see me as a girl. Mom says he'll start to notice me like that in the next couple of years. I totally wish he'd hurry up. It's super boring just being a friend.

"Where's the rest of your group?"

Mr. Pauley barks out a laugh. "I don't care one bit where Snappy Welles is, kid. He's a jerk. As for Carson, who knows? We haven't seen him since that dinner debacle last night."

I nod, then look at Ms. Ochoa. She seems to be the most talkative one.

She shakes her head. "I haven't seen him."

The table gets super quiet. I guess I'm not getting anything more out of them. Maybe Lydia knows something. I give them all a friendly smile. "Enjoy your breakfast."

After putting the coffee carafes back on the counter, I go to the kitchen. Lydia's stacking dishes in the dishwasher. When she sees me, she raises her eyebrows. "Did Marquetta find your dad?"

"As far as I know. She asked where he was, and I told her he was with Chief Cunningham. Do you know what happened?"

"She got a phone call from Traci and asked me to take over. Then she rushed out. Sounded serious."

I tell her about the two missing guests and how the others in the Band of Six haven't seen them. Lydia still looks a little skeptical, so I add, "Maybe something happened to one of them. That dinner was super tense."

"Your instincts have been good before, Alex. If you think something is going on, maybe you should look into it for the *Cove Talkers Newsletter*."

"Mom and Dad aren't gonna like that." I know 'cause I've been there. Done that.

"Since when has that stopped you before?" Lydia kinda smiles and winks at me.

"You're right. I should totally check this out. You can be my first interview."

"Why me? I don't really know anything about them."

"You cleaned the room for Mr. Welles. Right? And you've seen them around here."

"Well, I guess." She crosses her arms over her chest and leans against the counter. "What do you want to know?"

"What kind of stuff did Mr. Welles have in his room?"

"The usual. Clothes. Toiletries."

"Did he have a laptop?"

Lydia's eyes go up for a second. "Yes. He also had a small notebook."

"You mean something like a journal?"

"Yes. I suppose it could have been. I don't see him as the kind to write down all his thoughts, though."

I totally agree. Unless his thoughts were about other people. For sure. He could have been keeping notes on them. I could totally see him writing out all kinds of nasty stuff about everyone else. "Did you see what was in it?"

"No, Alex." She stops and winks at me. "I'm not like you. You might get in a little bit of trouble for snooping on a guest. I could get fired."

I roll my eyes and sigh. "I really don't wanna get grounded again."

Lydia snickers. "I think your dad's learned that grounding you is a waste of energy."

Okay. I guess he has, like, said that before. "How big was it?"

"How big was what? Oh, the notebook?" She holds up her hands to show me it's about four inches wide by six inches tall. That's smaller than the journal Marquetta gave me. "How thick was it, Lydia?"

"Not very. About like this." She holds up her thumb and finger. "Less than an inch. It had a leather cover. It's the kind where you could refill the paper when it's filled up. Why the big interest in the man's diary or whatever it was?"

"You saw how mean Mr. Welles was to his friends. Why would they come on a trip like this if they knew he was gonna be nasty the whole time? They might've been forced to come here. He could be blackmailing them. One of them got mad and killed him!"

"Whoa, Alex! Hold on. You just went from he didn't show up for breakfast to someone committing murder. I think you need to find some proof before you make all those accusations."

"Exactly." Oh yeah, and I know just how I'm gonna get it.

12

RICK

MARQUETTA LED THE WAY BACK downstairs. Adam and Rick followed. When they pushed through the butler door, Alex was talking to Lydia, whose eyes widened as she turned back to the dishes waiting to be put into the dishwasher.

"I'm sorry! I'm sorry! I got distracted," Lydia blurted.

Marquetta went to Lydia and put a hand on her back. "It's okay." A moment later, she added, "Really. It's fine."

Rick knew something wasn't right. Lydia was about as honest as a person could be. She'd proven herself a hard worker who never shirked her duties. If Marquetta had asked her to take care of the dishes and she hadn't, she had to have been distracted by something. Or someone. He gave Alex a sideways glance. There was one person who was a master at distracting Lydia. Alex. He'd bet anything she was concocting some sort of scheme. "What are you up to, kiddo?"

After a quick shrug, Alex tossed a glance at Lydia. "We were just talking about the Band of Six. Right, Lydia? How weird it is that they split up for breakfast."

"I see." Somehow, Rick didn't quite buy that as the whole story, even though it sounded plausible. And challenging it would put Lydia in the position of having to choose between protecting Alex and...what? Being caught in the middle of one of Alex's 'operations?' It seemed impossible that Alex had already heard the news about Snappy Welles. Just in case, he made a mental note to watch for signs that his daughter was sticking her nose into police business.

"Adam's joining us for breakfast, Lydia," Marquetta said. "Why don't we make up a huge scramble? Rick? You and Adam can go outside for a bit if you want."

Rick caught the look of disappointment on Alex's face. Aha. She had suspected something was up. How in the world had she heard about Welles already? Perhaps Lydia had been more than an innocent bystander. She was plugged into the town's rumor mill, a machine with an efficiency that never ceased to amaze him. "Good idea. Grab a mug, buddy. We'll go out back."

A few minutes later, Rick and Adam stood at the edge of the concrete patio gazing out at the Pacific Ocean. A mist filtered the horizon, softening the view. It was almost like looking through condensation on a glass window. At least the wind wasn't blowing this morning. And as the first rays of sun poked through holes in the gray sky, Rick felt the promise of a new day. Unfortunately, this one was being tainted by murder.

"This is novel. Are we hiding out here from Nancy Drew?" Adam asked with a sly grin.

"How many times have I asked you not to call her that?"

Adam raised his mug to his lips, took a sip, then winked. "Oh, I don't know. Maybe fifty? Sixty? A hundred?"

Cradling his own mug in his hands, Rick tried not to smile as he held his friend's gaze. A hundred was probably an exaggeration. Or was it? The grin Adam gave him said it all. This was definitely a losing battle. "You're never going to stop. Are you?"

"Nope."

Rick sighed deeply. He took a long sip from his mug. He should be happy that Alex was so precocious. That she had a good head on her shoulders. And that she was, in a sense, following in his footsteps. "You really admire her investigative skills, don't you?"

"That daughter of yours could open her own private investigation agency."

Rick blew out a long breath. The truth was, Adam was right. "I know. And I know that she knows something's up. Did you catch how guilty Lydia looked when we walked in?"

"I thought that was just because she was chitchatting and not working."

Rick shook his head. "Lydia's no slacker. And if Marquetta had asked her to take care of those dishes, she'd have jumped on it right away. No. Lydia knows we don't get upset over a little time spent talking. She's also going above and beyond to make sure Marquetta doesn't get overworked. I suspect she got distracted by Alex. If I know my daughter, she's already got a plan of some sort in the works. I just don't know what it is."

Adam laughed and said, "That's why we're relegated to clandestine meetings out here on the patio? To avoid being overheard?"

"Good grief, that sounds ridiculous." Rick craned his neck back and groaned. "Why couldn't my daughter just be interested in something less dangerous?"

"It's not in her DNA, Rick. I'll bet Alex skipped the playing-with-dolls stage and went straight to criminal investigations. Am I right?"

"Don't remind me."

Adam shrugged. He glanced over his shoulder at the house. "It wouldn't surprise me if she has this patio bugged."

"Don't give her any ideas. Please."

"Enough about the munchkin. Tell me what happened last night at dinner before Deputy Kama and I showed up."

"What didn't? Liz Ravel was flirting with Welles. When her husband and Welles almost got into it, Brid Ochoa defended Liz. Then Brid Ochoa's boyfriend went off on Welles. It was a real sideshow."

"From what little I saw, Welles must have been defiant and obnoxious through it all. Would you agree with that?"

"Absolutely."

Adam huffed and stared off into space. "It sounds like the guy was just asking for trouble."

"I think he'd have been happy to have gotten beaten up by the others. It would have given him one more thing to hold over their heads. Maybe he's willing to take their abuse just to keep them around. He obviously has a thing for Ms. Ravel. I wonder if she's the kind who's always attracted to the one she doesn't have."

Adam snorted. "That would be a pretty sick relationship."

"From what I've seen, the group dynamics are very screwed up. There's got to be something holding them together. Normal people don't keep putting up with that sort of thing for long."

There was a long pause while Adam watched the ocean. Rick chose to let his friend have the moment of silence and sipped from his mug while he watched a distant freighter crawl across the horizon. It had been months since the last time he and Adam had worked together. While that was good because it meant no crime, he missed the closeness that came from their teamwork. Theirs was a comfortable relationship, one that allowed them each to play to their strengths while filling in the gaps for their partner's weaknesses.

"Your turn," Rick said. "Tell me what happened last night. Where did Welles get run over by a car?"

"About a block from the Crooked Mast. It doesn't make any sense. His wounds from the accident were superficial. He must have walked behind a car that was backing out. He had some bruises but no broken bones. No concussion. When we found him, he was just...dead. Kama and I speculated that maybe he'd had a heart attack. Later on, when the ME arrived, she said everything pointed to asphyxiation."

"So, somebody backs out of their parking space and knocks the guy down. And when they don't kill him, they decide to smother him? That's pretty bizarre. Why not just back over him a couple more times? Where's the car? The driver?"

"So far, nobody's come forward to say that they hit him. I'd like to interview the staff at the Crooked Mast. I'm hoping one of them saw the accident."

"What about Ken's security cameras? Surely they must have picked up something."

"Nope. He's got the equipment. He hasn't had it installed because he's waiting for an electrician from San Ladron. That's all I have to go on so far."

"It's not much," Rick said.

"So, will you help me out?"

As much as Rick hated to see his friend become overwhelmed. There were so many things going on at the B&B. And now, they had a baby on the way. "I'll tell you what. If Marquetta's okay with me helping you, I'll do it. I really want to keep Alex out, though."

"You know that's not up to you. Right? If she wants to do some investigating, she'll find a way."

"I think Alex is going through some turmoil. She's been having second thoughts about being a big sister." Rick went on to explain how Alex was beginning to wonder about her place in the family. "I just don't want that leading her into making some sort of rash decision or taking excessive risks."

"Dream on, buddy. She's a little older and a little wiser, but she's still a kid. It's in their nature to do both of those things. Look, I think the best thing is to go back in there, be open and honest about Welles, and then ask her to let us do our jobs."

"You've got to be kidding me," Rick scoffed. He turned his attention back to the ocean. The slow, steady pace of waves marching toward shore had a calming effect, albeit not enough to make his decision any easier.

"She'll find out, anyway, Rick."

"You're right. What the heck? When all else fails, why not try reasoning with a headstrong thirteen-year-old?"

"When you put it that way," Adam chuckled. "Come on. Let's go see if we can keep Nancy Drew off the case."

The aroma of onions, potatoes, and garlic cooking filled the kitchen. Rick just stood and watched as Alex, Lydia, and Marquetta worked together. It was like watching art in motion.

"Should we offer to help?" Adam asked.

"Not a chance. We'll just get in the way. Those three have this down to a science. We just need to stand clear and appreciate the result."

Marquetta stopped, pointed at them from across the room, and called out, "Five minutes, you two. Sit at that table."

Precisely five minutes later, Rick and Adam were joined by Alex, Lydia, and Marquetta. The table sat six, so there was plenty of room. It didn't take long for the conversation to turn to the events that had brought Adam to the B&B. Rick noted that Alex and Lydia exchanged a glance when Adam mentioned the ME's initial analysis. Before he could ask Alex what plan she was working on, Marquetta laid down her fork and gazed at him from across the table.

"What's wrong?" Rick asked, panic inching into his voice. "Is it the baby?"

"No, the baby's fine." Marquetta took a deep breath and looked at Adam. "Is the reason you're here to ask Rick to help on the case?"

Adam winced. Kind of like a kid caught with his hand in the cookie jar, thought Rick.

"I know it's a lot to ask, Markie. You guys have so much going on right now."

Marquetta waved a hand in front of her. "It's fine, Adam. I know how important this is to the town." She looked directly at Rick. "You need to help him. If there's so little to go on, Adam's going to need all the help he can get to figure this out." She turned back to Adam. "I hope you're not offended, Adam. That's just the way I feel."

"Believe me, Markie. It's no problem. I'm happy to have your support. Rick? Are you in?"

Stealing another glance at Alex, then Lydia, Rick made his decision. "I told you if it was okay with Marquetta, I'd help out. There's something else I want to do before we get too far into this. I want to talk about the elephant in the room." He turned to Alex.

Alex scrunched up her face. Her brows furrowed, and she sat up straight. "What elephant?"

"You know exactly what your dad's talking about, Sweetie. I can almost see the wheels spinning in your head. Your dad and Adam are being more forthright about this than I expected. It's your turn. What are you and Lydia planning?"

13

ALEX

OH, SNAP! JUST WHEN I thought me and Lydia had a secret plan. I guess I should've known. Mom knows me so well. It's that whole soulmate thing again. The only bad thing about having a soulmate is it's too easy for them to guess what you're hiding.

"You're right," I mutter. "But it's not Lydia's fault. I made her answer my questions."

"No, Alex. I answered willingly. I'm an adult and could easily have told you no."

Lydia's got a super guilty look on her face, and that makes me feel even worse. I scrunch up my cheeks and turn to my dad. "I don't want to get Lydia in trouble."

"Nobody's in trouble, Alex," he says. "We just all need to put our cards on the table. As much as I hate to say it, I think we're all in this together. Now, what was your plan?"

I might as well just blurt it out. Besides, me and Lydia haven't done anything yet. "I wanted to read Mr. Welles's notebook."

My dad's eyes get super big, and my mom's jaw drops. Lydia squeezes her eyes shut for a second before she starts rambling in Spanish. I recognize a few of the words—they're the ones she uses when she's like having a total panic attack. "It's cool, Lydia. You didn't do anything wrong."

She takes a breath, then switches to English. "When I was cleaning Mr. Welles's room, I noticed that he had a laptop and a small notebook on the desk. Of course, I didn't touch his things, but when Alex and I were talking earlier, she suggested that Mr. Welles might be blackmailing the others in his group. She wanted to go into the room and read it."

Uh oh. That was a little too much information.

My dad starts to say something, probably to chew me out for having crazy ideas, when Chief Cunningham interrupts him by clearing his throat. "I'm not saying I buy into this theory of yours, Alex. On the other hand, the death of Snappy Welles is pretty far out there all on its own. Explain to me how you got from an auto accident to blackmail and, I assume, murder."

I go through the explanation like I did with Lydia. My dad looks totally skeptical. He never believes in my logic, and he's always telling me it's not logic. He calls it reckless thinking. Mom's got her elbow on the table and has her chin propped up, resting it on the back of her hand. Chief Cunningham just seems kinda blown away by it all.

"Rick? Got a question for you," the chief says. "Since your guest is officially not returning to his room, what's your next step? I assume you have someone new coming in. How long do I have before you clean out the room?"

"Welles was scheduled to check out Monday morning. Under the circumstances, I guess I can let you in at any time. Did you want to go up there now?"

"Actually, yes. And thanks for making this easy. Since you're giving me permission, I don't need to get a warrant."

I wanna do a fist pump 'cause the chief is taking me seriously. This is awesome! "Does this mean you think I'm right?"

"Not necessarily, Alex. I just think we need to be considering all of our options. Especially because if this man really did die from asphyxiation, that means he was murdered. And if he was murdered, someone had a motive. Blackmail would certainly fall into that category. The bottom line is I'm not saying you're right, and I'm also not saying you're wrong. We need a look at that notebook before we can make that determination."

Awesome. That's not a no. "Can I go get it?"

"No!"

Wow. All of them at once? Did they practice that or something?

Chief Cunningham clears his throat and says, "Your dad and I are the ones who need to do this. We are, after all, the official investigators on the case."

Oh, man. Just when I thought I was gonna get to do something fun.

14

RICK

FOR THE REST OF THEIR breakfast, Alex continued to speculate on the notebook and what might be in it. Like a virus spreading through a crowd, her enthusiasm gradually infected each of them until even Adam seemed anxious to get on with the search.

"Go, you two," Marquetta said when they'd finished eating. "I know you're dying to see what's in that room."

Before he stood, Rick clamped a firm hand on Alex's shoulder. "You, kiddo, stay here and help your mom and Lydia. I'll let you know what we find out."

Feeling slightly guilty for not helping with the dishes, Rick pulled out his master key and stood. Adam followed him upstairs. They turned left at the second-floor landing and walked quietly down the hall to the Admiral's Suite. Rick knocked first, then sheepishly looked at Adam. "Habit." He slipped his key into the lock and opened the door.

As the largest of the rooms at the B&B, the Admiral's Suite had its own separate sitting area. The space also served as the entryway to the room. An overstuffed chair with an intricately carved mahogany back and patterned sateen upholstery faced into the seating area, which included a small matching couch, a coffee table, and two smaller chairs. Like most of the furnishings in the rooms, these had been picked out by Rick's grandfather during a massive remodel a few years before his death.

Adam sighed as he gazed at the furniture in the seating area. "Captain Jack liked his dark woods, didn't he?"

"Yes, indeed. I've heard plenty of stories. I believe what Marquetta's told me the most. I'm convinced she's got the most accurate version. He remodeled the entire place for a woman he wanted to impress."

"Francesca." Adam nodded. "I've heard she loved antiques. I can see where she'd have liked this. It's kind of dark for my taste."

"I agree. We can't replace it. Not yet, anyway. We're focused on paying off the mortgage he took out to do the remodel. About the time we get that paid off, we'll probably have to do it all over again." Rick scanned the room. There were papers strewn everywhere. One corner of the bedspread had been pulled down, exposing only the top corner of the sheets. "How odd. Other than that turned-down corner, the sheets look like they haven't been touched since Lydia last made the bed."

"Seems weird because the rest of the room is such a mess," Adam said.

Rick nodded absently as he explored. "Mostly, it's just clutter. He was one of those guys who left everything out."

As near as Rick could tell, there were no stains, spills, or damage. In the bathroom, he inspected the combination shower/tub. He had to admit that Captain Jack, or whoever had picked out the tiles, had done an excellent job of coordinating colors. The diagonal pattern of beige tiles with dark and light green two-by-two-inch tiles interspersed throughout created a soothing elegance that guests who stayed in this room mentioned during their stay.

"That's all it is," Rick said as he finished his inspection. "Just clutter. I guess the guy wasn't destructive, just kind of messy. I don't see the notebook on the desk. That's where Lydia said it was. Right?"

"That's what she said. I've been looking around while you were checking things out. The only thing of any significance on the desk is the laptop. Has anybody been in this room?"

"It wouldn't have been one of us. Alex just found out about Welles, so she didn't have time to snoop. It certainly wasn't Lydia or Marquetta. None of the other guests had a key, so it had to be here. Unless...he didn't have it on him, did he?"

"No. We inventoried all of his possessions. There was no notebook. I'll check the sitting area. Why don't you look around the rest of the room?"

"Will do." Rick started with the nightstand on the turned-down side of the bed. Welles had left several personal items on top of the nightstand, including a comb, a sealed package of hand wipes, and a charging cord for a laptop. He skipped down to the top drawer. The only thing in the drawer was a prescription. He read the label. "Adam? Have you ever heard of a prescription medication called aripiprazole?"

Adam stopped his search of the seating area, shook his head, and held up his hand. Rick tossed the bottle to him. Adam read the label, made a face, then said, "I'll bet the ME knows. We'll call when we're done."

Rick moved on to the dresser. In one drawer, he found an envelope from a brokerage firm. Other than that, the only things he found in drawer after drawer were clothing and a few other personal items. No notebook. Surely Lydia wouldn't have mixed up her rooms, would she?

Moving on, Rick checked the closet. It was the same story there. His only other discovery was something he already knew —Welles had expensive taste in clothing. Even his tee shirts had come from high-end shops. From shirts and slacks to shoes, there wasn't a cheap item in the bunch.

"It appears our Mr. Welles liked designer brands," Rick said. "Did you find anything?"

Adam held up a checkbook. "It also appears he had some money. His checking account has over ten thousand in it."

"There was an envelope in the dresser from a brokerage. Maybe it's got a statement." Rick returned to the dresser and pulled out the envelope. He whistled as he scanned the transactions. "You might want to revise that assessment. Between all of these accounts, it looks like he's got more than five million with this brokerage. Based on the transactions, the guy had a substantial income. The smallest deposit I see is about ten grand."

"So, who was your Mr. Welles, Rick? Did he run a business? Or, maybe the munchkin's not so far off. It looks like we could have two possible motives—money and this missing notebook."

Rick handed the brokerage statement to Adam. "You should probably take this into evidence."

"Along with everything else. We'll inventory it all. We can put his clothes in the suitcase and box the rest. I want to make sure we don't miss anything."

"I'll go downstairs and see what I can find. You want me to bring up a notepad? Something bigger than that little thing you use all the time?"

Adam patted his breast pocket. "Nope. Might be the only lesson of any value I learned from my predecessor. Have something to write on wherever you go. Instant documentation."

"Sounds like a good system. Be right back."

As Rick descended the stairs, he thought about his interactions with Snappy Welles. The man hadn't been very nice. Was that how he got ahead? Made his money? Was he a vicious businessman? Or a shrewd investor? From the looks of that brokerage statement, maybe all of the above.

The minute Rick walked into the kitchen, Alex was right there waiting for him.

"What'd you find, Daddy? Did you find the notebook?"

"No. It wasn't there," he said resignedly.

Lydia did a double take and stared at Rick. "What? That's impossible. It was sitting there, right on top of the dresser."

"You're sure? The Admiral's Suite?" Rick asked.

"Of course, Rick. I wouldn't mix up my rooms."

"There was no notebook on or in the dresser, and not in the seating area either. The fact that it's missing tells me it probably would have been helpful. We're going to inventory all of Mr. Welles's effects. I need a box big enough for his things."

"You're in luck," Lydia said. "I just unpacked a shipment we got this morning. I put the boxes in the laundry room and was going to break them down. I'll get you one."

While Lydia was gone, Rick pulled a pad of paper and a pen from the desk. He instantly recognized the logo on the box Lydia brought back. They received one of those boxes every other week from a restaurant supplier in San Ladron. The shipment always included coffee and tea supplies, napkins, and condiments like sugar and creamer. "Thanks, Lydia. All right, you three, I'm on my way back to the Admiral's Suite." He handed the pad and pen to Lydia. "Write down everything you remember from when you were in that room. I'm starting to wonder if someone somehow got in there."

While Lydia wrote, Rick headed back upstairs. He found Adam packing Welles's clothing in the suitcase, his small notepad on the nightstand at his side. "Good. You can sort. I'll make a list," Adam said.

They went through all of Snappy Welles's personal effects. Clothing went in the suitcase; everything else was added to the box. By the time they were done, they had an extensive list of every item in their possession that had belonged to their victim.

Just as they were doing a final inspection of the room, Adam's phone rang. He checked the display, and his eyes lit up. "It's Doc Turner. I left a voicemail for her while you were downstairs." He punched the button on his screen. "Hey, Doc. You must have gotten my message."

As he listened, Adam's brow furrowed. At one point, he said, "No, we didn't find anything like that." After listening for another minute or so, he said thanks and hung up.

"Well?" Rick asked.

"That medication is an antipsychotic. He could have been undergoing treatment for bipolar disorder. If Welles was on that medication, it probably would not be the only one."

"So we should have found other meds?"

"Sounds like it."

Adam returned the phone to its holster and looked around the room. Rick followed his gaze. They'd gotten everything. There were no other personal items. From clothing to electronics to the one pill bottle, they'd gotten it all. They'd been over every inch. There were no other meds, not even a stray pill.

"Doc Turner thanked me for telling her because it's possible it could cause a false positive for amphetamines. She'll have preliminary results tomorrow. If she has to do further testing, it could take a few weeks. You know what that means, right?"

"Yeah," Rick sighed. "Finding out what happened to Welles is all on us. It's you and me again, pounding the pavement and digging into the victim's life."

"We should start with the ones that knew him—his so-called friends."

"I'm beginning to wonder if they're not more like mortal enemies. I'm also wondering if one of them broke in here and stole that notebook."

Adam walked back to the door, opened it, and inspected the lock. "There's no sign of forced entry."

"I know," Rick sighed. "Whoever got in here would have needed a key."

"And Welles had his on him when we found the body."

"Which means Welles must have had the notebook on him when he was killed. Do you think someone would have killed him to get that?"

Adam tapped his finger on his chin and gazed back into the room. He grimaced, then took a long breath. "I guess it all depends on what was in it. I want to get this back to my office before something else goes missing. Would you talk to your guests? Make sure they don't leave town until after we interview them."

Rick snorted. "And here I was, looking forward to them leaving."

15

RICK

RICK SAT AT THE HEAD of a table for six he'd set up in the middle of the dining room. The remaining five Band of Six members sat around the table. Their expressions portrayed a range of emotions—curiosity, irritation, and maybe even trepidation.

"Thank you all for coming down here on such short notice," Rick said, then watched closely as he delivered his next words. "The reason I wanted to talk to you was to let you know that Mr. Welles died last night."

Several muttered quietly, "What?"

The reaction he found most interesting was Liz Ravel's. She sucked in a breath, covered her lips with her hand, and her eyes brimmed with moisture. Her voice cracked with emotion. "Snappy's dead? When? How?"

Once again, it sure seemed like there was more going on between her and Welles than just friendship. Could there have been a romantic relationship between the two of them? Was that why her husband had gotten so angry the other night at dinner?

"There was an auto accident," Rick replied. "The Chief of Police has asked me to let you all know at once and then speak with each of you privately."

All eyes around the table zeroed in on Rick. He braced himself for an onslaught of anger and was surprised when the only one who said anything was the man who'd been remarkably quiet so far. Carson Coulson shot back a terse, "Why?"

"We'd like to reconstruct Mr. Welles's actions after the dinner at the Crooked Mast. Our goal is to find the car that hit Mr. Welles."

"So it was a hit-and-run," Coulson stated flatly. "Fitting way for Snappy to go. I'd say."

A movement at the door caught Rick's attention. Alex had just walked by for the second time since he'd started this meeting. Knowing his daughter, she'd positioned herself where she could overhear everything that was being said. "One moment, please." Rick pulled out his phone and texted Marquetta, asking her to check and see if Alex was spying on this group. He got a quick reply, after which the butler door from the kitchen opened.

Marquetta planted her hands on her hips as she stood in the doorway. From the look on her face, Rick had been correct— Alex was up to her old tricks. Marquetta crooked her finger, and that was followed by a frustrated huff.

When Alex passed by the dining room on her way to the kitchen, she stuck out her tongue at Rick. It was all he could do to keep from laughing. Rick gave Marquetta a thumbs-up as she ushered Alex into the kitchen. Confident that Marquetta would have signaled him if there were any other spies, Rick continued. "One of the questions the chief wants me to ask each of you has to do with dinner at the Crooked Mast. It appeared quite contentious."

Barnaby Pauley barked out a quick, "That's an understatement."

A couple of the others murmured their agreement, and Brid Ochoa said, "It was always that way with Snappy."

"Excuse me for asking what might be a stupid question. Is Snappy a nickname?"

The three men at the table smirked and exchanged knowing glances. "I'll say," muttered Pauley.

"I assume it had nothing to do with the way he dressed," Rick said.

Coulson stifled a sarcastic laugh, and Pauley glared at him.

"Will you two stop acting like a pair of delinquents?" Liz Ravel barked.

This time, she was the one who became the center of attention. Each of the others stared at her, and she retaliated with a defiant glare. She huffed, "What are you all looking at me for?"

Brid Ochoa, who was sitting in the adjacent chair, put a gentle hand on her shoulder. "Come on, Liz. You knew him better than anyone."

Liz sighed, looked across the table at her husband, and grimaced. "I don't think Barnaby wants me to talk about this."

It wasn't the answer Rick had expected and further cemented his suspicions that Barnaby Pauley was a jealous man. And perhaps with good reason. "There will be a lot of questions, Mr. Pauley. I need everyone's full cooperation."

"Is this a police investigation?" Pauley demanded.

"We are trying to find out who owned the car that hit the victim."

"Snappy Welles was never a victim. He's the one who victimized everyone else. You're right. It's a nickname. People started calling him that after he broke up with Liz. He was terrible to everyone. Especially her." Pauley stopped and fixed his wife with an irritated stare before he continued. "Anyway, behind his back, it became the standard joke. 'Here comes Snappy.' We all thought he'd get upset when he heard about it, but no, not him. Everyone was shocked when he didn't have a fit over being called that. The truth was that he liked it. It was like a badge of honor or something for him. After that, the nickname stuck."

"Are you saying he was proud of the fact that he wasn't nice to people?"

"That's not true," Liz protested. "He'd told me he didn't like the way he treated others. He claimed he couldn't stop himself."

"The man should've been on medication," Guy Silvan snickered. "They've got stuff to help people like that. Right?"

Rick waited for a reaction from the others. He was hoping one of them might reveal that they knew about the medication he and Adam had found in Welles's room. Not one did, not even Liz Ravel.

After a long silence, Guy scoffed, "What a bunch of wimps. It's no wonder he walked all over you."

Carson Coulson glared at Silvan. His British accent thickened as he ground out the words. "Don't sound so high and mighty, Guy. I did not see you walk away from the money."

"Shut up, Carson!" Brid shook her head. "You fool."

Rick did a double take. He looked directly at Coulson. "What money?" When the man looked away, and none of the others volunteered an answer, Rick hardened his tone. "What money?"

"Snappy was a very wealthy man," Liz said. "He was also very lonely. The truth is we'd all cut him off at one point or another because he could get so antisocial. Maybe because he couldn't keep us as genuine friends, he basically paid us to be his friends. He arranged this whole trip so we could do something 'fun' together."

The notion seemed preposterous to Rick. So why were all of them deliberately ignoring the others? They studied the tabletop or the ceiling or simply gazed out the window. Not one made eye contact, and that was enough to convince Rick he was on the right track. If they were all uncomfortable with the idea, it probably was the truth.

"Are you talking about the Silver Gulch tour, Liz?"

Liz cleared her throat, then murmured, "Not just the tour. The trip."

"This entire trip was being paid for by Welles?" Rick asked. No sooner had the words come out of his mouth than he realized the answer was right before him. Of course. The reservations had all been made by Liz Ravel, and they'd used Welles's credit card to pay for the rooms in advance. He'd always assumed the others had made arrangements to repay Welles individually.

"This was supposed to be our first trip together," Liz said. "Each of us had identified a passion of ours, and Snappy wanted to experience all of those. This trip was all about Brid's fascination with California's history. Our next one was to go watch Carson compete in a world archery contest." Liz glanced at Carson Coulson.

The man fidgeted with the bright red pocket square that stuck out of the breast pocket of his navy blazer. "I'm a professional archer. Snappy was one of my sponsors."

"Who are you kidding, Carson? He was your only sponsor." Guy Silvan leaned back in his chair and smirked at Coulson.

After a loud huff and a few words muttered under his breath, Coulson continued, "Snappy said he wanted to bring a cheering section for the Archery World Cup competition."

"I see," Rick said. Or, at least, he was beginning to. This entire relationship raised so many questions. Where did he even begin? "That's why you all put up with his abuse? Because you were being paid to?"

"God, aren't we a dodgy group?" Coulson snickered.

"Well put," Barnaby said. "We definitely take a medal for bottom feeders."

Nervous laughter circulated around the table. Rick didn't want to sound judgmental, but Paulson had hit the nail on the head. This group took the cake in so many ways. On top of it all, the mood around the table seemed less like remorse or shame than embarrassment over having been discovered.

"Liz, is that why you made all of the reservations? Because Welles was personally paying for all of your rooms? That was always the plan?"

Liz grimaced, then said, "Yes. I know that's not what I said when I registered. I kind of led you to believe Snappy was just paying to make sure we got all the rooms we needed. Sorry."

Rick contemplated Liz's reaction. Her regret seemed genuine. And from a business standpoint, did it really matter who was footing the bill? It was only now that their roles had changed that it made any difference. "Liz, I'm not judging you or the others. At the time you booked, the only thing I needed to make sure of was that your rooms would be paid for. Now that this is a police investigation, we have to follow the money."

"Understood." Her voice faltered as she asked, "What else do you need to know?"

"You said this trip was all about Brid's interest in California history. If you were the one Mr. Welles was closest to, why didn't he start with something you wanted to do?"

"I refused. I told him I'd walk away from the whole thing if he didn't do everybody else first. Brid's my best friend, so I recommended he start with her, and he agreed."

Brid Ochoa sucked in a surprised breath through parted lips. "What? That's why we did this? And you didn't tell me?"

"I'm sorry."

Under other circumstances, Rick would have been happy to let these two talk this out. Unfortunately, the other-circumstances rule didn't apply now. He needed answers. Quickly. And this group had proven themselves to be professionals at taking conversations down rabbit holes. "You two can resolve this later," Rick said firmly. "Ms. Ochoa? Why Silver Gulch?"

"I'm a librarian, and I came across the history of Gentleman George when I was doing some research for one of our patrons. I also like physical challenges and individual sports. Most of my time off, I spend hiking. The concept of survival training kind of interests me, so when I read about the orienteering challenge, I thought it would be a great way to kill two birds with one stone. The problem was, it wasn't something I could ever afford to do, so when Liz told me Snappy's latest scheme, I figured, why not?"

"What do you mean, latest scheme?"

"We'd done things before. It was always something Snappy wanted to do. It was usually pretty boring. Like that dinner at the sky lounge in LA."

"And the Dodgers game," Guy Silvan said.

"And the opera," Liz added. "That was actually the last one where he chose the activity. After that fiasco, I told Snappy he needed to change things up. You know? I wanted him to ask what the others were interested in. That's when he decided to turn the tables on us and have us pick the things we liked."

In all his days of reporting on crime in New York, Rick had heard a lot of crazy stories. He'd talked to hookers, con men, and thieves. He'd even done a story once about paid online friends. Those all paled in comparison to this arrangement. Snappy Welles and his deal with the Band of Six was definitely the strangest thing he'd heard in a long time. And something told him there was more to this little arrangement than this group would willingly divulge.

16

ALEX

"AM I GONNA GET GROUNDED?" I ask.

Mom sits on the stool next to mine. The corners of her mouth turn up a little into a smile as she shakes her head. "You seem awfully eager to have that happen, Sweetie."

"No! I just thought...so why did you make me come in here?" That didn't come out right. I love it here in the kitchen. Especially when I'm working with Mom, she's made learning how to cook a lot of fun. She also says I could be a world-class chef someday if I wanted. "What I meant was that I just wanted to hear what the Band of Six was gonna say to Daddy."

"I know, Sweetie. I know. It's just that your dad and I are worried about you getting yourself involved in another murder investigation. You promised the last time that you were done with this sort of thing."

"I'm not investigating! I'm researching a story for the *Cove Talkers Newsletter*."

"And maybe figuring out who murdered Mr. Welles while you're at it?" Her eyebrows knit together, then her dimples disappear and her smile turns into a firm line.

Oh, man. She knows me way better than anyone else. Deep down, I guess that's what I really want to do. I scrunch up my face. Tug on my tee shirt.

"Alex, you're only thirteen, but you are getting older and need to start thinking about consequences. You nearly died the last time you got involved in one of these investigations. I couldn't bear it if something happened to you."

I shudder. Every once in a while, especially when I'm alone, I can still feel that man's hand on my arm. The rush of fear when he grabbed me. I realize I'm trying to rub away the feel of his grip when Mom takes my hands in hers.

Her eyes are kinda sad as she looks at me. "It still bothers you. Doesn't it?"

The legs of an imaginary spider crawl down my back. They send a shiver down my spine, and I can't look at Mom. How many times had she warned me? I whisper, "Yes."

Then, her fingers are under my chin. She's lifting my face. Looking into my eyes. Instead of anger, I see worry. Or maybe she's sad for me. "Your dad and I don't want to stop you from following your passions. We also won't let you do something if you're exposing yourself to danger."

"But Daddy helps Chief Cunningham. Why can't I?"

"For starters, your dad is working with Adam at the mayor's request. And Adam's there to protect him. Besides, do you really want to be a policeman? You do realize you don't just get to be a detective right away. Don't you? Adam spent years reading water meters and writing parking tickets. He only got to be chief of police because he got a lucky break. Is that really the life you want?"

"Well, yeah. I don't wanna read water meters. That sounds boring."

Mom laughs. "Funny. That's what Adam always said. And he hated writing parking tickets."

Now it's my turn to laugh. "So if I just stick to reporting, you'll be okay with it?"

"As long as you're not putting yourself into dangerous situations."

I look over at the stove. Mom taught me to make my first grilled cheese sandwich there. It was an epic fail—and my dad still ate it. He said it was good and that I'd gotten it extra crispy. Who would do that except a dad? I know he'll support me no matter what I want to do. I know Mom will, too. It's just so hard to decide. How do you figure out your life when you're just a kid?

"Sweetie? Look at me." Mom puts her finger under my chin again and smiles at me. "You don't have to make any big life decisions yet. You've got years before you'll have to do that. What I do know is that you're just itching to look into the Band of Six. Right?"

I nod.

"And you know a lot about social media. Right?"

"For sure."

"So what do you think you could do to help you write your story? Assuming that's what you want to do."

I get it. I could do what I've done before. "So it's okay if I check them out online?"

"You just need to do it in a way that they don't know about it."

"No problem. That's easy."

Mom bites her lower lip and fingers the necklace that me and my dad gave her. "There's one thing you need to think about. People say a lot of things online. Things they don't always mean. And sometimes, things they know are outright lies. You need to be able to sort out the fact from the fiction."

She's totally right. "How am I gonna do that? I don't know them. And if I only see what they post...."

"You remember what I've told you about gossip?"

"That repeating it can hurt people."

"And it's not always true."

"Oh." I draw out the word when it hits me what she's telling me to do. "You want me to check everything out so I don't print a lie."

"It's not up to me to make you check your facts. I want you to think about one thing, though. Don't you want your story to be accurate? Isn't that what your dad always used to do with his stories? Didn't you help him do that late at night?"

I scrunch up my face again. "I usually fell asleep. It was boring."

"You were four."

True. And now that I'm older, I can work on my own stories. And make sure I get them right. "I get it. Thanks, Mom. I love you so much."

We reach out and hug each other, but when she pulls away, she's got a worried look on her face. When I ask what's the matter, she hesitates, then blows out a breath.

"I probably shouldn't tell you this. It's something I overheard when the Band of Six first checked in. I don't know if it's of any value. It has to do with Carson Coulson."

Omigod, is she gonna give me a lead? "What is it?"

"Mr. Coulson didn't want to come on this trip. When I was taking him up to his room, I noticed that he had an unusual bag. I asked him what was in it, and he told me it was his archery equipment. He said that he should have stayed home to get in some practice rather than coming here."

"Oh." That's kinda disappointing. It's not much.

She pauses, looks toward the door, and lowers her voice. We're like the only two here. I wonder if maybe she's worried that my dad will walk in.

"He also told me that Mr. Welles was his sponsor and that he'd been forced to come here. He said he's had enough of Welles and wants to find a new sponsor. I asked him how hard it would be to do that. He claims it would be very difficult unless he could find a way to break his existing contract."

"Oh." This time, I don't sound disappointed at all. I get it. If Mr. Coulson got rid of Mr. Welles, he wouldn't need to break his contract. He might have had a big motive. "That could be huge."

"It could also be he wasn't telling me the whole story."

"Like when Billy Thornton tried to blame me for what happened at the mine and only told Mr. Boyd that I called him stupid."

"Exactly."

I look at Mom. She's smiling like she knows she's sparked my curiosity. "So if he didn't want to come here, why did he do it?" I ask.

"That will be for you to figure out. I suspect it had something to do with Ms. Ochoa because he made another comment that she'd 'talked some sense into him.'"

"Do you think there was something going on between Ms. Ochoa and Mr. Welles?" All of a sudden, I've got a million questions about their relationship, too.

"I don't know, Sweetie. Remember, I didn't tell you this so you could jump to conclusions. I told you so you could find the real story. Don't just make one up."

"You're right. I'm on it! Thanks for the tip."

Just then, the butler door opens, and my dad bursts in. He's shaking his head and looking super frustrated. When he sees us, he says, "Good. I'm glad you're together. We need to talk."

17

RICK

"WHAT'S WRONG, RICK?" MARQUETTA ASKED.

"When it comes to those people? Everything. I've never seen such a dysfunctional group of adults. Pauley, Silvan, and Coulson don't even want to be here."

"We got that impression." Marquetta shot an involuntary glance at Alex, then gazed at Rick. "I was also just telling Alex what Mr. Coulson said when I checked him in. I hope you don't mind."

"I guess it depends on what you were telling her."

"Snappy Welles was a corporate sponsor for Carson Coulson."

Rick shrugged. That was no big deal. "I just learned that myself. It's probably nothing, but it prompted me to call Adam. I just got off the phone with him. Alex, are you doing a *Cove Talkers* story?"

"For sure. Why?"

"Does it have anything to do with the auto accident or the murder?"

Alex shot a sideways glance at Marquetta, who shifted uncomfortably before turning her gaze to Alex. Rick's jaw tightened. It felt as though his heart had stopped beating for a moment. He'd guessed correctly.

"Well...."

"Let me make this easy," Rick said. "Adam agrees with me that we don't want you interfering in the investigation. It's just too dangerous."

"Daddy!"

"Hear me out. I'm not telling you to stay out completely. I know that's impossible. The other thing is Adam wants to harness some of your energy."

Marquetta's eyes widened. She started to say something but stopped when Rick winked at her.

"Huh?" Alex said, then stared at Rick.

Good. For once, he'd surprised her. It didn't matter if she wasn't thoroughly pleased with the option they'd come up with. At least it was a way to let her do something while also keeping her safe.

"We want you to see what you can find out about Mr. Coulson as a competitor in the World Archery competition."

Alex's eyes widened, and that made Rick chuckle. He held up his hands. "I know. How crazy does this get? You're getting a green light to do what we know you're going to be doing anyway. The stipulation is that anything you learn is relayed back to Adam and me. No exceptions."

"What about the auto accident? And the murder? I wanna write about that stuff for the *Cove Talkers Newsletter*."

"And you can. That's not a problem. We'll give you all the facts once we have them so you can write your story. You just can't do it before we wrap up the case." Rick noticed Marquetta holding back a smile. Matter-of-factly, he said, "What are you so pleased about? You know something."

"That's part of what I was telling Alex. Mr. Coulson had quite a bit to say about Mr. Welles when he checked in. It seems odd to me, especially because there appears to have been no love lost between the two of them."

"He told you that?" Rick looked at Marquetta, once again amazed at how much information she got out of people. "It was like pulling teeth to get what little I got. Well, did you also know that the rest of the Band of Six were on the payroll?"

"Whose payroll? Are they his employees or something?"

"More like, or something. From the little I got, it sounds like all of them were being paid to be friends with Welles."

"Excuse me?" Marquetta gaped at Rick.

"You can do that? That's awesome!" Alex broke into a grin that went from ear to ear. "You mean, I could, like, have a job being somebody's friend?"

"That's a thing?" Marquetta asked.

"In answer to your questions, yes and yes. You've both seen how difficult Welles could be. From what I can tell, the man didn't have real friends, so he started paying these people to do things with him. They've gone to dinners and baseball games. This trip was because Brid Ochoa is interested in California history."

Rick could almost see the wheels turning in his daughter's head. And when Marquetta looked at Alex, he was sure they were thinking the same thing.

Marquetta pointed a finger at Alex and said, "Don't you even consider the possibility of becoming someone's friend for money."

It was Rick's turn to suppress a smile. She'd beat him to the punch.

"Why? It sounds like fun."

"Because you're letting someone else control your life. Believe me, Sweetie. You might think it sounds fun today, but look at what these people have been putting up with."

"Marquetta's right, kiddo. I'm telling you, this group is dysfunctional."

Alex frowned and cocked her head to one side. "What's that?"

"Messed up," Marquetta said. "They've let Mr. Welles completely ruin their lives. At least, temporarily. And look where it got them. Someone killed their meal ticket. Now, I'll bet none of them know what to do. Besides, who would you rather hang out with? Sasha and Robbie? Or Billy Thornton because he paid you money?"

Alex made an ugly face. "Billy Thornton doesn't have any money."

"Maybe not today," Marquetta said. "Who knows? Maybe he's got a rich uncle. Kind of like when your dad inherited the B&B. What if he suddenly wanted to pay you to hang out?"

"Ewww. No way."

Thank goodness for Billy Thornton, thought Rick. He made such a great example. "Just focus on being you, kiddo. Both Marquetta and I want you to be true to yourself. Don't let someone else take over your life or make decisions for you."

"It does sound kinda messed up. And I wouldn't want to be friends with Billy Thornton no matter how much money he had."

"Exactly, Sweetie. Now, I think it's best if you tell your dad what we agreed to before he came in."

As Rick listened to Alex explain what she was going to do, he realized that her involvement could save him and Adam some time. If she found something, she could point them in the right direction. In a way, it was like letting her scout the trail. "Okay, that goes along with what we were thinking," he said when she finished. "I'll tell Adam we're all on the same page."

"Rick, this whole friend arrangement doesn't sound remotely normal. How did Mr. Welles find five other people to go along with this?"

"You're asking a very good question. And one I don't have the answer to yet. It struck me as a very strange agreement. At some point, we need to look into the others. If Welles was paying all of them money, maybe they've all got some sort of secret that they're hiding."

"Do you think he was blackmailing them, Daddy?"

"There's one problem with that theory, Alex. If Welles was blackmailing the others, why would he be paying them? No, there's more to this whole arrangement than meets the eye. I have a feeling that it's all somehow tied to Welles's death."

"Unless Mr. Welles got into an argument with someone after he got hit by that car. Maybe the owner?" Marquetta raised her eyebrows. "Have you considered that?"

"We're considering all options at this point. I'm not saying the Band of Six are all suspects. What I'm saying is they all had a very curious relationship with Welles that might shed light on his life...and ultimately, his death. Right now, I have to call Adam."

Rick pulled out his phone and dialed. Adam answered almost immediately. After Rick explained the agreement he'd come to with Alex, Adam said, "See? Told you it would all work out."

As far as Rick was concerned, 'working out' was a relative term. He still wasn't so sure this little plan of Adam's wasn't going to backfire. "We'll see."

"Right. And if she does well with Coulson, we can consider having her do some checking on the others."

What? That wasn't what they'd agreed to. They'd talked about letting her do this on one person. Rick turned away from Alex and Marquetta and lowered his voice. "What are you doing, Adam? We agreed on Coulson. That was it."

"Sorry, Rick. Mayor Carter showed up, and I made the mistake of telling her what we'd decided. She thought it was wonderful and told me she wanted to expand it to the rest of the Band of Six."

Rick groaned. Francine Carter. Of course. A truckload of enthusiasm, and not always a lot of caution. "I need to talk to her. My first concern is my daughter. I don't know if I can go along with this."

"I know what you want to do, Rick. Let it go for now. I got her off of charging full speed ahead, and if we can wrap up the investigation quickly, you may not need to get into it with her."

It was true. Conversations with the mayor seldom went well. Francine was almost an unstoppable force, with the important qualifier being the word 'almost.' As long as you had leverage, Francine could be stopped. So, for now, Adam was right. It was best not to disrupt the agreement he'd achieved. He'd wait. Unless the mayor pushed for Alex to be more involved. In that case, he'd do whatever he needed to make sure his daughter wasn't exposed to danger.

"What do you want to do next, Adam?"

"Let's start by talking to Francine about the altercation she saw in front of her shop. Can you meet me at Scoops & Scones in ten minutes?"

Finally, something that wasn't involving Alex. The trick would be making sure they steered the conversation away from Alex altogether. "Sure. See you then."

18

RICK

THE TINKLING OF THE MINIATURE bell attached to the front door of
Scoops & Scones felt almost like the clanging of the bell in a
boxing match. This was one of Alex's favorite places in town. It
was a fact Mayor Francine Carter knew well. It seemed obvious
to Rick that Alex's palate was maturing. She'd started branching
out into a wider variety of flavors, another behavior Francine
had noticed on previous trips. This was not a tasting trip or a
social call. This was strictly police business. Nor was it an
opportunity for the mayor to recruit Alex to do more police
work.

"Morning, Madame Mayor," Rick said as he entered.

Francine Carter looked up from the box she was wrapping
and returned the greeting in her usual piccolo tones. "Oh, hello,
Rick! To what do I owe the pleasure?"

"Adam was going to meet me here. He said something about
you seeing a confrontation."

Just then, the bell tinkled again, and Adam strode in. "Sorry,
I got a call from Mrs. Cantwell on my way out."

"How is Flora?" Francine asked in what sounded like an
almost gleeful tone. "As obnoxious as ever, I presume."

"She was calling to tell me that Tommy Cat found his way
home." Adam glanced at his watch. "In the one hour and fifteen
minutes since he disappeared."

Francine rolled her eyes. "That cat has cost this town far too much money. I should just hire a catnapper and make him disappear for good."

"Now, now, Madame Mayor. She's one of your constituents."

After giving them an evil smirk, Francine lowered her voice. "That old bat hasn't voted in years. Every time an election comes around, that stupid cat goes missing." Francine shrugged. "Worrying about her is just too much bother. Let's talk about the important matters at hand. Rick, you mentioned a confrontation. Are you referring to the one between those guests of yours?"

"Yes. Did you get their names?"

Francine patted the back of her perfectly coiffed curls and pulled her shoulders back. "Of course. One was Snappy Welles, and the other was Barnaby Pauley."

Rick's first thought was that he was glad it hadn't been Carson Coulson. Then again, Pauley? Seriously? Maybe he should be the next person they talked to. "Was this just something verbal, or did it get more serious?"

"I dare say I'm sure it would have become more serious if I hadn't intervened!" Francine actually bent her knees, crouched down, and clenched her hands into fists. "As sure as I'm standing here, those two men were ready to engage in fisticuffs."

Oh, brother. Francine did love her drama. "But they didn't actually strike each other. Right?"

"No. They did not. As I said, I stopped them."

"I guess it's a good thing you were there." Somehow, Rick kept a straight face as he delivered the compliment, knowing that the trick to getting more out of Francine was always one part acquiescence and one part massaging her ego. Unless he was mistaken, he suspected the answer to his next question was going to be a solid yes. It would just take a bit of urging to get there. "Did you, by any chance, hear what they were arguing about?"

Francine forgot about the boxer's stance and looked away. She rolled her eyes and acted as though she wasn't sure how to answer. "Well...."

"It would certainly help our investigation," Adam said. "You know how valuable that type of information can be."

"I might have...heard something. But it's not because I was being nosey. They were just being so public about everything."

Rick shot a glance at Adam, who sighed and grimaced before he said, "Nobody's calling you nosey, Madame Mayor. And I'm sure you're right. If they were arguing on the street, who knows how many others might have overheard them? And as a witness to a potential incriminating incident, you have a responsibility to report what happened."

"Since you put it that way." Francine pursed her lips, seemed to notice that Adam had his notepad and pen at the ready again, and smiled to herself. She lifted her chin slightly and enunciated her words clearly. "The upshot of it is that Pauley's company is going broke, and he was trying to get more money from Mr. Welles."

Too late, Rick realized he'd failed to hide his shock. His mouth was open, and Francine was smiling at him, obviously pleased with herself. "Barnaby Pauley is already on Welles's payroll, and now he wants more money? How deep in debt is this guy?"

"Deep," Francine said smugly.

"Are you sure? How do you know that?"

Francine fingered the back of her neck and gazed at the ceiling. "Oh. Alright. Since you insist. I heard from Michelle at the bank that Pauley went in to get cash. He tried to write a company check. When she verified the funds, he didn't have enough in the account to cover it. Michelle said that Pauley was embarrassed and got very flustered. He rushed out and said he'd get the cash elsewhere." A moment later, she added, "It wasn't even that much money."

Rick noted that while Adam made notes about Francine's statement, every now and again, there was a glimmer of skepticism in Adam's expression. He also wondered how much of what they were hearing was fact and how much was conjecture. Between Francine's tendency to embellish and the fact that he didn't consider Michelle the most reliable witness, there was a lot to wonder about with this story. However, if Pauley's check had bounced, then maybe he had gone back to Welles. "You're saying this argument between Pauley and Welles was because Pauley wanted to borrow money, and Welles refused?"

"Indeed! From what I heard, Welles believed Pauley mismanaged his company and his money. He called him a 'ridiculously inept businessman' and threatened to cut him off."

"That certainly sounds like something Welles might say," Rick said. It also sounded a lot like a motive for murder.

Adam nodded and added, "Was there anything else, Madame Mayor?"

"There was, Chief. Pauley became very irate and made his own accusations against Welles." Before either of them could say a word, Francine held up her hand with her fingers splayed. "I know. You want to know what he said. He called Welles a terrible excuse for a boyfriend. When Welles asked what that meant, Pauley claimed he'd never let money come between him and his wife like Welles had."

"Wait. What?" Rick blurted. Had Liz Ravel been with Welles before? Was that why she was so familiar with him? "Welles and Liz Ravel were a couple?"

Francine's eyes widened, and Rick detected the hint of a smile as she spoke. "Apparently. Yes. From the sounds of it, those three had quite the convoluted relationship. They are, or were, quite the *ménage à trois. N'est-ce pas?*"

Adam nodded while he made another note. Rick wished that he had a notebook so he could hide, too. "More convoluted than I realized. Was there anything else?"

"That was when Welles said he didn't need Pauley as a friend and that he was going to cut him off. I was just sure the two were going to get into a fistfight on the street right then and there. I marched up to them and told them to stop acting like juveniles, or I'd call the police."

"What did they do?"

"They stormed off in opposite directions."

Adam lowered his notepad and said, "And the next thing you know, they're all at dinner at the Crooked Mast, after which Welles is murdered. It sounds like Mr. Pauley has some explaining to do."

"It does," Rick said. "The thing is, Pauley wasn't the only one who was upset with Welles at that dinner. It was all of them. I do have to wonder about Liz Ravel, though. I had no idea she had once been Welles's girlfriend."

"If that's what they were," Adam countered.

"You should talk to this Ms. Ravel and Mr. Pauley immediately," Francine said.

"We intend to, Madame Mayor. Rick, why don't we start with Ms. Ravel? I'd like to have a little more background on this relationship between her and Welles. That way, if Pauley tries to hide something, we'll know about it."

Francine's eyes lit up, and she raised her hands to her sides. "Oh, that's brilliant. I love it when the devious minds of law enforcement get one step ahead of the criminals!"

How tempting it was to remind Francine that this was not a TV mystery. Of course, trying to tell the mayor anything was like trying to herd cats—nice in concept, almost impossible in practice.

19

ALEX

IT'S AWESOME THAT CHIEF CUNNINGHAM wants my help. I'm gonna do the best job possible. This is my chance to show my dad how much I've learned. I totally want to make him proud, so I'm gonna follow our motto here at the B&B. Always excel. My dad says you always gotta have a plan to do that, and I've got one!

Mr. Coulson's social media profile wasn't hard to find. There were only two people with the same name, and the other one looked like an old guy who was about a hundred years old. He was nothing like the man who is staying here.

It helps that Carson Coulson is into archery. There's no way there'd be more than one person with that name who does the same thing. Right? According to the profile, he's in some big world tournament coming up in a few months. And this Carson Coulson says that he expects to win the men's recurve competition. That's so much like Billy Thornton. Always bragging. Everybody in school knows he says a lot of stuff that's totally never gonna happen! I wonder if Mr. Coulson is the same way. Maybe I could find out how many tournaments he's won.

I do a search for international archery tournaments. The website that comes up first looks like it's some sort of national organization. There's a link on the site for tournaments and one for national results. Cool. That's what I want to know. How good is Mr. Coulson? There's one way to find out.

The link takes me to a page with results for different types of tournaments. There's one for National Recurve Men. That's the one he's gonna enter. Awesome. So what is it? I Google it. As soon as the page comes up, I get it. Recurve is a type of bow. This has been super easy so far.

The list is really long and it includes names of men from all over the country. I finally find Mr. Coulson at number 84. Seriously? There's no way he's gonna win. Why would Mr. Welles sponsor someone who's better at bragging than winning? I ought to ask my dad about it. He might know.

While I'm thinking about the sponsorship thing, I go back to Mr. Coulson's profile. There was a post I skipped over before. I start reading. It's not about archery at all. It's about the dinner at the Crooked Mast.

"That's so bogus," I say after I finish.

According to what he wrote, Mr. Coulson sent his dinner back because his steak was tough. Maybe I'm prejudiced because I like the Crooked Mast. In all the times we've been there, we've never had anything bad. I'll bet this guy's just super picky. Or maybe he likes being annoying. I know exactly how to see what happened at that dinner.

Mary Ellen Herbert was their server. She'd know for sure if there was anything wrong with the food. I'm gonna ask her what she thinks. There's also a post about their trip to the Silver Gulch mine. It totally sounds like that was another disaster. Except for Billy Thornton, everybody in school thought Mr. Boyd was super funny and cool. But Mr. Coulson says he was rude and annoying. Probably 'cause Mr. Boyd assigned teammates again. I don't think Mr. Coulson knows what teamwork is. Actually, that's not much different than the rest of the Band of Six.

My jaw gets super tight as I read on. It's nothing more than a rant about how Mr. Boyd put Liz Ravel and Brid Ochoa with Barnaby Pauley and how Mr. Coulson got stuck with Mr. Welles and Guy Silvan. It sounds like nobody got along, and they all argued. That made Mr. Boyd mad. He even chewed them out for acting worse than the group of kids he'd had there that morning. That's funny. We were better than the Band of Six!

The rant just goes on and on. It's totally ridiculous and makes me bite my knuckles to keep from yelling 'liar, liar' at my computer. I wonder if any of it's true. According to Mr. Coulson, it took like five minutes for that nasty Mr. Welles to start complaining. And then Mr. Welles said he was gonna work alone because he couldn't stand the others anymore. Does that mean he threatened to stop sponsoring Mr. Coulson? That he was gonna stop paying for him to compete? He probably would have cut him off as a friend. And that would have made Mr. Coulson want to get rid of him before he changed their deal!

There are six photos included in the post. The first one shows all of the Band of Six. Most of the others are of the teams, but there's one of a hillside. In the background are two people. When I zoom in on the photo, I can make out that it's Mr. Welles and Liz Ravel. Holy cow.

They're hugging each other. Could her husband have seen this? And how did they get together? They were on different teams.

Okay. This is my find. My lead. I'm also gonna check out Liz. I'll keep it on the down-low. My dad's not gonna be happy about it 'cause I might've just broken the case!

March 9

Hey Journal,

I got a big problem. I promised my dad I'd only investigate Mr. Coulson. That was before I found what could be a relationship between Mr. Welles and Mr. Pauley's wife. There's a photo of her hugging Mr. Welles. No wonder her husband gets so jealous. Just so I don't miss something important, I have an obligation as a reporter for the Cove Talkers Newsletter to look into it.

To get the right story, I'm gonna have to interview Mr. Coulson and Ms. Ravel. I'll bet I can get close to both of them without them getting suspicious. I'm gonna need to be super sneaky. If my dad finds out what I'm doing, he'll go apoplectic. Cool word, right Journal? I looked it up after I heard Ms. Ochoa say it. She was talking about her boyfriend with Ms. Ravel. She said he got super angry at Mr. Welles 'cause of how he was bragging so much about that new watch of his at the Crooked Mast. What do you think, Journal? Could Ms. Ochoa's boyfriend have gotten so angry that he killed Mr. Welles over the watch? Yeah. Maybe.

I have to go soon, but there's one more thing. I heard from Sasha that she heard from one of the other girls that she overheard Billy Thornton is out to get me after what happened at the mine. All I can say is Billy better watch out. If he tries to bully me, he's gonna be sorry!

xoxox

Alex

20

RICK

RICK AND ADAM FINISHED THEIR conversation with Mayor Carter, then walked back to the police station. On the way, they rehashed what the mayor had told them and decided it was worth looking into a possible conflict between Barnaby Pauley and Snappy Welles.

"Barnaby Pauley had a couple of reasons to dislike Welles," Rick said as they passed The Bee's Knees. "For one, Welles wanted Pauley's wife to get a divorce and come back to him. Then again, maybe he wasn't even worried about the divorce. It could be that Francine's right. Pauley's business is going under, and Welles wasn't being very empathetic about it."

When they were in front of Crusty Buns, Adam stopped and gazed inside. "It almost sounds like Welles was cutting off a couple of his so-called friends. If these people were dependent on that money, the thought of losing that support system could have driven one of them to desperation. Why don't we see just how dependent they were?"

Rick followed Adam's gaze and realized he was watching Barnaby Pauley, who sat alone at one of the small tables toward the front of the shop. "You want to start with Pauley, not Liz Ravel?"

Adam shrugged, then winked at Rick. "Sometimes, buddy, you just gotta play the cards you're dealt."

Not when they're bad cards, thought Rick. He resisted the urge to say that, mostly because Adam had become a much better investigator since they'd started working together. In the beginning, Adam's lack of experience made him highly dependent on Rick. Gradually, he'd been venturing off on his own. Now, Rick supposed he'd better get used to the idea of Adam wanting to call the shots. He was, after all, the chief of police. And it wasn't a terrible call. What the heck? They probably should just seize the moment.

Barnaby Pauley was busy reading the screen of his phone as Rick followed Adam toward the table. It wasn't until they were standing about a foot away that the man seemed to realize he had company. "Oh, hey, Rick. And you must be...." Pauley leaned forward and eyed Adam's name tag. "Oh. Chief Cunningham. I heard that you two worked together on occasion. Since you're standing at my table, I guess this means you want to ask me some questions?"

"That's correct, Mr. Pauley. Rick and I are investigating the death of Mr. Welles."

Pauley shifted from one side to the other in his chair. Within a matter of seconds, he was frowning. "Is there something specific you wanted to know?"

Adam pulled out his notepad and pen, flipped open the pad of paper, and waited with the pen poised over the pad. "What was your relationship with the deceased?"

"We were, um, friends."

"That's all?" Adam quirked an eyebrow at Pauley.

Rick had to admit the man was looking extremely uncomfortable. Pauley forced a smile and looked up at Rick. "We were kind of business partners, too. You understand how it was. Right, Rick?"

Adam didn't wait for Rick to respond. His voice took on a more determined edge. "We've discussed your friendship arrangement, Mr. Pauley. I'm talking about your business. What was the nature of those business arrangements?"

"Mr. Pauley, we've heard how the two of you argued in front of Scoops & Scones," Rick said. "Don't be ashamed if you were having business problems or needed additional capital. It happens. That's nothing to hide—unless there's something else."

Pauley was immediately on guard. He leaned forward in his seat and peered at Rick. "Like what?"

"Were your business dealings with Mr. Welles legal?" Adam asked.

"Of course they were!"

"Then why are you so evasive, Mr. Pauley?"

Rick suppressed a smile. Adam had mastered the role of the small-town cop with zero tolerance for shenanigans. It felt good to let him show how irritated they both were with Pauley and the other members of the Band of Six. Even better, that irritation was having the desired effect. The man looked like he was ready to crumble. Rick leaned a little closer and tried to sound encouraging.

"Please, Barnaby. Just tell us the truth. I'm sure you don't have anything to worry about. Do you?"

Pauley took a sip from his mug, then nodded. "Alright. You already know that Snappy was paying all of us to be nice to him. As desperate as he was to not be alone, you would've thought the guy might've been nicer to people. From what I hear, each deal was different. In my case, he invested heavily in my business. Mostly, it was at Liz's urging. Snappy didn't want to help me. But he'd do anything for Liz. She was with him for a few years until she got tired of his focus on making money. He basically was going at it 24/7. The guy never seemed to take a break. Eventually, it drove Liz away."

Rick made a mental note, probably the same one Adam was writing down—each deal was different. He'd also noticed the tone of superiority when Pauley had said Welles's money interest had driven Liz away. The man was smug about it. Why? "How did you and Liz get together?"

"Right place. Right time. Liz was vulnerable. I've been in love with her since we first met. So when she dumped Snappy, I was there to pick up the slack."

Really? What was this, a work marathon or something? "That doesn't sound very romantic."

"Romantic?" Pauley snickered. "No. It never was, not with Liz and me. Everything was always a compromise. A negotiation. Unfortunately for me, I think the only man Liz ever truly loved was Snappy Welles. Maybe, now that he's gone, she'll start to get over him."

Rick and Adam exchanged a glance that said it all. If anything, Pauley was not helping his cause. In fact, based on what he'd just said, he had a strong motive to kill Welles. Rather than asking, though, Rick chose to come at the question slowly. "So, how long after Liz broke up with Mr. Welles did you two get married?"

"About three months."

"That was quick," Rick blurted.

Pauley's cheek twitched. He cleared his throat, then said, "Well. Maybe. They broke up last May, and Liz was feeling low. I got Brid and Guy to meet us for drinks. I told her I'd pick her up and drive her home. We went for a walk on the beach after drinks. That's when I got up the nerve to ask her out. At first, it was kind of awkward, but gradually we grew more comfortable with each other. A few months later, we decided we were good for each other and got married. It was a spur-of-the-moment type thing."

The whole thing sounded more like another business deal than a marriage to Rick. Not that he was an expert. He'd been too young when he married Giselle and hadn't realized what he was getting into. Rick's career and Giselle's had pulled them in different directions until they were living separate lives.

"Do you think this relationship with Liz is going to last?" Rick asked.

"Of course it is!" Pauley exploded.

Rick raised his hands in front of him. The relationship Pauley had described hadn't sounded much like love, nor did it appear he was willing to let that relationship be analyzed. "Sorry, Barnaby. That came out wrong. I didn't mean to imply anything about you and Liz. It's just that Mr. Welles seemed to be paying a great deal of attention to her." And she to him, he thought.

"Snappy never got over her. It galled him that she was with me and not him." One corner of Pauley's mouth curled up, and though he tried, he couldn't hide the smirk. "He couldn't stand that I had something he couldn't have."

The hairs on the back of Rick's neck prickled at Pauley's attitude. He sounded more like he was talking about his favorite toy than his wife, and, the more he bragged, the more he loosened up. And wasn't that what they really wanted? It was time to drop the formality and encourage the man to talk. Maybe even let him incriminate himself.

"I get it. Liz is a real catch, right?" Rick winked at Pauley and gave him a conspiratorial smile.

"Yeah. She is."

"So Welles was giving it another shot? Do you think he was trying to impress her by throwing his money around? Maybe make her miss the time she'd spent with him?"

"Of course. The man was an idiot, and Liz saw him for what he was." Pauley smirked again.

"And what was that?" Rick asked.

Pauley grunted. "Well, a spoiled brat with too few scruples and too much money."

"Some of which he invested in your business," Adam said.

"Which lets me out as someone who wanted him dead. I was getting more out of Snappy when he was alive than I'll ever see now that he's gone."

"Unless it wasn't money you were interested in," Adam said.

"What's that mean?"

Adam took a small step forward. His voice turned hard. "I'm wondering if you decided to eliminate him so that he'd stop going after your wife. You might have gotten a little insecure. It's entirely possible you decided that getting him out of the way was more valuable to you than his money. You might have decided to save your marriage, even if it would cost you your business."

Pauley's smug expression fell. His hazel eyes, which had held Adam's gaze moments before, suddenly flitted away. Hunted, thought Rick. He looks worried. Obviously, the man had realized his attitude—at least for the moment—had made him a prime suspect.

"No, no. It wasn't me." Pauley licked his lips as he stroked a three-day growth that did nothing to improve his looks. The only thing it did was make him look scruffy. "Chief...um, maybe I got a little carried away there. You guys kind of laid a trap for me. Don't you think?"

"You're the one who laid the trap, Mr. Pauley." Adam's voice held the same hard edge, and he hadn't glanced away after he'd made his accusation. "Where did you go after the dinner at the Crooked Mast?"

Pauley hesitated for the briefest moment. Rick wondered why the man had to think about where he'd been. It was when his eyes darted up to the right that any sympathy Rick might have had shifted to suspicion. Maybe he was trying to make something up.

"I went for a walk," Pauley blurted. "Liz was ticked off at me, so I just walked down to the harbor."

Adam nodded and jotted something on his notepad. He'd most certainly want to check on Barnaby Pauley's alibi, but a walk at the harbor would be almost impossible to verify that late in the day. Even if they couldn't verify the man's alibi, Rick wasn't so sure Pauley was their killer. From what he'd seen, unless Welles had told Pauley he was pulling out all his support, Pauley would never want something to happen to his cash cow. And then there was Liz's comment about her husband. He was starting to think that what she'd really meant was that Pauley didn't have the stomach to commit murder. Especially something as gruesome as strangulation.

"Barnaby, come on. Let's be honest. What about the others in your group?" Rick asked. "When we first met, you made a comment about them having a desire to kill Welles. Did any of them have reason to want him dead?"

After taking a moment to digest the question, Pauley swallowed hard. "I...I don't know. Maybe. There's always this underlying tension in the group. And Snappy, as you know, wasn't a very likable guy. He rubbed everybody the wrong way."

It was a smart answer, thought Rick. Point the finger at everybody and nobody at the same time. He and Adam had their work cut out for them.

21

ALEX

AFTER PUTTING AWAY MY JOURNAL, I lock my door and go to the top
of the stairs. From where I'm standing, Mr. Coulson's room is
down the hall. It's just a couple doors away. That's all. But the
idea of actually going into his room gives me an itchy feeling. It's
like I've got ants crawling all over me. I chicken out and go down
the stairs instead. Besides, my dad would totally ground me if he
found out I went into a guest's room to investigate. Right?

I don't wanna upset my dad or Mom, so I'm just gonna have
to talk to Mr. Coulson when he's not in his room. And I'm totally
fine with that. If I get lucky, he'll be in the living room sitting by
the fire or something.

My shoulders slump when I get downstairs and there's
nobody around. I can't even ask if anyone's seen him. Now
what? I check the dining room. He's not there, either. It looks
kinda like Lydia's been here recently. The carafes are all full, and
the condiments are stocked. There are plenty of tea bags and
sugar and everything else. Lydia must have been here. Maybe
she's seen Mr. Coulson. I'll bet she's in the kitchen.

When I push through the butler door, I'm disappointed
again. No Lydia. I groan and look up at the ceiling. "Why me?"

A second later, Lydia pokes her head out of the laundry
room. "Hey, Alex? What's wrong?"

Awesome! She's here. "I've been looking for you."

"I'm just finishing up with the towels. Come join me." She ducks back inside.

It looks like Lydia's got everything super organized. She's folding the last of the towels and has the others ready to be put away. "Hey, have you seen Mr. Coulson? I have a question about a story I'm working on for the *Cove Talkers*."

Lydia's eyes get wide. "That man is some kind of crazy, Alex. He brought a bow and arrow with him." She cocks her head toward the backyard. "He's out back shooting at targets he brought with him. He's barely wearing any clothes, too!"

I go to the window and look outside. What Lydia said about his clothes isn't exactly true. He's wearing a red shirt like golfers wear and khaki shorts. "He's dressed, Lydia. Some of the kids at school wear shorts all year long."

"Not me. I get too cold. It never gets that hot in Seaside Cove."

"That's true, but it never snows, either. That's one thing I do kinda miss about New York. It was always totally awesome when the first snow came. We had snowball fights and went sledding."

"Sounds like fun." The lines at the corners of Lydia's eyes crinkle as she gives me a little smile. "Do you miss it?"

Sometimes. It's been a couple years. And it all seems so far away now. I shrug. "I dunno. Maybe. It's just that there are so many things I like here."

Outside, Mr. Coulson takes an arrow from a holster thingy at his side. He's using one of those recurve bows. When he pulls back, it's in one smooth motion. He aims for a few seconds, then lets go. The arrow goes straight into the target.

Lydia leans closer to me and lowers her voice. "When the others were talking, they said he visualizes that the target is Mr. Welles! Can you believe it?"

"Really? Do they think he's like a psychopath or something?"

Lydia furrows her brow. Her eyes look sad. "Young people your age shouldn't know about those kinds of people."

"I know." The reminder gives me the creeps again. Lydia's right. Kids shouldn't know about crazy killers. I wish I didn't. "So what do you think? Is he?"

"I don't know, Alex. You shouldn't be alone with him. He could be dangerous."

"This is something I gotta do alone. If you want, you could watch from the kitchen window." Actually, I kinda hope she will. I'd feel better knowing there was an adult I can trust watching.

"How long do you think this will take?"

"Not long."

"Okay. Marquetta asked me to get a few things done, but I'm sure she'd rather have me make sure you're safe. You go talk to him. I'll watch."

"Don't let him see you!"

Lydia's lips curl up into a lopsided smile. She winks at me. "I understand."

As I walk out the French doors, I glance over my shoulder. Lydia gives me a thumbs up. Even though I want her watching, it's kind of embarrassing to have someone guard over me. It makes me feel like a little kid again. My heart is pounding like crazy. Thumping against my chest even though I know this is totally safe. Even though it's been months since I've done something like this, the memory of having a man want to kill me is still there.

From the kitchen, it was like watching someone shoot a bow on TV. It seemed so distant. Here, in the open, watching him slowly pull back the string and take aim, I feel more exposed. Almost like he could turn at any second and shoot me instead of the target.

He seems to concentrate longer this time, and when he finally releases his grip, the twang of the bow makes me jump. The arrow flies across the yard. There's a thud when it hits the target. It sinks deep. It's not a direct hit like one of the others. It doesn't matter. The sound still reminds me of death. I try to swallow my emotions, the fear that's building inside. What if that had been a person?

Mr. Coulson hasn't seen me yet. And I wanna talk to him before he shoots another arrow, so as he's reaching down to pull the next one out, I call out to him. He jerks his head in my direction. He's got a mean look on his face. I've seen it before. It's like he's angry. Or determined. To kill someone.

He lowers the bow to his side, and the look disappears under some sort of mask. "Sorry. I was quite focused on my target. Were you standing there long?"

"Not too long. You're really good, Mr. Coulson. I guess that's why you're in competition." I expected the compliment to make him happy. Maybe make him smile. Instead, he gives me a cold stare.

"You're Alex, right?"

Wow. Nothing. I didn't expect him to be so cold. Maybe Lydia's right. Maybe he is a psychopath. I nod. "I read about you online. You're like in a world competition. When did you start?"

He brushes back his gray hair with his free hand. All of a sudden, he gives me a friendly smile. That's something else psychopaths can do. Right? Switch on the charm. His brown eyes no longer look evil. They look almost friendly. "I've been practicing a long time."

"That's awesome. Is it something I could do?" Not that I have any interest in shooting arrows at targets.

He looks down at the bow hanging at his side. It kinda dangles from a string. He reaches up and rubs his palms together, then blows warm air on them. After taking a deep breath, he purses his lips and seems to relax a little.

"I was about your age, I suppose. I was having some problems in school. Couldn't get along well with other kids. One of my teachers told me about archery and offered to give me some lessons. Ever since then, I've been hooked. I love the fact that it takes complete concentration to do well. Archery is not one of those sports where you can phone it in."

A few minutes ago, he didn't even know my name. Now he's telling me about his whole entire life. I don't trust him. "I'm working on a story for the *Cove Talkers Newsletter*. Would you mind answering a few questions?"

"I take it that's your local paper?"

I give him what my dad calls the sanitized version of what the newsletter is all about. Mr. Coulson doesn't need to know that the newsletter can get super gossipy.

"Sure. I'm used to dealing with the press." He winks at me and adds, "Both big and small."

"Thanks, Mr. Coulson. How long did it take before you won your first tournament?"

"It was in college. I went to school on an archery scholarship. I was fortunate and had an excellent coach who saw my potential."

I'm not sure what to say next. How do I get him to talk about Mr. Welles? That's when I see the logo on his shirt. Welles Development. Awesome. "So, was Mr. Welles your sponsor?"

Mr. Coulson clenches his jaw, then glances down like he's trying to hide the look on his face. The anger is back. I can see it.

"You noticed the shirt," he says. "Snappy was my sponsor. What about it?"

"How does the sponsor thing work?"

"Why?"

"It would be good for the story. You know, background. The life of a professional athlete kind of thing. Most people don't know what it's like." Whoa. That was pretty awesome. I must be getting really good at this reporter thing. Then again, I can't tell from the look on his face. Is he gonna answer? Or not?

22

RICK

RICK WATCHED A GROUP OF three men who had been sitting at a table near Barnaby Pauley prepare to leave. The legs of their chairs scraped on the wooden floor as they rose. Though Rick and Adam were unfazed by the loud noise, Pauley flinched and gritted his teeth. Good, thought Rick. He even felt a small sense of satisfaction knowing that one of the Band of Six was getting a little taste of 'obnoxious' in action.

Popular with locals and tourists alike, the only time when Crusty Buns wasn't bustling with activity, the only time when it wasn't noisy, was when the store closed. Rick had thought it a terrible place to interview someone the first time he and Adam had done it. To his surprise, the commotion around them seemed to work to their advantage. Sometimes. This appeared to be one of those times.

Rick glanced around the restaurant, didn't see Liz Ravel, and said, "So tell me, Barnaby, where's your wife right now? I'm surprised she's not with you."

"She's with Brid. They went back out to that Silver Gulch Mine. Brid's really into California history." Pauley gritted his teeth, then continued. "She wanted to talk with Boyd since he's 'an expert' on the subject." Pauley made finger quotes in the air. "Personally, I think that Roy Andrew Boyd is spouting more nonsense than he is truth. It's not my place to tell Brid what's what. Let her figure that out for herself."

Rick looked at Adam, not sure if he'd see it as a valuable way to spend time or not. "Do you want to go out there and talk to her?"

"Sure. We can go check it out. Mr. Pauley, I may have more questions for you later, so don't leave town." Adam fixed Pauley with a determined stare. "Got it?"

"Am I a suspect or something?" Pauley stammered.

"Right now, you're just a witness, but I don't want to chase you all over the state to get answers. Do you understand?"

"Yeah. Okay. Sure. I guess we're here for another day anyway. Right, Rick?"

"Right, Barnaby. That you are." As he and Adam walked away, Rick thought Pauley was looking both scared and lonely. He waited until they were outside the store before asking, "How much of what he told us do you believe?"

"Not much. There's something not right with this whole arrangement between him and our victim. Why? Do you think he's being straight with us?"

"No. Not at all. I think he's only telling us part of the story. The part he wants us to know about. He's hiding something. In order for us to find out what that is, we'll need to dig up more information. Here we go again, peeling back the layers of the onion one by one. I wish there was a way to do it faster than one layer at a time, but I've never found one. My problem is that I've got new guests coming right after this group leaves, so we'd better dig quickly."

Adam shrugged. "I know. For now, let's just let Mr. Pauley sweat."

In less than fifteen minutes, they were nearing the end of the drive over a washboard dirt road. Rick chuckled at how the kids' voices had quavered as the car jounced along like a giant vibrating machine.

"What's so funny?" Adam asked.

"I was just thinking about Friday's drive out here with the kids. They loved this part of the road and played that old game of opening their mouths and saying, 'Ah.'"

"I did the same thing when I was a kid. Got the biggest kick out of it." Adam snickered as he gazed out the windshield.

Short as the drive was, it still felt like they'd traveled miles by the time they arrived at the small dirt parking lot for the Silver Gulch mine. There were three vehicles parked in the lot. A white Toyota Corolla, an old dark green pickup truck, and a black Ford SUV. "I recognize the white Corolla. It belongs to Liz Ravel. And that old pickup; wasn't it here the other day?"

"Yeah. It must belong to Roy. Which means he's got another customer. Let's hope he'll make himself available willingly."

Boyd making himself available turned out to be a nonissue. The man was busy chatting up Liz Ravel and Brid Ochoa while his other customers wandered the hills. "Mr. Boyd," Rick called out as they approached.

It took a moment for Boyd to recognize them, but when he did, he smiled and nodded. "Well, if it isn't the city slicker and the sheriff. To what do I owe the honor, gentlemen?" A wide grin spread across Boyd's face as he strode forward, his hand extended in greeting.

Both Liz and Brid covered their mouths to hide their chuckles. Rick was sure they wouldn't be yucking it up once they learned why he and Adam were here.

When Rick shook Boyd's hand, he found himself squeezing hard to prevent Boyd's iron grip from crushing his.

"I'll be darned," Boyd said. "Mr. Atwood, I didn't take you for a man with a solid handshake. That's pretty good for a city slicker. And you, Sheriff, you've got quite an impressive grip yourself."

"Mr. Boyd, you can call me Chief, or you can call me Chief Cunningham." Adam moved closer to Boyd until he was standing nose-to-nose. "But if you call me Sheriff again, you'll be calling your bail bondsman."

Rather than appearing intimidated, Boyd laughed and slapped his thigh. "Heck fire, Chief. I knew I liked you. And you can call me Roy. Both of you."

"Sounds good to me," Rick said. "We might have a few questions for you. However, we actually came out here to see Liz and Brid."

The color in Liz's cheeks drained, and she pulled back slightly. "Us?"

"You know they're going to want to talk to us, Liz. They'll want to know about our relationships with Snappy. Right, Chief?"

"Exactly, Ms. Ochoa," Adam said. "We'd like to speak to each of you individually."

Boyd screwed up his cheeks, raised his left hand, and wagged one finger as he spoke. "Chief? The ladies came out here to talk to me about California history, and Brid had a few more questions. Maybe we could finish our conversation while you talk to Liz."

"Oh, thank you, Roy! That would be great." Brid looked at Adam with a hopeful expression. "Please, Chief? Roy has so much information. I'd hate to miss the chance to pick his brain. If you want, Liz can drop me off at your police station. Is that okay? Can we talk there?"

Adam grimaced and scanned the area. "I guess we can make it work."

Rick followed Adam's gaze. He was right. While the distractions at Crusty Buns often worked to their advantage, Rick wasn't so sure about interviewing two witnesses in the middle of a quiet parking lot. Voices could carry. Body language would be easy to read. All reasons why this needed to be done before these two had more time to compare notes.

"Sounds like a good idea," Rick said. "Brid gets her time with Roy, and we get to speak with Liz."

Adam nodded firmly, then looked at Brid. "Sounds like a plan. Ms. Ochoa, we'll talk to you back at the station. You two can follow us into town."

"Wonderful!" Brid gushed, then promptly grabbed Roy Andrew Boyd by the arm and pulled him away. As they walked, she prattled on like an excited child in a toy store. "Now, Mr. Boyd. I have so many questions about how these old silver mines worked."

Liz laughed quietly as they left. "She gets so wound up over California history. You should have seen her the first time we met. I invited her to talk to my class because she had a program about early California she'd prepared for the library. She had my kids so pumped up with stories about stagecoach robberies and road agents that I thought I'd have to give them all a time-out."

"She does seem very enthusiastic." Rick noticed that Liz's earlier apprehension had faded. He hoped to keep that apprehension from returning by letting her talk more about a comfortable subject, so rather than launching straight into questions about her relationship with Snappy Welles or her husband, he decided a small detour was in order. "How did you hear about her?"

The corners of Liz's lips curled up, and she gazed over to where Brid was peppering Roy Andrew Boyd with questions. "There was a book I wanted to check out from the library. My local branch told me it would take a couple of days to get the book through an interlibrary loan, so I just drove across town to pick it up. When I walked in, I saw these posters about a program on early California. The clerk sent me upstairs to talk to Brid—she works in Reference. Anyway, she said she'd be delighted to talk to the kids. We really hit it off, so I asked if we could meet for coffee to strategize."

"And you two just kept meeting after that?"

"Oh, yes! We had such a great time talking that we decided to do it again. We've been friends ever since. Sometimes, it feels like she's the only one who really understands me." Liz craned her neck and let out a deep sigh. "Thank goodness for Brid. She helped me get through the breakup with Snappy. That's what you really want to talk about, isn't it? My relationship with him."

Rick nodded solemnly. "Unfortunately, it is. Tell me. Just out of curiosity, what was the book?"

"Healing relationships with the ones you love—or something like that."

"Was that for your relationship with Mr. Welles?"

"Yes. And, no, it didn't work. Snappy was always so focused on money. If he wasn't working on a scheme to actually make his next million, he was thinking about how to screw over the person he was dealing with. Quite honestly, it just got to be way too ugly for my taste. I began to hate who I was just because I was with him."

"When did that breakup occur?" Adam asked.

"It was almost a year ago, Chief."

"And you married Mr. Pauley a few months later?"

"That's right. I guess you might say I jumped out of the frying pan and into the fire. Brid can tell you. Marrying Barnaby was a huge mistake."

23

ALEX

OH, MAN. WAITING FOR MR. Coulson to answer my question is awful. My dad always said that once a source refused to answer one question, it got easier for him to say no to all the others. I cross my fingers, swallow hard, and wait.

After looking off at the ocean for a minute, he looks back at me and points a finger at me. "Let me tell you something, Alex. Everyone thinks professional athletes have this cushy life. That we train a little and spend the rest of our time going to fun parties and schmoozing. The truth is that your life isn't your own. You're at the beck and call of your sponsors, your agent, and even your fans. It can be very stressful and terribly draining."

Whoa. That wasn't what I expected. What's he want? A pity party because he gets to shoot a bow-and-arrow for a living? "Was Mr. Welles your only sponsor?"

"Yes. We signed an exclusive deal, and that was mostly at the urging of Liz. She was instrumental in getting Snappy to dole out some serious cash. I think he only did it because he thought it would help him win her back." He laughs. "Snappy never did figure out that Liz couldn't stand him anymore. She was just using him for his money. I can't blame her. In all the time they were together, he didn't pay attention to her. It was only after she got fed up with the way he was treating her and left that he even tried. He was wasting his time."

It sounds like they must have been friends for a long time. "How long have you known her?"

"About five years." He stops, thinks for a second, then says, "Almost six."

"Has she ever done anything to break the law?"

Mr. Coulson snorts, then laughs. "Are you kidding? Liz is as straight as they come. She's a schoolteacher, not a Mata Hari."

I don't know what that is. Not that it matters. What's important is that it doesn't sound like she'd break the law. "So why'd you all come here, Mr. Coulson?"

"That was all Brid and Liz. Snappy took the credit, despite the fact that they're the ones who arranged everything. Liz was the one who convinced me to come along. She said it was a way to 'do more together.'" He kind of sneers at the last words, like he thinks this is a waste of time.

"You didn't want to come?"

"None of us really wanted to be here except Liz and Brid. Those two just wanted more time together. I'm telling you, it's all part of the game. Once they convinced Snappy to pay for the trip, I was obligated."

"So Liz and Brid are really close?"

"Oh yeah. Between the two of them, they probably know everything about everyone in this little clique."

Awesome. If they have all the dirt on everybody, I should totally be talking to them. Even though my dad and Chief Cunningham are probably doing that, I bet I can get more out of them just by playing innocent. "Mr. Coulson, if you were gonna pick someone in your group as the one most likely to kill Mr. Welles, who would that be?"

He crosses his arms and gives me a Billy Thornton smirk. "Aren't you the little Nosey Parker?"

He snorts, then leans toward me. The look on his face is mean and makes my skin crawl. It's all I can do not to back up or wave to Lydia for help.

"So you want me to dish on the rest of the group, do you? Well, in my opinion...." He pauses to lick his lips, then says, "I don't think any of them could do it. They're all too weak and spineless. We're also way too dependent on Snappy's money. None of us wants to kill the golden goose."

Rats. That's not the answer I wanted. Somebody's got a secret they're trying to keep. A secret that's worth way more than money. So far, I haven't been able to figure out what Mr. Coulson's secret could be. That doesn't mean I won't. "What about Mr. Pauley? Or Mr. Silvan?"

"Guy Silvan is just a stick of dynamite waiting to explode. He's got a short fuse, but he's the kind who's all bluster and no action. If it came right down to it, he couldn't kill. And Barnaby Pauley wouldn't have done it because he knows Snappy dying would devastate Liz. "

"I thought you said she hated Mr. Welles."

"She does, but here...." He stops and pounds his fist lightly over his heart. "She's still in love with him even though she hates what he is and how he treats her. She doesn't want to be with him, but she can't help herself. It's truly a love-hate relationship." He takes in a breath and gazes at a passing wisp of fog. "You haven't asked me about one person, Alex."

Uh oh. He's got that smile on his face again. The creepy one. Do I dare ask? What'll he do? I shoot a glance at the kitchen window. Lydia's there. He can't do much 'cause Lydia will come to help me. "You're right. So? Did you?"

"If I had, why would I confess to you? Especially when you're being watched from the kitchen window."

Oh, snap! I never should've looked that way. Now what do I say?

"Don't worry about it, kid. I've heard about your reputation as an amateur sleuth. How you helped solve some other murders. Let's drop the pretense about an article for your little local rag and get to what you really want to know. Did I kill Snappy Welles?"

I've got those little creepy crawly spiders all over my back again. Or maybe it's just the cold from the wind. Or—who am I kidding? I can't show him I'm scared. I tell myself to be strong and forceful like my dad does when he's dealing with a difficult guest. Strong. Forceful. I also can't be threatening. I look straight at Mr. Coulson. "Did you?"

He nods to himself as he scowls at me. "You got gumption, kid. I'll give you that. This interview's over."

24

RICK

RICK HUNKERED DOWN IN HIS jacket against the chill from a gust of wind. Even though it was the middle of the day, wisps of fog were already drifting in from the ocean. He pursed his lips and watched Liz Ravel's face. Sure, he'd noticed the tension between her and her husband at the Crooked Mast dinner. And now that he thought about it, he'd seen it at other times. When they arrived, there had been darting glances. At breakfast, they'd often sat apart. No one incident had seemed significant at the time, but now that Liz was openly expressing her regrets about her marriage, it all made sense.

"I'm sorry, Liz. Are you leaving Barnaby?"

The world felt like it had gone silent as Liz's eyes misted over. Her jaw tightened, and she stared vacantly at nothing. Rick rubbed the back of his neck, a heaviness settling into his chest as Liz wrestled with an answer.

Overhead, a hawk circled. Floating on the air currents as it watched and waited for prey to appear. How patient they were. How silent. And deadly. The thought intensified the heaviness. He knew this was the right thing to do. Like all the others in the Band of Six, Liz Ravel was a suspect, and he dared not forget that fact.

Waiting wasn't going to work. He reached out and touched Liz's arm. "Are you okay?"

Her eyes glistened with tears. "You can't tell Barnaby this."

"He won't hear a word. This is a confidential investigation." It wasn't entirely true. He and Adam had often played one person's testimony against another's. In this case, he had a feeling what she was about to tell him was not about the case, and that was a different story. "Please. It might help us to find Mr. Welles's killer."

She bit her lower lip. Her head bobbed up and down quickly. "Okay. I was just thinking about how I got into this mess. I suppose I was on the rebound when I married Barnaby. No... that's not true. I knew what I was doing. And I think I was just trying to get back at Snappy. I wanted to make him jealous and show him that he wasn't the only man I could love."

No surprise there, Rick thought. Not given their previous conversation with her husband. She was carrying some sort of burden, though. And from what Rick could see, it weighed heavily on her. Could he get her to reveal it?

"Go on."

"It didn't work," she blurted. Rubbing her forehead with her fingers, she let out a derisive laugh. "Do you know what Snappy did when I told him I was going to marry Barnaby? He told me to go ahead. He said I'd be sorry. That Barnaby was a complete loser who could never satisfy me. I stormed out on him, but deep down...I think I knew he was right. There really was only one man I could love."

"Snappy Welles?"

Rick waited patiently as she seemed to ponder the question. Finally, she croaked, "Yes. I think I always will be in love with him. I pretended to be in love with Barnaby. I fooled everyone except myself." She shot a glance off to where Brid was chatting up Roy Andrew Boyd. "And Brid. She figured it out."

And her husband. He'd figured it out, too. Rick had seen it all too often on the crime beat in New York—a jealous spouse or lover turned into a killer by raw emotion. Had Welles died due to his involvement in some sort of weird love triangle?

"Does your husband know how you feel?"

"No," she shot back.

Really? Standing on the outside, her feelings now seemed so obvious. Either Liz didn't see that, or she just didn't want to give Barnaby credit. Then again, who was he to judge? He'd done the same thing with Giselle during their few years together. No wonder she seemed so angry with her husband most of the time.

"Liz, I appreciate you telling me this. It helps to explain a lot. You know, I was married once before. We were young and in love. She always wanted to be a Broadway star and chased her career relentlessly. After we had Alex, I stopped seeing the signs. The late-night meetings with producers—the rehearsals at odd hours. I also let my anger cloud my judgment. So, I'll ask you this—are you being honest with yourself? Do you really believe he doesn't know?"

She closed her eyes, squeezing them tight as she seemed to try and force away the truth. When she looked at Rick, there were tears in her eyes. "How could he not?"

"I think the truth is that we choose to lie to ourselves. My first marriage fell apart because my wife and I had different interests. So I understand how Barnaby might be so focused on competing with Welles that he forgets to see you or listen to you. Do the two of you ever talk about where your lives are going?"

She cast her eyes downward. Her laugh felt forced, as though her anger were simmering just beneath the surface. "We don't talk much. When I first broke up with Snappy, Barnaby tried to talk to me. The funny thing was that he never really understood me. His idea of consoling me was taking me out to do things. Since we got married, even that's stopped."

"Why did you two come on this trip together? Why not just come up here with Brid?"

"Brid couldn't afford it. That's why we needed Snappy. He could pay for it. Easily."

"What about your husband? He didn't want to come?"

"He didn't. It was only after he learned that Snappy would be here that he decided to join us." Liz laughed again and looked up toward the sky. "I think he was worried Snappy might try to get me back or something."

Rick nodded sympathetically. If only she could realize what her husband felt. Sadly, he felt he couldn't tell her. "Does Barnaby not trust you?"

"It's hard to know what Barnaby feels. He's always so closed off about things."

"I'm sorry to keep asking you about your relationship with Barnaby, but I think the two of you need to talk. Unless you've already decided to get a divorce. Have you?"

"Barnaby wouldn't want that."

"I wasn't asking about him. Would you?"

"I...don't know." There was a long pause during which a gust of wind kicked up a small dust devil out in the parking lot. Finally, Liz added, "If things don't get better...probably."

If he hadn't done the same thing with Giselle, he might not understand. Because of his own mistakes, he got it. Her inability to destroy a bad marriage in exchange for nothing made some sort of perverse sense. "I understand. Liz, do you believe that if your husband found out how you feel that he might hold it against Mr. Welles?"

"He might."

"How perceptive is your husband, Liz?"

"Not very. Obtuse would be more like it."

There it was, the blindness. He'd been there, done that, too. Once he'd figured out what had happened with Giselle, he hadn't given her credit for much of anything. It hadn't been his finest moment, but he hoped he'd learned from it. "If he had figured this out, do you think he might have had something to do with Mr. Welles's death?"

Liz blew out a long breath. This time, as she stared off into space, she clutched her arms around her as though she were cold. Her mouth opened, then closed. After that, her jaw set with determination as she studied Rick's face. "I think I'm not the best judge of what Barnaby is capable of."

It was the type of response Rick had been dreading. The shutdown. He'd get nothing more out of her now. In fact, it would be best if they kept the two women apart until they'd finished both interviews. Otherwise, Liz's shutdown might taint Brid's attitude.

"Adam, I think...."

"I know, Rick. Ms. Ravel, we're going to need to speak to Ms. Ochoa before we let you two go."

Liz shrugged and waved her hand in front of her face. "Brid already knows all of this. I just don't want any of it getting back to Barnaby."

"We'll do our best not to reveal anything unnecessarily," Adam said. "You should be aware that you have told us a few things that directly affect our case. We'll also be talking to Ms. Ochoa, which could bring us back to this subject."

Liz shot a glance in her friend's direction. "That's one thing about Brid; she'll give you her opinions straight up. It's one of the attributes I love about her."

"You two are very close, aren't you?" Rick said.

"I swear, she's my other half. It's like we have a sixth sense about the other one. We both know when something's not right. At this moment, I can tell that even though she's excited to be talking to Mr. Boyd, she's worried about me. She's probably wondering how much I'll tell you. And whether I held back anything."

"Did you?" Adam pressed.

"No. I told you everything. Be nice to her, please? She's the one person in our group that I can say with one-hundred-percent confidence didn't kill Snappy."

"Why is that?"

"She's too nice." Liz gave Adam a weak smile.

He cocked one eyebrow, then said, "One last thing. Where were you after the dinner at the Crooked Mast."

"I walked back to the B&B with Brid." She glanced over at her friend, then quickly added, "I was there for the rest of the evening."

Rick recalled walking through the living room when they'd gotten home from dinner. He hadn't seen either of them. Had they gone up to one of their rooms? "Were you with her the entire time?"

Liz's nostrils flared as she glared at Rick first, then Adam. "Are you suggesting I went back and killed Snappy?"

"We're merely asking you to account for your whereabouts, Ms. Ravel," Adam replied.

Liz stiffened, glanced over at Brid, and grimaced. "I get it. Everyone's a suspect. I was with Brid. The entire time."

Rick wanted to believe her. He even might have if it hadn't been for the way she'd avoided his gaze right after she'd said the words. Her action had him thinking the worst—could she be trying to provide an alibi for both of them?

25

RICK

LIZ SHIVERED AND RUBBED HER hands over the goosebumps on her arms. Her white, collared blouse with short sleeves was no match for what was turning into a chilly afternoon. She gazed over at the parking lot. "Why don't I wait in the car while you get with Brid? All this talk about Snappy has me feeling kind of depleted."

"I'm sorry this is so stressful for you," Rick said. "Maybe when you get back to the B&B, you can have a hot cup of tea. I'd suggest bundling up and going out to the rose garden. It's very soothing out there."

"I just might do that." Liz rolled her eyes. "Or maybe I'll just take a nap."

"There's always that," Rick said with a smile.

While Liz returned to her car, Rick and Adam approached Brid Ochoa and Roy Andrew Boyd. In some ways, Brid seemed the exact opposite of Liz. Where Liz had dark, curly hair, Brid's was straight with a little natural curl. Brid wore large glasses that gave her a very bookish appearance; Liz wore none. And Brid's pale complexion gave her an almost anemic appearance compared to Liz's caramel-colored skin. Despite their physical differences, the two were obviously fast friends. Two like-minded souls who had found each other. Rick only hoped this investigation didn't tear them apart.

"This little lady's done her research," Roy Andrew Boyd said with a wide grin. "It's nice to meet someone else with an interest in history."

"Oh, my gosh." Brid's face lit up as she prattled on. "Mr. Boyd is a wealth of information. Did you know that Wells Fargo stagecoaches alone were robbed nearly 350 times from 1870 to 1884? Fourteen years! I didn't realize they continued all the way up until 1916! Can you believe it? I have to put this into my presentation."

While Rick found her little information dump interesting and her enthusiasm infectious, their investigation had nothing to do with stagecoach robberies from more than a hundred years ago. "Brid, we need...."

"And Mr. Boyd was telling me all about claim jumpers. He said this mine was originally owned by a family who was running low on food. They had almost nothing left when they finally found a vein. On the way to the assay station, the Hasp brothers killed the husband and stole his silver. The man's wife and brother had nothing left, so they were forced off."

"The Hasps were a low lot," Boyd said, a healthy dose of irritation in his voice. "I've done my research, and I know that they did the same thing on at least three other claims. They never did amount to much because they were always more interested in quick money than actually working a mine."

"And they died young? Right?" Brid said.

"One of them did. Got himself shot while trying to do the same thing to a man who had better aim. Actually, it was probably just pure luck. Most of those men were better at digging than shooting. Gentlemen, it looks like you've got yourself some questions. Would you like me to leave you alone for a while? My other customers are coming back, and I need to give them their money's worth."

"Go right ahead," Adam said.

With a tip of his hat, Boyd slipped away to greet his customers. His voice boomed as he approached them, further convincing Rick that the man should have been on stage.

Adam waited until Boyd was out of hearing range, then said, "Ms. Ochoa, we'd like to talk to you about Mr. Welles. We have a number of questions about his relationship with members of your group. As we understand it, you were actually the one who inspired this trip. Is that correct?"

Brid pushed up the nosepiece of her glasses, sliding them up from her nostrils to the bridge of her nose. "Yes. Liz and I got to talking about things to do together. She knew about my interest in stuff like this, and when I saw a story online that the Silver Gulch Mine was going to open up, I told her it was something I'd like to do. She thought it was a great idea, but we didn't have the money."

"That's why Mr. Welles was paying for the trip?" Rick said.

"That happened later. I'd never met Snappy. I mean, I knew that Liz had broken up with him. She'd been devastated. To me, he was just this random guy who'd hurt her. I'd never actually seen him. I guess it was about a month later that I realized there was this guy who always showed up at the library at the same time as Liz. He was too well dressed to be homeless. The other thing was his timing. It was way too coincidental. I asked him if he had a research question, and he said he was interested in old California mines. We got to talking, and I said something about coming up here. He asked who I was going with. When I told him, he said he knew Liz. That's when I got suspicious."

"Suspicious? Of what? That he was stalking her?" Rick asked.

"Totally. I called her and told her what had happened. She said she wasn't worried, that she knew how to handle him. The next time we saw each other, she said it was time to give Snappy a little payback."

"Do you know what she meant by that?" Rick asked.

"She said she was going to take his money and give him nothing in return. So she contacted him and told him she wanted him to pay for the trip for six people. I was surprised when he said yes, but Liz wasn't. So, here we are."

Brid's revelation certainly shed new light on what Liz had told them—actually, more like what she hadn't told them. Could it be that this trip had nothing to do with Liz still being in love with Welles? Was it nothing more than a way to exact some form of revenge? "Let's go back to when you called Liz and told her about Mr. Welles's visit. Did she seem to be upset by it?"

Brid shrugged. "Not really. She was like, Snappy's a jerk, and he'll never change. We might as well use that to our advantage."

"Do you think she was mad? Or do you think she was pleased that he was still paying attention to her?"

Brid's eyes narrowed as she seemed to think about the question. "I'm not sure. Now that you mention it, it is like kind of perverse that she would be willing to come on this trip with both him and her husband. That is kind of weird. Right?"

If she thought only that one thing was weird, they had altogether different interpretations of the word. Everything about the Band of Six seemed weird to Rick. Rather than answering, Rick waited. As he'd expected, Brid continued without prompting.

"And, what's even stranger is that we talk all the time. We share everything. Well, most everything. When I asked her about Snappy, I got the impression she was holding back." She shot a look toward the parking lot. "I knew Liz was unhappy with Barnaby, but we never like talked about her getting back together with Snappy."

"What about Mr. Welles? Did he ever say anything about wanting to get back together with her?"

"Oh, for sure. He made it very clear what he wanted. I think that's why he was so willing to put up the money for this trip."

Rick kept seeing the image of the Band of Six at the Crooked Mast. Everything that had happened during dinner suddenly took on a different meaning—Welles showing off his new pocket watch, Liz sitting next to him, and her husband's accusations.

Adam's voice intruded on Rick's thoughts, pulling him back to the present. "What are you thinking, Rick?"

"Welles inserted himself back into Liz's life after he'd told her to go ahead and marry Barnaby Pauley. I can see him having regrets, but the fact that he went about things surreptitiously leads me to believe he was trying to manipulate her. He had to know when he started talking to Brid about the trip that Liz would hear. He also knew they didn't have the money. The man obviously liked to play games with people."

"You know, that's right!" Brid again pushed up her glasses. "He didn't say anything the first time I told him where we were going. It was the next time he came in that he made a comment about it being an expensive trip. I told him we were going to have to save up for a long time to be able to do it. That seemed to make him kind of happy."

Rick nodded. The pieces fit. Welles had wanted Liz and Brid to come here, perhaps thinking he could seduce her if Liz could get her away from her husband. Then Barnaby decided to tag along and the game became more complex. "Do you know how Liz got Mr. Welles to pay for everything?"

"You mean, did she agree to sleep with him? I don't know. It was one of those things Liz wouldn't talk about."

Another secret? Another layer of the onion? "How did the others become involved?"

"Simple math, More people meant more money. Liz wanted to make Snappy pay big."

"That's what she said? Those were her exact words?" Rick asked.

Brid made a face and tugged on a strand of dark hair. "Actually, she said she wanted him to pay dearly."

"Do you think she was referring to just money?"

"I...I don't know." Brid paused, then quickly added, "Snappy had plenty of money, so it's hard to believe that was her only motive. It could be she asked Barnaby to come along to make it more personal for Snappy. He didn't want to at first, but once he heard that Snappy would be here, he changed his mind. Liz is also the one who suggested I invite Guy. And since Guy's been trying to get in good with Carson, we invited him, too."

"Maybe you could clarify something for me. The other night at the Crooked Mast, you were paying a lot of attention to Mr. Welles. Did that have something to do with Liz?"

Brid's jaw tightened momentarily. Then, the anxiety was gone. "No. It was because he was showing off an antique pocket watch he'd bought at an auction. I just wanted to see it up close." She flipped a hand dismissively and glanced away. "That's all it was."

Really? Then why had she just tensed up? From what Marquetta had told him, Brid's behavior that night had been more than just someone showing idle interest. If only he hadn't been admiring the sunset with Alex and had paid more attention to the Band of Six at the time. His breaths came faster. It really felt like he was getting close to something important. What if he pushed just a little harder? "To be honest, you seemed more than mildly interested in a watch."

"No. No. That's all it was." Brid's shoulders were hunched slightly forward when she crossed her arms in front of her.

"Honestly, Rick. I think you're reading something into a perfectly normal situation."

"I'll be blunt, Brid. There's not much about your group I'd consider normal."

Brid laughed. "That's us. One big unhappy, dysfunctional family. I blame most of that on Snappy. He's the one who kept stirring the pot."

Could that be the reason someone had killed him? Because he'd stirred up trouble once too often? "What was your impression of Mr. Welles? Do you think he was just a nasty man, or could his 'nastiness,' for lack of a better term, have been driven by a purpose? Could he have been deliberately trying to manipulate the group?"

"I'm totally sure of it." Brid nodded and let her gaze drift in the direction of the white Corolla where Liz still sat. "My guess is that he was using everyone else to put pressure on Liz and Barnaby. I'm a hundred percent sure that his end game was to tear them apart so he could get her back."

That, at least, tracked with what Liz had said. And quite possibly, he'd been close to succeeding. Or had he? What about that agreement Liz hadn't wanted to talk about? "Do you think Welles's plan was working?"

"I don't know. Liz wouldn't say. It's like she's bottling it up inside."

"I thought you two shared everything."

Brid's brow furrowed as she gazed towards her friend, who had rolled down one window and sat staring out at the dirt parking lot. "That's mostly true. Liz and I can talk about almost anything, but there are limits."

"Such as?"

"How she convinced Snappy to pay for the trip for one." Brid bit her lower lip and sighed. "What she did after the dinner at the Crooked Mast for another."

Rick exchanged a quick look with Adam. At last, they'd come to Liz's alibi. "What do you mean?"

"Just disappearing on me like that."

"Didn't you and Guy walk back to the B&B together?" Rick asked innocently.

"No. Guy stormed off after Snappy. I caught up with Liz. Then we walked most of the way to the B&B. When we got to where you guys have that little park, she saw Barnaby pull into the marina parking lot. She said she needed to talk to him and left."

"Wait. Barnaby didn't walk back to the B&B?" Rick said.

Brid shook her head. "No. He and Liz drove to dinner."

Rick cut a glance at Adam, who was nodding to himself as he made a note. Well, well, they'd caught Barnaby Pauley in another lie. The trick now was to keep all the players apart.

Most likely, as soon as Brid and Liz had a moment alone, they'd compare stories. Liz would realize her fake alibi had fallen apart. They had to get to her before that conversation took place. With that, maybe they could finally find out what had really happened after that dinner.

26

ALEX

Hey Journal,

This is totally weird. I talked to Mr. Coulson. He gives off a creepy vibe. One second he's like super friendly, then he's totally spooky. I don't know which one is the real him. Maybe it's both. I guess just 'cause he's kinda creepy doesn't mean he killed Mr. Welles. Right?

One of the things he said has me thinking I should check out the two girls in the group. I found the social media profiles for both of them. They post a lot of photos of themselves together. Liz put up a photo of them when they got to Seaside Cove, and she said that she felt like Brid was her only true family. Mr. Coulson said the two of them share everything. I wonder if he's right. I sure hope me and my baby brother are gonna be that close!

I'm hoping to see if I can get one of them alone so I can ask some questions about Creepy Coulson. Maybe they'll tell me more. Right now, I need to talk to Mom. She's always got the best intel in the world 'cause everybody tells her everything.

Bye for now,

Alex

* * *

I'm not sure where my mom is, so I start looking for Lydia. She'll know for sure where I can find her. Since Lydia's probably in the kitchen or the laundry room, that's where I go first. There's no sign of her, though. That means she's probably cleaning one of the guest rooms. I look out the window to check for Creepy Coulson. He's not practicing anymore. I'm gonna keep my distance from him just in case the creepy vibe is the right one.

That means I still have to find Lydia. If she's in one of the guest rooms, she shouldn't be too long. Wait! I can check for the vacuum. It'll be in the supply closet, in the hallway, or I'll hear it in one of the rooms.

On my way upstairs, I look for Mom. I don't see her anywhere. Maybe she's taking a nap? That's become kind of a thing for her to do these last few days. She could be in either the master bedroom or in my dad's office since he's not here. The big couch in there is her favorite 'cause it reminds her of when she was little. She says she used to go in there when Captain Jack was supposed to be working. She'd fall asleep on the couch, and when she woke up, he always had his head on his chest and was sound asleep at his desk. It always makes her laugh when she tells that story!

Oh, snap! The vacuum's in the closet. Now I'm gonna have to wait for Lydia to come out of a room. I walk along the hall, kinda whisper-calling to her. "Lydia!" Rats! No answer. "Lydia!"

I jump when the door to the Mainsail Room opens right when I'm in front of it. Lydia whispers, "Alex, what are you doing out here?"

"Looking for you," I whisper back.

Her eyes flick from side to side like she's trying to figure something out. "Why are we whispering?"

"I didn't want to cause a problem with any of the other guests." Especially Creepy Coulson. "I don't know why we're still doing it."

She laughs, then pulls me into the room. "Here, you can help me. You do the dusting while I finish in the bathroom. We can talk while we work—I've got something to tell you."

While I finish the dusting, Lydia takes the towels that she's left on the bed and goes into the bathroom. As we're working, she tells me that Mr. Grayson from the Crooked Mast and his wife are getting a divorce. That's a total bummer 'cause their daughter Maxie is my friend. I also really like Mr. Grayson. I met his wife when she came to Mom and Dad's wedding, and she seemed super nice, too. It's sad that they're not getting along.

After she finishes telling me about the Graysons, I tell her about my talk with Mr. Coulson.

"You stay away from him, Alex. I told you that man's not right in the head."

"I know," I say as I move a book one of the guests left on the nightstand. It's got a cool image on the front of men holding up a stagecoach. The title says it's the true story about early California road agents. Those are the same guys Mr. Boyd told us about. I set the book down while Lydia finishes straightening the towels. We're super particular about how they're folded for the guests. "The room looks great, Lydia." While she finishes up, I pick up the book again. This time, a pamphlet about finding birth parents falls out onto the floor.

"Who's staying in this room?"

"Ms. Ochoa and her boyfriend." Lydia comes over, takes a look, and shrugs. "I guess one of them was adopted. You should put that back."

"It must be Ms. Ochoa. The book has to be hers 'cause she's into this kind of stuff." There are notes inside the pamphlet. And a letter. I smile at Lydia, and her jaw drops open. She shakes her head.

"Alex! Don't you dare. That's private!"

It's too late. I'm hooked. I gotta know. "Lydia, these notes are Ms. Ochoa's. You're right. She was adopted. Her note says her mother was Milly Ravel." I scrunch up my face. "That's the same last name as her friend. Holy cow! This letter is addressed to Liz Ravel."

"Alex! Put that back. Right now! You'll get me fired."

"Why? It's not locked. It was just sitting here." I give Lydia a big smile. "And the papers fell out when I was dusting."

"You are incorrigible. She could sue your dad for violating her privacy."

I pull out my phone and take pictures of the note before I put it back where I found it. "How's she ever gonna know?"

Lydia starts muttering to herself in Spanish. I don't know what she's saying, but there's no way it can be good.

27

RICK

IT DIDN'T SURPRISE RICK THAT both Barnaby Pauley and Liz Ravel
had lied about what they'd done after the dinner at the Crooked
Mast. He had to admit that he might have been more surprised
if they hadn't. He and Adam had Brid Ochoa wait to one side
while they discussed how to proceed.

"Then we're agreed," Rick said. "We talk to Liz right now
and give her a chance to tell us the truth. And, I agree with you,
if she doesn't come clean right away, then you'll have to take her
in for questioning. Adam, I think she's just afraid. You know
how people get. They get embarrassed and do something stupid.
I'm sure that's all this is."

"Could be, buddy. The problem is she lied during a police
investigation. Let's not lose sight of that important fact. Ready?"

Was there any other choice? This was the tricky part. If Liz
wasn't a guest at the B&B, this would be far easier. Roy Andrew
Boyd wouldn't have this dilemma. If his venture succeeded, he'd
have an ideal job. Surrounded by towering pines and scrub
brush, he'd have no tricky decisions over how hard he should be
on one of his customers. Rick pulled in a deep breath. "For the
record, Adam, I am not looking forward to this. Let's go."

Brid approached, a tentative expression on her face. "I
assume you want to talk to Liz again? About after the dinner?"

"We do," Adam said. "We'll need you to wait in the car while we talk to her."

"Would you mind if I went and talked to Mr. Boyd instead? I have more questions for him, and I may not get back out here."

Adam's green eyes darted off toward Boyd, who was coming their way with his other two customers. "Sure. I don't see a problem with that. You will, however, need to keep your distance from Ms. Ravel."

"I'll get Liz," Rick said. He walked toward the car, thankful that Adam wasn't rigid about when and where to interview people. While the Silver Gulch Mine was hardly an ideal location for these types of interviews, at least this wasn't happening at the B&B. That made it easier to balance his dual roles as innkeeper and police consultant.

Liz got out of the car just as he was nearing her door. "You want to talk to me again."

"I think you know why."

She looked down and scuffed the dirt of the parking lot with the toe of her shoe. "I lied. It was stupid."

The crunching of footsteps reminded Rick that there were other people within hearing distance. He looked over at the couple that was leaving, then shot a glance at Liz. She seemed content to wait for privacy. Rick waited as the man spoke across the rooftop of their SUV to his companion.

"Interesting. Not much out here. Not what I thought it would be."

"Honey, this place is a bust. It's just a couple of old, closed-off mine shafts. Let's go do something fun."

Rick didn't hear the man's reply. He didn't need to. Based on body language alone, the man agreed completely as he got in the car.

"She's right, you know?" Liz said. "Brid thinks this place is cool because she's into history. The reality is, there's not much here."

Looking around, Rick tried to do an unbiased assessment. Boyd's display of artifacts was interesting but hardly overwhelming. "You're right. This is a good activity for local kids or people who are into a lot of old stories. Otherwise, it is a disappointment."

"It helps if you have a good imagination," Liz added.

"Yeah. That, too." Sadly, Rick realized he had to agree. Unless Roy Andrew Boyd did something to bring the Silver Gulch Mine up to the same level as his personality, this mine might go under for the second time around. Rick changed his earlier assessment. Maybe the man was going to have a lot of stress after all. He cleared his throat. "Liz, I think I understand why you did it. We still need to talk to Adam and straighten this out."

By the time they were back to where Adam was standing, Brid was again chatting up Boyd.

"Ms. Ravel," Adam said. "You told us that you walked back to the B&B with Ms. Ochoa after the Crooked Mast dinner. That's not true, is it?"

"I'm sorry, Chief," Liz said. "It just sounds so bad."

"What does?" Adam pressed.

She grimaced, then gazed at the sky. "The truth. Brid probably told you that we walked together. That was only until we got to that park on Front Street. I saw Barnaby's car pull into the marina parking lot. He got out and went to sit on that bench just near the entrance to the docks. I knew I needed to talk to him. I didn't lie about the fact that things aren't working out for us. I wanted to tell him that, and I didn't want anyone talking me out of it. If I waited, it would only get more awkward back at the B&B, so I went down to talk to him."

"Liz, it's a bit of a walk from Marina Park down to the docks. Was he still around when you got there?" Rick asked.

Her eyes brimmed with moisture, and she sniffled. "He was. Barnaby can be very difficult to get along with. He likes it when everything is in harmony, and he hates confrontations, so this trip has really put him over the edge. When he gets like that, it takes forever for him to cool down."

"Did you two argue at the marina?"

"In a way. It was more like a one-sided argument. I got there and told him I was thinking of ending things. He got this really dark look on his face and started yelling at me. He said Snappy was trying to tear us apart. And that Snappy was ruining his business. He also said he had to stop Snappy because he wasn't going to let me go, and he wasn't going to lose his business, either."

"Did he say anything else?" Rick asked.

Liz pulled in a deep breath, then nodded. "After he stopped his rant, I told him I'd already decided we should get a divorce. He started calling me all kinds of names and said that Snappy had turned me against him and that he was going to get even. There was something else, too. He was just sort of—I don't know —wallowing in self-pity. The thing is, he wasn't taking responsibility. He was blaming it all on Snappy."

"Anything else?"

"No. He just got in his car and drove off."

"What happened when he got back to the room? Did he tell you where he'd been?"

"He just said he'd been driving around. I wasn't surprised that he was still angry. That's just the way he is."

Adam jotted down a note, then fixed Liz with a deliberate stare. "What about after you learned Mr. Welles had been killed? Did he say anything then?"

"No. And I was afraid to ask. Chief Cunningham? I'm just sure Barnaby didn't do it. He's not a killer."

"Correction, Ms. Ravel. You don't think he's a killer. For his sake, I hope you're right. Either way, we're going to need to know where your husband went and what he did after he left you. And, for the record, what did you do after he left you at the marina?"

"I was so distraught that I just stood there watching the water even though it was already starting to get dark. After that, I walked back to the B&B. I was out by the gazebo until it got too. After that, I went up to my room and waited for Barnaby."

"And what time was it when he showed up, Ms. Ravel?"

When Liz didn't answer right away, Rick coaxed her gently. "Liz?"

"About eight-thirty. He said he was cold and tired and just wanted to go to sleep. He was shivering so bad that we just turned out the light and went to bed. I guess I was completely drained because I conked out and didn't hear anything until morning."

"Liz, unfortunately, I don't have any other rooms available right now. Are you okay with your current situation?"

"It's fine. It's not like Barnaby and I are at each other's throats all the time. If things get really bad, I'll talk to Brid. Maybe I can move in with her." She shrugged. "I guess Guy could stay with Barnaby."

"However you want to work it out is fine with me. I just want you to be comfortable during your stay. You said that Barnaby thought Mr. Welles was trying to ruin his company. Do you have any idea what he meant?"

"I'm not a hundred percent sure. Snappy has a reputation for destroying his competitors."

"Your husband wasn't a competitor," Rick said. "Why would he want to ruin a business in which he was an investor?"

"When it came to personal vendettas, Snappy didn't care about money. He always said that he made his fortune by being ruthless, and he treated his personal life the same way. If he took a dislike to you, he'd go to any extent to hurt you."

"And he'd taken a dislike to your husband because of you?"

"I don't know that for sure because he never admitted it, but it wouldn't surprise me. Snappy was one of those people who'd say one thing and do another."

Frustrating. That's what this case was. They had an unpredictable victim and five unpredictable suspects. It was beginning to feel like an impossible situation. "Certainly, there was animosity between your husband and Mr. Welles because of you. Did your husband say if there were any other reasons Mr. Welles wanted to destroy the company?"

"Rick, I think we'd better ask that question directly to Mr. Pauley," Adam said.

"Yes. And we will. Right now, I'm worried that if there's something he's ashamed of, he may try to hide it." Rick looked deliberately at Liz, who again dropped her gaze to the dirt beneath her feet. He was pretty sure she got the point.

"I don't know that Snappy wanted to destroy the company as much as he always wanted to be the winner. He always wanted to best Barnaby. It happened all the time. I suppose in his perfect world, Snappy would have forced Barnaby out of the company and taken it over. It was just like that stupid pocket watch. That happened right before we came up here. Snappy outbid Barnaby at the last minute just so he could say he'd won. Then, of course, he had to rub Barnaby's nose in it."

"And you think Mr. Welles did that on purpose?" Rick asked.

"I know he did. He told me when we were out at the mine and he was showing it to Mr. Boyd." She shook her head and looked off to the side. "Levi's Folly. Talk about a ridiculous name."

And a ridiculous display of childish behavior. No wonder Welles was dead.

28

RICK

Liz Ravel rode in the back of Adam's 4x4 on the drive to the Seaside Cove police station. From the moment Adam closed the door on her, Rick sensed her fear. Suddenly locked into a cage with no possibility of escape, she seemed to realize the gravity of her situation.

Though the drive was about the longest in Seaside Cove, it lasted less than fifteen minutes. Despite the relative shortness of the drive, with one of his guests sitting glum and silent in the back, those were some of the longest fifteen minutes Rick had ever felt.

Located on the east end of Main Street, Rick had attributed the nondescript pea-green police station with its matching green-and-white striped awnings to bad architectural design the first time he'd seen it. In a town filled with beautiful Victorian and Craftsman homes, this square box with square windows with only the awnings for ornamentation simply didn't belong. At the time, he'd had no idea how much time he'd be spending inside that building.

As Adam set up the recorder, Liz grew increasingly sullen. Rick tried to reassure her that she wasn't a suspect, but she wasn't buying it.

"I lied to you, Rick. I shouldn't have done it, but I did. And now you can't trust me."

"Just tell the truth now, Liz. That's all you have to do. Everything else will work itself out." He hoped.

"This changes how you're looking at Barnaby, too." She glared at Rick; her brown eyes were intense, her tone accusatory. "It does. Doesn't it?"

"Yes. It could put him in jeopardy as far as the investigation goes. The facts are the facts, Liz. Snappy Welles is dead. You saw your husband driving toward the scene of the crime at about the time of death. And there was a great deal of animosity between your husband and the victim."

Liz's hard facade cracked. Tears welled in her eyes. Then she drew a ragged breath. "I'm sorry. It's not your fault we got ourselves into this mess. I shouldn't take out my frustrations on you. Let's get this over with, okay?"

Adam plugged in the recorder, which had to be about the oldest piece of electronic equipment Rick had seen in years. He sat next to Rick, punched the button to start the recorder, and dictated an introduction that identified those in the room along with the date and time. "Ms. Ravel, we need you to tell us about the dinner at the Crooked Mast. Earlier, you said Mr. Welles was showing off a pocket watch that he claimed to be known as Levi's Folly. Is that correct?"

"Yes."

"Can you describe this watch?" Adam asked.

"It was gold. Gaudy. Snappy was bragging about how many diamonds it had. It had a white face. Why are you asking me? He would have been carrying it in his pocket when he was killed. It was there. Right?"

"No, it wasn't," Rick volunteered before Adam could respond. He knew Adam probably wouldn't want to answer the question, but he didn't see the harm. Besides, treating this as a two-way exchange of information might actually get them more.

"What?" Liz exploded.

Adam grimaced, then said, "We inventoried all of Mr. Welles's belongings. There was no watch in his possession."

"Somebody stole it?" Liz gaped across the table at them for a second, then shook her head and composed herself. "I'm sorry. If it wasn't there, then this is probably the first you've heard of it."

"Yes, it is," Adam admitted. "Now, we have more questions."

The rest of the interview involved far less drama. Liz seemed to be over her initial shock about the missing watch. Her reactions alternated between anger, sorrow, and sheer numbness. By the time she left and pushed through the front door, she looked like a woman with a purpose.

"What do you suppose she's going to do?" Rick asked.

"I don't know, but she's one unhappy camper."

"I guess, given the nature of your job, you're used to people not being their happiest when they leave here."

"I have to admit that it was a lot easier back in the days when I was just a part-time deputy and part-time meter reader."

"Look, I have an idea. Why don't we check with Howie Dockham about this Levi's Folly?"

"Even better. I'll let you talk to Howie. Madeline is probably working today, and I'm sure she'll be delighted to see her favorite son-in-law," Adam said with a smirk.

"Oh, please. Don't do that. She says that every time I see her."

"Okay. You're off the hook. While you go see Howie, I'll go back to see what Mr. Roy Andrew Boyd can tell me about this famous pocket watch. I'll bet he knows more than he said when he was telling the kids about it. I'd like to have a better idea of what we're actually looking for."

To the side, the mini refrigerator kicked on, its gentle hum filling the room. "Sounds like a plan. I should get going. It's Saturday afternoon, and it's getting late. Howie's probably going to be closing soon."

On the way to Howie's Collectibles, Rick watched for Liz Ravel. She'd been so upset when she left the station that he expected to find her somewhere along the way, just standing and staring off into space. When he didn't see her, he assumed she'd gone back to the B&B. If that's where she'd gone, he hoped her mood would settle down by the time she got there. They didn't need another Band of Six flare-up.

29

ALEX

AFTER WE LEAVE THE MAINSAIL Room, I ask Lydia if she wants to read the notes and the letter I found. She shakes her head and backs away.

"I want nothing to do with this, Alex. I'm warning you; reading someone's personal property is wrong. No good will come of this. You should delete those photos."

She's kinda right, but if I'm gonna get my story, I need to read what Brid wrote. Part of the problem is I don't even know what my story is now. I thought I knew what it was until I found the booklet and the letter. I'm not so sure now. "Lydia, it's like my dad used to say when he worked at the paper. I'm following a lead."

"A lead? For what?"

"I dunno yet. Do you need any more help?"

"No!" Lydia raises her hands in front of her. "I need to get these rooms finished, and I don't think I want you anywhere near any of them."

"Okay. No problem." I turn around to go to my room. I feel kinda bad 'cause Lydia doesn't deserve to get in trouble, and now she's all worried I might get her fired or something. I'm thinking of going back and apologizing to her when I hear what sounds like someone crying. At the bottom of the stairs is Brid

Ochoa. She's got both hands on the banister and looks like she's bracing herself.

I start down the stairs. "Ms. Ochoa? Are you okay?"

She looks up at me and sniffles. "I've just gotten my sis—I mean, my best friend, in trouble with the police."

By bending down, I can look into the living room and see that the room's empty. The fire's going. It looks super comfy. Thank goodness none of the guests are around. I take the last few steps and put my hand on hers. There's a lot of hurt in her eyes when she looks at me.

"C'mon. We can talk in the living room."

I lead her by the hand, kinda like Mom does to me when I'm feeling down. She shuffles behind me, then sits. I take her hands in mine and lean with my shoulder against hers. She's short, so we're almost the same height. My dad says I'm growing like a weed. He's totally exaggerating, but I am starting to look more like an adult than a little kid.

"What happened?" I guess I'm thinking more like an adult, too, and that makes me feel even worse about Lydia.

She tells me about the trip to the Silver Gulch Mine and how my dad and Chief Cunningham showed up and started asking questions. When she tells me that Ms. Ravel lied to the chief about what happened, my insides tighten. She's totally gonna be in a lot of trouble for that.

"So that's why they took her to the police station? To question her some more?"

"The chief said he wanted a statement. He's getting ready to talk to Barnaby."

That can only mean one thing—Chief Cunningham thinks someone's lying. My dad's always telling me you've gotta have the truth before you can see the whole picture. He's totally right. But Mr. Pauley? A killer? I don't think so.

"Why do you think you got Ms. Ravel in trouble? She's the one who lied."

"I didn't know Liz hadn't told them that she saw Barnaby that night. I'd do anything for her, and I wouldn't have told them if I'd known."

I give her elbow a nudge with mine. "I get it. Once my baby brother gets older, I can't imagine ever telling on him. I bet we'll get in trouble all the time. The cool thing is we'll do it together."

"I envy you. I always wished I had a sister when I was growing up. The truth is, I was adopted and never knew who my biological parents were."

Omigod. This could be what I need. It would solve the problem for Lydia and for me. I tell her about my real mom and how she never really wanted me. "We kinda have some stuff in common."

She nods slowly and takes a long breath. "Call me Brid. You're right. We have a lot in common."

"Because you were adopted, did you have a sister you didn't know about?"

"Yes, I did. My birth mother wasn't married when I was born. The reason she gave me up for adoption was that she'd met a man named Simon Ravel, but he didn't want kids. He was willing to marry her if I wasn't part of the picture."

"Wow. That's cold."

"That's a good way to put it. That was Simon Ravel, a very cold man. At least you'll know your brother right from the start. There won't be any secrets. And you'll have a home where both of your parents want you."

She still hasn't said anything about the letter. Biting my upper lip, I wonder if I'm going to need to get more direct and tell her what I found. "Can I ask you something personal?"

She laughs and bumps my shoulder with hers. "I kind of thought that's what we were doing?"

"Well, yeah. Was Simon Ravel your real dad?"

"No. Why do you ask?"

"You mentioned him before. And while me and Lydia were cleaning your room, I saw a book about finding your birth parents. Since Liz has that last name, I wondered if she might be your sister." I hold my breath, not sure if she's gonna get mad or what. Lydia's right. This could be a lot of trouble for me.

Brid sniffles again. "My mother said my biological father was a very nice man who died a few months after they met. I was fortunate in that I was able to reconnect with her. When I finally found her, she told me Simon Ravel had died several years before. That's when she told me that giving me up was the biggest mistake of her life."

I'm tempted to tell her how much work it was for me to get my dad and Marquetta together, but that might get us off track. Instead, I ask, "So what was it like? Reconnecting with your real mom?"

She laughs. "It was wonderful and terrible and uplifting and depressing all at the same time. There was so much pain she'd been holding inside. It was the secrets that were eating away at her. Did your biological mom keep secrets?"

Secrets? Yeah. I guess you could call it that. I can feel my insides tightening again. Even though Marquetta's my mom now, it still hurts sometimes when I think about how we got here. "She wanted to be a big actress on Broadway and had a boyfriend who was supposed to help her career. What kind of secrets did your mom keep?"

"There were so many. She didn't tell Simon Ravel she'd never been married. Instead, she told him she was a widow and that her husband had been killed during a military-training accident. It's true, that's how he died, but they never were married. She also hid the fact that she tried to find me a couple of times. The biggest one of all, though, was she never told my sister about me."

"That's Liz?"

"Yeah." Brid closes her eyes, presses her lips together, and blows out a breath. It makes a funny noise that actually says a lot.

"You haven't told her. Have you?"

"I haven't had the nerve. I don't want to ruin our relationship."

Now what? This is awful. I wish I didn't know.

"What's wrong, Alex?"

I look over at the fire. The flames from the gas log are flickering, giving off a nice, warm glow. Despite the coziness around us, I feel a chill from the guilt of what I've done. How many times have Mom and Dad told me it's important to respect people's privacy? They've asked me how I'd feel if someone read my journal. Now I know exactly. Just like this. No. Worse.

"Brid, there's something I have to tell you."

She pulls her hand loose from mine and pushes up her glasses. The sadness in her eyes disappears, and she looks right at me. She doesn't say anything for a few seconds. When she does, her voice is firm.

"You read it. Didn't you?"

I close my eyes and nod. "I'm sorry. I shouldn't have." I start to make an excuse. To tell her the lie that I made up with Lydia, then stop. "It was wrong. Are you gonna tell my dad?"

There's another long silence, and this time she's the one who watches the flames. Gradually, I see the tightness in her jaw relax. Then, there's a little bit of a smile. "Actually, I'm relieved. I wrote that letter because I had so many things to tell her that I didn't want to screw up. What you read is probably my twentieth draft."

"Have you told anybody? What about your boyfriend?"

"Oh my God, are you kidding me? I'd never tell Guy something like this." She takes in a long, slow breath, then lets it out. "You're the only other person in the world who knows this. It feels good to get it out. To say the words. Milly Ravel was my mother. Liz is my sister." Her smile grows, and then she says it again.

A woman's voice croaks, "What?"

Angry footsteps stalk across the hardwood floor. I rush over just in time to see Brid's sister slam the front door behind her. Rats! Neither of us had been paying attention to where we were or what was going on around us.

"Brid, that was Liz. You have to go after her!"

Instead of moving, she just sits there on the couch looking like she's scared to death. "What do I do? What do I say?"

Who cares? As long as she says something. I rush back, grab her hand and pull. It's like she's in a daze. At least she stands. Then she looks at me and frowns.

"Just talk to her. Tell her the truth. Now, go!" I push her towards the door.

She looks at me, nods, and then rushes out after her sister.

30

RICK

RICK WASN'T SURPRISED THAT HOWIE'S Collectibles was busy when he entered the small store. Barely a visit went by that one of them at the B&B didn't refer a visitor here. Between the collectors, bargain hunters, and curiosity seekers, Howie's business was nearly constant.

Madeline Weiss greeted him with a wave and broke away from her customers. "Rick! How's my favorite son-in-law?"

"I'm fine, Madeline. And how's my favorite mother-in-law?"

"Touché." She winked, then lowered her voice to a conspiratorial level. "Having the time of my life."

Since Madeline had moved back to Seaside Cove, she'd been much happier than when he first met her. She'd put on a few pounds, and her job at Howie's Collectibles, along with her relationship with the owner, seemed to agree with her. Though there had been no discussion of it, Rick wondered if there might even be wedding bells in the future of Howie Dockham and Madeline Weiss.

"Just so you know, Marquetta's still doing well. And Alex, she's, well, as enthusiastic as ever."

"Wonderful!"

"Actually, I'm here on police business," Rick said reluctantly.

Madeline's smile fell. She huffed, then said, "I heard we had another murder in town. You're helping Adam?"

"Yes. I need to grab a few minutes of Howie's time."

Madeline looked over her shoulder, saw that Howie was just finishing up a sale with two women, and said, "You'd better hurry. It's a busy afternoon. Just jump in after he finishes that sale."

While Rick waited, Howie finished his spiel about a piece of amber jewelry one of the women had been admiring. The woman plunked down her credit card and was gushing about her latest find to her friend. As they passed Rick on the way to the exit, her friend said, "Get me out of here before I spend my next two paychecks on things I don't need."

Rick went to the counter, then said, "Afternoon, Howie. Another happy customer, I see."

"That's all we have," Howie chuckled, then cocked his head to one side. He rolled his wheelchair over to a small desk and waited for Rick to join him. "We'll talk here just in case Madeline has to make a sale. Let me see if I can guess why you're here. There's been a murder, and you're here to see me, which probably means you need information about an antique." He paused, looked at Rick over his wire-rimmed spectacles, and smiled. "How am I doing?"

"Pretty darn good. I'll give you double bonus points if you can tell me which antique I'm interested in."

Without missing a beat, Howie responded. "My guess is it would be Levi's Folly."

Rick knew Howie was connected in the art and antiquities world, but he'd never expected him to get this right. "How did you know that?"

Howie brushed the dark gray diamond pattern on his sweater. "As the saying goes, elementary. There was an auction only a short time ago in which there was a lot of interest in that particular piece. Multiple bidders and all that. The piece sold to a new collector from Los Angeles. Suddenly, you have a visit from a group of tourists from LA, and the first thing they do is go to the Silver Gulch Mine, which is basically the home of the last owner of the watch."

It took a moment for Howie's summation to sink in. When it did, Rick was left with multiple questions. "You're amazing. How did you know about the group of tourists?"

The answer was obvious the moment Howie glanced in Madeline's direction. He wrinkled his nose. "A little birdie told me."

"Marquetta told Madeline about our guests?" Marquetta was not the type to gossip. She heard plenty, but she never repeated it. Alex, on the other hand, was a completely different story. "I can't believe it."

"That's because it wasn't Marquetta. I said a little birdie."

"Oh. Alex. That makes a lot more sense."

Howie's gaze cut across the store to where Madeline was chatting up a customer. "I assume you know where she gets it from."

"Yes. I think I do," Rick sighed. It was one of the big differences between Marquetta and her mother. It was almost as if their listening-to-talking ratios were reversed. While he couldn't stop Madeline from gossiping, he could at least try to deal with Alex. "So Alex comes in here?"

"A couple of times a week. Whenever her grandmother's working."

"That's going to make this very difficult. Alex adores Madeline, but she's got to learn about our guests' right to privacy. I'll deal with it."

Howie made a zipping motion across his lips. "You didn't hear it from me. Now, on to more interesting things." He tapped on his keyboard, then turned the monitor to face Rick.

The screen was filled with the image of a pocket watch. It was stunning and gaudy and, in Rick's opinion, completely impractical. "That's it? That's Levi's Folly?"

"The picture makes it look much larger than it is. It's a miniature watch, barely three-quarters of an inch in diameter. It was a marvel when it made its debut at the 1851 World's Fair in London."

Rick did a double-take and stared at the image. "Levi's Folly was at the Crystal Palace Exhibition?"

"It's rumored that Prince Albert himself wanted to buy it. That, however, is unsubstantiated. What is known is that the case is 18-carat yellow gold with 390 rose-cut diamonds. Its precision movement was one of the most advanced in the world for the time." Howie stopped and gazed up at Rick with a smile. "One of the other interesting rumors is that it's said that this watch is cursed."

"So we've heard. Do you think it's true?"

"I don't believe in curses, but it is interesting how the watch seems to disappear for extended periods. Twenty or thirty years at a time. For a pocket watch, it's got quite the flamboyant history."

"Including time at the Silver Gulch mine after it was stolen from Levi Clark?"

"Ah, Gentleman George. Yes, he is considered one of the owners. And one of our more colorful residents. He used those hills as a hideout."

Rick studied the photo of Levi's Folly. Who would have thought something so small could cause so much trouble? And possibly even result in murder. He pointed at Howie's screen. "So that's what it looks like? It really is kind of gaudy."

"Beauty is in the eye of the beholder, Rick. This photo is from the page put up by the auction company that brokered the sale. Apparently, Mr. Welles liked it enough to buy it out from under a couple of other bidders. What I've heard is that there was a great deal of interest until the price went above $75K, then the bidders started dropping off. My friend didn't give me the exact sale price. He only told me it was significantly north of that. I'd guess about a hundred thousand."

Rick stared again at the photo. The watch had not been in Welles's room, nor had it been on his person. Could this have been a robbery that went wrong instead of an intentional murder? He pulled out his phone and dialed Adam's number. His call went to voicemail.

"We need to talk. Howie's just given me new information that could change everything about our case. Meet me in my office when you get this."

31

ALEX

SITTING ON THE COUCH AND looking at the tall windows and polished wood of the floors and banister, I see the love and care that went into remodeling this old house. In the wintertime, it feels kinda drafty, but it's the place I've grown to love. And when we have a guest like Brid who gets to kind of meet her sister for the first time—I totally wanna be a part of it. That's why I'm torn between going after Brid and letting her have the time alone with her sister.

Getting up, I go to the door and peek outside. There's no sign of either of them, so I step out onto the porch. I didn't see them go around the side of the house, so Liz must have walked into town. Out on the sidewalk, I look that way. That's when I see two figures on one of the benches in Marina Park. That has to be them.

I bite my lip. Should I go? Why not? I've still got my story I need to work on. I run upstairs and grab my coat. The closer I get to the park, the more sure I am that the two people on the bench are both women. And then I can make out features. It's them. They don't notice me until I wave. Then they wave back and motion for me to join them. When I'm close enough for them to hear me, I say, "I'm glad to see you two are getting to talk."

Liz Ravel wipes away a tear that dribbles down her cheek and looks at me. "Alex, Brid tells me you helped her find the courage to talk about our relationship. Thank you from the bottom of my heart."

I bite my lower lip as the heat rises through my chest and into my cheeks. "You're welcome."

"My parents always told me I was an only child. I had no idea that Brid was my sister. I always felt like there was something missing in my life, but I just thought it was me. That I was...broken. Thank you for helping to make this happen, Alex."

It feels awesome knowing I had something to do with reuniting two sisters. And then, for some reason I don't understand, the feelings of longing boil up inside of me. "I felt lost, too, when I was little. It was because of my birth mom. I always thought she wasn't around 'cause of me. Marquetta made me realize it wasn't my fault."

"I know, right? When I figured out we were sisters, I realized why I'd always felt we were connected," Brid says. Then, all of a sudden, her face darkens, and she peers at her sister. "I hope I didn't get you in trouble with the police."

Liz shakes her head. "It was my own fault. I panicked. In a way, I'm glad they found out. I don't feel as guilty now." She reaches out to take Brid's hand. "Thanks for being there for me when I needed you."

"Guy had just stormed off after Snappy when I saw you arguing with Barnaby outside the Crooked Mast. I figured you'd need someone to talk to. That's why I caught up to you."

"I'm just glad you were there. It was so comforting having someone to talk to." Liz lets out a heavy sigh and leans back against the bench. "And then I rushed off on you. I'm sorry."

My heart beats a little faster. Could this be another lead? More good stuff for my story? For the investigation? "Where'd you go?"

Liz looks at me and Brid, then she finally says, "I've already told Chief Cunningham what I did. You know what? I'm done protecting that man. I've realized Barnaby is not who I thought he was. He's as vain as Snappy and can be just as childish. After we argued outside the Crooked Mast, he stormed off to get the car. For some stupid reason, he'd insisted we drive to dinner. I waited for him to come back and even called out to him a couple of times. When he didn't, I figured he was still on his cellphone."

"Was he still mad about what happened at dinner?" Brid asks.

"You know how Barnaby is. Once he boils over, it takes a long time for him to cool down. It was the same thing when I talked to him down at the marina. He kept going on and on about Snappy and me and how we'd deceived him and how he was going to get even. You must have heard him. He was awful."

Brid nods and looks at me. "She's right. He was terrible. Guy had gone off after Snappy. That was why I joined you when I did. I was upset about what Barnaby said to you. And I'm not even married to the man."

"I think that's the moment when I gave up on any kind of relationship with him." Liz rubs her hand over her forehead and sighs. "I didn't know he'd tried to run down Snappy."

I can almost picture the accident in my head. Mr. Pauley's angry with Liz, so he walks back to get his car and backs into Mr. Welles. Maybe it was on purpose. Maybe it was an accident. But somebody strangled Mr. Welles. If Mr. Pauley hit him with his car and wanted to finish the job, why wouldn't he just run over him again? "Did you tell this to my dad or Chief Cunningham?"

"Not all of it." Liz kinda winces. "I left out the part about the argument outside the Crooked Mast because I don't think it was relevant to the investigation."

Wow. Some people never learn. When my dad and Chief Cunningham find out Liz and her husband had an argument right after dinner, they're gonna be really ticked off. "You've gotta tell my dad about the argument."

"Oh gawd, do I have to?"

Really? She's asking me? I'm, like, thirteen. "For sure. You can't filter out stuff just 'cause you don't want them to know about it."

"Alex is right. The best thing is for you to be honest about everything."

Liz hangs her head. "Okay. I will."

"Were you the only ones who drove to dinner?" I ask.

"I think so."

"I'm sure of it," Brid says. "Guy and I walked, and Carson and Snappy were just ahead of us."

Oh, snap! I think I just cracked the first part of the case!

32

RICK

RICK THANKED HOWIE FOR HIS time, then wended his way through the obstacle course of shoppers and display tables to the exit. He'd just stepped onto the sidewalk when his phone chirped with a call from Alex. A little stab of fear pierced his heart before he answered for one simple reason—Alex never called him unless she was in trouble. "Hey, kiddo, are you okay?"

"I'm fine, Daddy. I'm at Marina Park with Brid and her sister. You gotta come talk to us."

"Wait a minute. Brid has a sister? And she's here in town?"

"Kinda. It's Liz. They're related. I found out 'cause there was a book on road agents in Brid's room, and when me and Lydia were dusting, a letter to Liz fell out. When I asked Brid about it, she told me the whole story. We also know who ran down Mr. Welles."

Not sure what to say, Rick just listened as Alex rattled on, her words coming out in a rush the way they did when she got excited. When Alex stopped talking, he simply said, "I'll be there in five minutes."

Rick speed-walked to the park in a daze. In some ways, he felt like he'd just been hit by a truck. A letter fell out of a book when Alex was dusting? Seriously? One of these days, Alex's curiosity was going to get them sued. It wasn't that much of a surprise that Alex was on a first-name basis with the guests.

Again. How was it that she could so easily insert herself into their lives? Perhaps it was because guests still saw her as an innocent child. He knew better. She was anything but innocent.

Alex stood near one of the two benches in the park. Brid Ochoa and Liz Ravel sat on the bench in front of her. Upon entering the park, he realized the two women were holding hands. Brid's eyes were red and swollen. Liz held a wadded-up tissue in her hand. Sisters? A warm glow slowly rose through his chest. Obviously, this had been an emotional reunion. His cheeks tightened as he gazed at Alex. She'd meddled. Again. The reality was that her meddling had made someone's life better. Oh, great. Now he was doing it, too.

He gave Alex a tight-cheeked smile, then said, "Maybe what you need to be when you grow up is a professional meddler."

Alex rolled her eyes and shook her head. "Daddy, don't be silly. There's no such job." A moment later, her jaw dropped. "Is there?"

Brid and Liz both laughed, and Brid said, "If there isn't, there should be."

Alex's cheeks flushed with a rosy glow. She crossed her arms over her chest, gave Rick a firm nod, and lifted her chin. "Maybe I will!"

Rick winked at Alex, then turned to the two women. "Congratulations, you two. I guess you're closer than you realized. Also, Alex tells me you know whose car hit Mr. Welles. Is that true?"

Liz told him about the argument she'd had with Barnaby outside the Crooked Mast and how agitated he'd been. When she finished, she added a quick, "I didn't actually see him do it."

"I'll call Adam." He stepped away, dialed, and when Adam answered, recapped everything that had happened.

"I wish these people would just tell us the truth the first time," Adam grumbled. "Okay, here's the deal. After we talked to Ms. Ravel the last time, I had Deputy Kama check your guests' cars for damage. She checked them all very carefully. We struck out. None of the cars had any damage. That's not unusual in a low-speed accident, which means it's going to be impossible to prove without a confession or a witness."

Rick glanced at Alex, who was watching him eagerly, probably hoping for a compliment about helping to solve the crime. She was in for a disappointment. "Thanks, Adam."

"Wait. There's something else. We also have a change in the cause of death. It turns out Welles didn't die from asphyxiation. He actually died from a heart attack. The ME says someone did try to strangle him. They apparently compressed the carotid artery just long enough for him to suffer cardiac arrest before asphyxiation set in."

"Does this change anything as far as the case goes?"

"We're still looking for a killer, although Nancy Drew may have come through for us again."

Rick lowered his voice to ensure that Brid and Liz didn't hear him. "Are we keeping this information quiet?"

"I think so for the time being. We can strategize, and I'll fill you in about my conversation with Mr. Boyd when you get here."

"Right. Be there in a little bit." He disconnected the call, thanked Alex and his guests for their help, then explained that he had to leave. Alex, of course, tried to pester him about the call. "I'll tell you later, kiddo. Right now, I have to get back to Adam's office."

Rick darted away before Alex could hit him with any further questions. Half a block later, he was following the curve of the roundabout and ready to head up Main Street to the police station when he saw the open front door of the Crooked Mast. On a hunch, he went inside, where he found Ken Grayson talking to a couple of his staff.

"Hey, Rick. What brings you in so early? We won't open for dinner for another forty-five minutes. The bar's open, but I doubt that's why you're here."

"You're right, Ken. I'm actually here on police business. I wondered if any of your staff happened to be on break when there was a hit-and-run involving Mr. Welles."

Ken raised his eyebrows and looked at the two servers. "Ladies?"

Mary Ellen Herbert put her hand on her heart. "Oh, my word. When did this happen?"

"We think the accident was shortly after they left. So, that would be around seven or so. Did you see something?"

"I did take a break then. I was just so upset over the whole dinner. Anyway, it wasn't so much that I saw something, but I heard someone start yelling. Obscene language. It was awful. Right after that, a car drove away."

"Do you know what kind of car? Or the color?"

"The streetlights had come on. But you know one of those lights has been burned out for months. All I can tell you is it was dark."

"Was it big? Small?"

"Big. Yeah. One of those SUVs. Oh, and it headed in your direction. I thought maybe it was one of your guests."

They'd need a lot better description than that. At any given time, there had to be dozens of dark SUVs in town. Only a few of the residents drove them; they were way too impractical on the town's small streets. The vehicles were popular with tourists, and every day they poured into town, jamming the streets and flocking to the quaint downtown area. And then there were always those who stayed overnight. Just at the B&B, there were four guests with vehicles fitting that description. And three of those were in the Band of Six—Welles, Barnaby Pauley, and Guy Silvan. They all drove large, dark SUVs.

Rick hoped for something more specific as he asked, "Is there anything else you can tell me about the car?"

Mary Ellen shook her head. "I wish." She avoided Rick's gaze for a moment, then sighed. "I feel kind of awful about not saying something sooner. I heard about that man getting killed. I guess I didn't say anything because he was such a jerk. I'm sorry. The truth is that I didn't want anything to do with him. I should have called Adam right away."

"It's okay, Mary Ellen." Rick reached out and put a consoling hand on her shoulder. He gave it a reassuring squeeze. "Really. It's okay."

Especially because what Mary Ellen had seen would hardly stand up in court under any kind of cross-examination. It might, however, with a little cautious delivery, serve as the catalyst to force a confession out of Pauley. Even if Alex was right about having solved the first part of the case, it wouldn't solve the murder.

"Did anyone else see anything?" Rick asked.

The other server shook her head. "Not me. I was covering for Mary Ellen while she was on break."

"Me, either," Ken said. "I was still dealing with the fallout from that debacle of a dinner. I'm considering banning the rest of them from the Crooked Mast. Especially that clown Coulson."

"Why's that?" Rick asked.

Ken snorted. "This happened before you arrived. The guy ordered a small rib eye steak, well-done, then when it was delivered, he threw a fit. He claimed he'd ordered a large, medium-rare."

"What a jerk," Mary Ellen huffed. "He poked it a couple of times, then claimed we were trying to poison him with overdone shoe leather. He made such a stink that Ken decided to comp him."

"Come to think of it, he did the same sort of thing at breakfast. Marquetta was ready to wring his neck. The man's pretty demanding. And not very considerate. Let's get back to the accident. Did you see anyone else, Mary Ellen? Could there be other witnesses?"

"Not around here. I was the only one on break at the time. And I didn't notice anyone over near where it happened. And right after the car drove away, I came in."

Rick thanked the three of them for their time and turned to leave.

"Got a second?" Ken asked.

"Sure." Rick felt a little twinge of hope. Did Ken know something he didn't want to say in front of the others?

Ken looked at the two servers and said, "We'll talk later." He rubbed the back of his neck and waited for the two women to leave. "This isn't about the case. I haven't said anything to anyone else, but there's something I've wanted to tell you. Mostly because we're in the same boat."

Rick cocked one eyebrow, curious. This wasn't like Ken. He normally didn't mince words. "What's up?"

"Abby and I are expecting," he said sheepishly.

"Oh, you mean unexpected expecting?" Rick grinned.

Ken snickered and nodded. "Yeah. This was definitely unexpected. After Maxie was born, the doc told Abby she couldn't have another child." Ken smiled, then continued. "I'm telling you because we've both got teenage daughters and now we're both going to have our second. We just told Maxie the other day, and she's not one hundred percent happy about it. I can't blame her. She's been the center of our world for thirteen years, and now that's all going to change. How is Alex dealing with it?"

"Our situation's easy," Rick laughed. "Alex has been pushing for this ever since she decided Marquetta and I should get married. My suggestion is to just make Maxie a full partner in the process. Maybe if you involve her in the planning and the decision making, she'll realize her role will be changing but be just as important."

"Good idea." Ken sighed and watched his workers for a moment. "Nobody else in town knows. The one possible exception is Marquetta. Abby may have talked to her because of the situation. Anyway, we've wanted to keep it a secret because Abby's been seeing a specialist in San Ladron. The doc feels there could be complications with the pregnancy or the delivery. We've been making a lot of trips out of town, and people are talking, as usual."

"Is it okay if I tell Marquetta about this?" Rick asked. "I don't want to violate your privacy."

"Sure. Go ahead. If she doesn't know already, I'm sure she can keep a secret."

Rick left the Crooked Mast and crossed the alley to the small parking lot where the accident had occurred. He went to the exact spot where the body had been found and looked across the alley at the back of the Crooked Mast. This spot was close to a hundred feet from where Mary Ellen would have been standing. The lighting was old, and with one of the bulbs out, it would have been very difficult to see much of anything.

Taking a right, Rick walked the half block to Main Street. There was a streetlight on that corner that was visible from the back of the restaurant. Retracing his steps, he walked the alley in the other direction. He quickly realized that if someone had been on this end of the alley, Mary Ellen would not have seen them. It was the perfect location in one sense—someone could have witnessed the accident and then walked to Welles while he was down. They would have had the opportunity to either help— or kill—and never be seen.

33

ALEX

AFTER MY DAD LEAVES, I stay in the park for a few minutes with Brid and Liz. They have a lot to catch up on, and it's super cool to see two sisters find each other. When the wind picks up, the two of them decide to go to the Rusty Nail for dinner so they can talk more. I know Mom's gotta be wondering where I am, so I walk back to the B&B to check in before dinner.

Just as I'm about to go up the walkway to the front door, I see Creepy Coulson closing the back end of a black SUV. I don't wanna run into him alone, so instead of going through the front door, I take the gravel path along the side of the house and hide behind the big old tree. Here in the shade, the wind feels super cold, especially now that the excitement of seeing Brid and Liz reconnect is over. Oh, man. It's freezing out here. Shivering, I wait until Creepy Coulson takes the walkway up to the front door. I give him a couple minutes, then rush to get inside.

March 10

Hey Journal,

What an awesome day! I brought two sisters together! They didn't even know they were related. Well, one didn't, and the other did. Now they get to learn even more about each other. We even figured out who was driving the car that hit Mr. Welles! The bummer is my dad was super secretive about something after he talked to Chief Cunningham. He left right away, so I totally know he's onto something. After he was gone, I stayed in the park with Brid and Liz while they started telling each other how they grew up.

Then I came back to the B&B and found Creepy Coulson's car. Bummer, Journal. It's too bad he's not the one who ran down Mr. Welles. He's creepy enough that I'd like to see him get in trouble for something. Maybe the murder? I could write what I know for the Cove Talkers Newsletter. Do you think that if I write the article so it sounds like I've got proof, he might confess? It'd be awesome if I could prove he was the one who killed Mr. Welles!

Right now, I have to go downstairs to help Mom finish dinner. We're having spaghetti and meatballs! Yay! It's one of my favorites! Creepy Coulson's gonna have to wait, but I've got my eyes on him!

Xoxo

Alex

Walking through the butler door to the kitchen is like walking into heaven. Spaghetti sauce is simmering on the stove. Over on the counter near the oven, there's a loaf of bread that's been sliced in half. It's ready to go under the broiler. Yay! Mom made garlic bread, too. Awesome!

Mom's at the stove stirring the sauce and smiles at me. "Hey, Sweetie, I'm guessing you're getting hungry."

"I am now." I go to her, wrap my arms around her and give her a hug. "I love you, Mom." I emphasize the last word. I guess I always knew Marquetta would eventually be my mom, even if she and my dad didn't know it.

"I love you, too, Sweetie. What brought that on?"

"I dunno. I just realized how long it took to get you and Daddy married."

She laughs and kisses me on the top of my head. "You did have to work pretty hard to make that happen. Have you washed up?"

"Yes. Is there anything I can do to help?"

"No, Lydia helped me with the sauce and meatballs. I had her take about half of it home."

I stare at the stockpot. Half? That's a lot of sauce and meatballs. I guess Lydia would need it 'cause she's got three boys and her husband to feed. "Wow. You two must have made a lot!"

"Lydia said we made enough to feed a small army." Mom takes a deep breath and sighs. "It was a lot of work."

"Why don't you sit for a few minutes and let me take care of things?"

Mom hugs me and kisses me again. "I have a surprise for you." She sits on one of the stools at the kitchen island, takes a sip from her glass of water, and watches me. "Before we get into that, tell me about your day. What have you been up to?"

Where do I even begin? And how much should I tell her?

34

RICK

IT WAS NEARLY FIVE WHEN Rick walked into the police station. Adam sat behind his desk, intently focused on his monitor. When Deputy Kama greeted Rick, Adam glanced up, waved, then returned his attention to what he'd been reading.

"What is so interesting?" Rick asked as he approached.

"I've been doing background checks on your guests. I've found something interesting. No criminal records for any of them, which is what I'd expect. Socials all check out for everyone. And credit records don't show anything unusual except for Guy Silvan. Basically, there are no former addresses or employment prior to ten years ago. Before that, it's like he didn't exist."

"You're telling me he was a ghost prior to that time?" Rick muttered. There was only one situation where that would be considered normal. "What you're telling me is that the man is not who he says he is. Do you think he was in witness protection?"

"I'm not sure. We'll have to talk to him. I am curious, though. According to Ms. Ochoa, Silvan disappeared after dinner."

"Okay. Why don't I check with Marquetta to see if he's at the B&B?"

"No need," Adam said. "He's about to walk through the front door."

Turning in his seat, Rick spotted Guy Silvan standing in the doorway talking to Deputy Kama. The deputy pointed at a nearby chair, then came to Adam's desk. "He says he's got something he needs to talk to you about, Chief. Do you want me to bring him back?"

"You bet I do. Put him in the interview room."

"How about if I go get him?" Rick said.

"He's all yours," Deputy Kama said. "I've got a few things to clear up before my shift ends."

Adam cocked his head to the open door of the combination break room, storage room, and interview room. "Meet you in there, Rick."

Silvan sat in a gray straight-backed chair with metal legs near Deputy Kama's desk. He stood abruptly as Rick approached and rubbed his palms on his pants.

"Mr. Silvan. Your timing is impeccable. We were just discussing the need to talk to you."

"Brid texted me a few minutes ago. She said you were interviewing all of us and that it would be a good idea to be proactive." He glanced around and shuddered. "I've got to tell you, police stations give me the creeps."

"Why's that?"

"I've got hoplophobia." When Rick gave Silvan a quizzical look, he added, "An irrational fear of guns. I can't even watch a movie where there's a lot of shooting. I get all freaked out."

Another phobia Rick had never heard of. It seemed like there was one for everything these days. "That must be difficult," Rick said as he ushered Silvan into the room. Sure enough, the man stiffened when Adam joined them. "Mr. Silvan's afraid of guns."

Adam looked down at his sidearm and said, "Sorry. Tools of the trade. Have a seat, Mr. Silvan. That way, you won't see it."

They all took a seat at the table, Rick and Adam on one side and Silvan on the other. Silvan's jaw visibly tightened as he glanced nervously around the room. "Brid said you wanted to interview all of us. That's why I'm here."

Rick looked at Adam with raised eyebrows, unsure if he wanted to dive straight into the 'where were you ten years ago' question, or if he wanted to stick to current events.

Adam shook his head slightly. He pulled out a yellow pad of paper and placed it in front of him. He then interlaced his fingers and leaned forward, planting his elbows on either side of the notepad. "Let's talk about what happened after the dinner at the Crooked Mast. We're trying to determine the whereabouts of each person. Where did you go after you left the restaurant?"

"I was super angry. I think I've put up with Snappy's arrogant behavior for too many years, and it just got to me. So I walked back to the B&B, got in my car, and drove out to that parking lot near the lighthouse."

Rick narrowed his gaze at Silvan. Terrific. Here they went again. Silvan was either flat-out lying or leaving out part of the story—the incriminating part that put him at the crime scene. It seemed crazy for someone to go to the lighthouse after dark. There was very little lighting. The trail out there would be treacherous in the dark, and there was no view. It was also crazy to lie to the police, yet these people seemed to be making a game of it. Didn't they understand that they'd all be found out sooner or later?

Adam made a note on the yellow pad and looked up. "I see. And what did you do there?"

He snorted. "I sat. And fumed. I thought about all the things I should have told Snappy over the years, and eventually, I calmed down. I was probably there for a couple of hours. Brid was in the room when I got back to the B&B."

"Did anyone else see you come in?" Adam asked.

"No. The lobby was empty. Brid can tell you what time I got in. She was in bed reading."

Rick pursed his lips as he watched Silvan's face. There was another possible scenario. Silvan went after Welles as Brid had told them. He'd seen a car run into Welles and, instead of helping him, had killed him. He'd spent the next two hours at the park trying to come up with a story that would keep him in the clear.

Rick looked over at Adam, who was tapping his pen against the notepad. He, too, seemed to be frustrated by Guy Silvan's statement. "Thanks for coming in, Mr. Silvan. You should be aware that I've been conducting background checks as part of our investigation."

Silvan stiffened, then blurted, "So you consider me a suspect?"

"We're casting a wide net right now and looking at everyone who knew Mr. Welles. When I looked at the report, I discovered there's nothing on you prior to ten years ago. Why is that?"

There was a long pause, then Silvan said, "It's actually very simple. My parents dropped out of society in the sixties. They lived most of their lives off the grid. I was raised on a farm, and it wasn't until my dad died ten years ago that you might say me and my mother reentered society."

Adam nodded absently as he made a note. While Silvan waited, Rick noted his breathing. Fast and low. It was a classic sign of a man under duress. The story was BS. It had to be. "Where's your mother now?" Rick asked.

"She died just over five years ago."

"I'm sorry," Rick said, then looked at Adam.

"Enjoy your stay in Seaside Cove, Mr. Silvan. If we have any additional questions, we'll let you know."

Silvan's movements as he went to the front door were those of someone trying not to look rushed, but the fact that he barely noticed Deputy Kama as he made a beeline out of the office bothered Rick. Deputy Kama joined Rick and Adam. "Tough one, Chief?"

"It is."

"Amy?" Rick asked. "Did Mr. Silvan even glance at your gun as you passed him?"

"No. He looked like he couldn't get out of here fast enough. Why?"

"He claims he's afraid of guns, and yet he passed within a foot of yours without even a sideways glance. That seems odd to me. Tell me something. Wasn't your shooting incident in LA about a year ago? I recall that you had a similar fear when you first came here. Were you hyperaware of them at the time?"

Amy's jaw tightened. A stocky, five-foot-six brunette who kept in shape thanks to a regimen of running and Vinyasa yoga, she was an intimidating force when she put on her game face and ordered you to stop doing something. That was why Rick could only imagine how tense the situation that resulted in her shooting a man must have been.

"It was a year and a half ago, actually. And yes, for a long time, I couldn't even look at a gun. I would have been very aware of getting that close. On the other hand, nothing about this murder makes any sense."

"In your time as a court officer in LA, did you ever see a case like this?" Adam asked.

"That's a hard comparison, Chief. I was only involved in one murder trial. And by the time it got to court, everything had been sliced, diced, and laid out in a neat presentation. In comparison, this is messy and chaotic. There are just too many unknowns at this point." She glanced over her shoulder at the door. "Look, Chief. I need to be taking off. I sort of have a date."

Rick's jaw dropped for a brief moment. She sort of had a date? Oh, he got it. She was embarrassed. Or worse, she might be moving. "Is this guy local?"

As soon as the words were out of his mouth, Rick regretted them. They felt presumptuous. Amy seemed to take the comment in stride. She laughed. It was one of the few times Rick had actually seen her smile. "As a matter of fact, he is. He moved here a few months ago. He was a stockbroker who made a couple of brilliant calls and decided to take the money and run. We both feel the same way about stress, so we hit it off pretty good."

"So I'm not going to lose my deputy?" Adam asked.

"Not likely, Chief. I like my job, and I love this town."

Adam sighed and smiled at her. "In that case, Deputy Kama, have a good time. Enjoy your date."

As Amy hurried toward the door, Rick noticed a distinct change in her bearing. Normally, she carried herself in a very deliberate manner, the strength from her physical training obvious. This time, as she made her way out the exit, she appeared lighter and more free.

"She look different to you?" Adam asked.

"I was just thinking the same thing," Rick said.

"The joys of love," Adam mused. "By the way, Guy Silvan walked in before I could tell you. Marquetta has invited us over for dinner."

"You and Traci?"

"Yes." Adam laughed, then stood. "Apparently, she's decided the only way she might get to spend time with you is to get me there, too."

"And the only way to get you there is to offer you food."

A sheepish grin crossed Adam's face. "Well, it helps that she invited Traci, too."

"They have known each other all their lives."

"And we are getting married next month."

Rick noticed the same sort of change he'd seen in Amy just moments before. A warmth filled his chest. This was the type of life he'd never known existed until moving to Seaside Cove. In New York, it had always been go-go-go. Here, they could live and enjoy time with friends, even in the midst of a murder investigation.

35

RICK

IT WAS AFTER SEVEN BY the time the last noodle had been twirled
and the last meatball skewered. With seconds of spaghetti and
meatballs under his belt, even Adam, who Rick often compared
to an eating machine, seemed sated. The wine, a Zinfandel with
notes of blackberry, cherry, and cinnamon, was now only a
memory. Rick had even given Alex a small taste of the Zin. He'd
breathed a sigh of relief when she told him it tasted like vinegar.

They sat in the dining room around two four-top tables that
Alex had combined. By unanimous consent, they'd avoided all
talk of the case and Alex's story. Even Alex, as much as she
wanted to talk about the case, had seen the wisdom in keeping
the Band of Six from overhearing the discussion. Now, however,
with dinner behind them, Rick knew it was time to deal with the
business at hand.

Marquetta leaned back in her chair and rested her hands on
her rounded belly. She sighed, then looked toward the butler
door. "Why don't you and Adam talk in the kitchen while Traci,
Alex, and I take care of the dishes?"

"Nope," Traci said. "Alex and I are handling the cleanup, and
you're going to supervise."

The laugh lines around the corners of Marquetta's eyes
crinkled with her smile. "I like that."

"Let's clear this table in record time." Rick stood, brought over the cart they used to ferry dishes, condiments, and supplies between the kitchen and dining room, and began to load it up. With all of them pitching in, the tables were cleared and returned to their original placement in a few minutes.

After rolling the cart to the kitchen sink, he and Adam went to the table at the back of the kitchen to talk. Traci and Alex began washing dishes while Marquetta perched on a barstool at the island. Rick had just sat when he heard Alex's voice.

"Mom?"

"Yes, Sweetie?"

Speaking very clearly and loud enough for Rick to hear, Alex said, "Did I tell you that Daddy got called out for talking when he was supposed to be chaperoning?"

"Did he, now?" Marquetta glanced down the length of the kitchen. Rick could feel the delight in her voice. "My, my, Mr. Atwood. Who knew you could be such a bad boy?"

"Well, I guess my daughter is a snitch." Rick shot back playfully.

Adam cleared his throat and spoke as if he were giving an order. "In Rick's defense, it wasn't all his fault. We were talking about serious business."

Traci laughed as she picked up another dish to wash. "Oh, brother."

Marquetta turned on her stool and looked at Adam as if she were scolding a child. "Adam Cunningham, don't try to BS me. I've known you since fourth grade, and I know every single one of your tells. You are making this up just to cover yourself."

Rick snickered. "Nice try on the save, buddy. I think you're busted, anyway. You might be the police chief in this town, but Marquetta knows everything about everyone. Don't even think you can get away with something." He lowered his voice so only

Adam could hear him. "Besides, I already told Marquetta about this. We're just letting Alex have her fun."

Adam's lips pursed, and he nodded knowingly. "Gotcha. You're right about Markie; she's the queen of intelligence."

"Wait a minute." Rick turned in his seat and called across the room to Marquetta. "What have you heard about the Band of Six? Anything?"

"I thought you'd never ask." Marquetta eased herself off the barstool and looked at Traci and Alex. "Well, girls, I think I'm being asked for some professional advice. You two have this under control?"

"No problem," Alex chirped. She winked at Traci. "We're cool."

Traci raised a soapy hand from the dishwater. "This is the last one, anyway. Please, do me a favor. Go help my fiancé solve his case so I can have him back, would you?"

Rick pulled out a chair for Marquetta. As she sat, she sighed. "Those barstools sometimes get to be a little too uncomfortable."

"Noted," Rick countered. "We'll compensate. Now, you look like you've got something big you're holding inside."

Marquetta looked down and again rubbed her belly. "That's a baby, Rick. In case you haven't noticed, we're having one."

"Haha. You know what I mean."

"You just made it so easy. I couldn't resist."

"You're not the same woman I married. The woman I married would never make fun of her husband."

"Oh, I'm the same woman, just bigger and better." Marquetta's eyes widened, then a grin spread across her face. "That was a kick. A big one. Somebody's getting tired of cramped quarters. Okay. Let me get serious for a minute. Adam, I'd forgotten all about this until I saw Carson Coulson this afternoon. He was talking to someone on the phone. Actually, it was more of a rant. He was going on about a disagreement he'd had with Mr. Welles. It had something to do with a competition. Apparently, Mr. Welles thought Mr. Coulson was being demanding and inconsiderate."

"Nothing new there," Rick muttered.

"Do you know what competition?" Adam asked.

"No, but I think Alex might know about it." She turned and called to Alex. "Sweetie, didn't you talk to Mr. Coulson about his next tournament?"

"For sure." Alex and Traci finished at the sink and approached the table. Traci exchanged a look with Marquetta as she sat next to Adam. While Rick couldn't tell what the look meant, he was certain he and Adam were about to find out. Alex also looked eager to share some tidbits when she took the seat opposite Marquetta's. "It's an international archery competition. I talked to him about it when he was practicing the other day."

It wasn't much to go on. Still, that line of questioning might help expose some of the group's other secrets. Maybe. At least, that's what he hoped. And then there was also Marquetta's sly smile. Apparently, she had at least one more detail she wanted to share.

"That's not everything, is it? You're holding back on us," Rick said.

"Nothing much, just that Guy Silvan is divorced," Marquetta said flatly.

"Wait! What? There was no mention of him even being married in his background check. How do you know about this, Markie?" Adam demanded.

"Well...I, um..."

Rick couldn't recall the last time he'd seen Marquetta so reluctant to answer a question. Unless she was protecting someone. He turned quickly to his daughter. "What have you done, Alex? Have you been snooping again?"

"It wasn't her," Traci blurted. "It was me. He was in the store looking for a gift to send to his daughter. He said he hadn't seen her in years because his ex had cut him off. His daughter has a birthday coming up, and he wants to send her something special."

"So much for background checks," Rick said.

Adam glared at Rick, but the irritation quickly turned to resignation. "Traci, if you're the one who had the information, why is Marquetta telling me about it?"

Traci batted her blue eyes at Adam as she pushed back a few strands of reddish-blonde hair. "Well, we've talked about me not getting involved in your work, and I didn't think you'd want me being a witness. Originally, I was going to tell you. Then, Marquetta called and invited us to dinner. That's when I asked her if she would tell you about it. I'm sorry, Adam."

"Sounds like a simple misunderstanding," Rick said.

Adam leaned over and kissed Traci. "I get it. Rick's right. This is just a misunderstanding, and it's not your fault. It's mine. I was pretty adamant, wasn't I?"

"Yes, babe, you were. I didn't want to do anything to hurt our relationship, so I figured if I could stay out of it, everything would be easier."

"In front of witnesses, I'm telling you, Traci Peterson, that I love you, and I never want you to feel like you need to hold back. That goes for our relationship as well as my work. Okay?"

"Got it. Holding back. Over. In that case, there's nothing like first-hand information. Right?"

Adam sat straighter, and his eyes widened. He swallowed hard. "As long as it really is first-hand. Is there something else you want to tell me?"

Traci wrinkled her nose, and her tone went up a notch. "I might maybe have overheard something else. I also kind of have an observation and an opinion. Do you want those, too?"

Rick glanced at Marquetta, who winked at him. "We need everything we can get, Adam."

"I agree. Of course, babe. What have you got for me?"

"You know how people will say and do things when they think they're alone or being anonymous? Well, Mr. Silvan had no idea who I was, and he seemed to consider me just some random part of the background. After he got done talking to me, he made a call to his mother."

"Wait." Adam held up his hand with his fingers splayed. "His mother? Are you sure?"

"Of course. He said, 'Hi, Mom' when the person answered the phone. Why?"

"I'll tell you in a minute. Go ahead."

"Well, he told her he called to see what his daughter might like for her birthday."

Rick, who'd been sitting with his chin propped up on his knuckles and his elbows on the table, huffed and shook his head. "Huh. He sure didn't mention any of this to us."

Traci shrugged. "Basically, he was talking freely as long as I was the only one in the store. It probably helped that I pretended to ignore him while I was working. The thing is, it got weird as soon as his girlfriend showed up. He got very secretive and said, 'I have to go.' He pocketed his phone, and when his girlfriend asked him about the call, he lied and told her he'd been talking to a friend of his back in LA. It was like he didn't even want her to know he'd called his mother. That's pretty weird. Right?"

Adam stared at Traci, his shock evident. "There's a little bit of a problem with that whole story, Traci."

"What's that?"

"A few hours ago, Guy Silvan told us his mother has been dead for five years."

36

ALEX

Hey Journal,

Chief Cunningham and Traci are still downstairs visiting. After we finished talking about the case, they all moved into the living room so they could sit by the fire. It totally sounds like the Band of Six has a lot of secrets! Before, I thought maybe Creepy Coulson was the killer, but now I'm thinking it could be any of them, especially now that Chief Cunningham said Mr. Welles had a heart attack. I still don't wanna believe Brid or Liz could have done it. They wouldn't, would they?

I'm having a super hard time figuring out what's supposed to go in my story and what's not. When it was just Mr. Coulson, it was easy. Now, there are all these secrets coming out, and it's all super confusing! Gotta go, Journal. I think Mom just knocked.

Xoxo

Alex

"Come in!"

Mom opens the door and pokes her head in. She's hiding something behind her back. It looks like a present. It's got purple and teal wrapping paper and a white bow. "Hey, Sweetie, I see that you've got your PJs on."

Mom totally knows my favorite colors. And that I love presents. I wanna know what she's hiding. "What's in the package?"

"I guess I can't hide anything from you, can I? No matter how big I've gotten."

I smile at her. She wasn't trying very hard. "I think you wanted me to see it."

"Okay, you're right. I did. This is just from me to you." She holds out the package. "It looks like you've been writing in your journal."

"I just finished. I'm done for tonight." I take the present from her hand and put my journal in the desk drawer. Wow. A gift from Mom to me. I lean forward and hug her. "This is awesome. Thank you."

"You don't even know what it is." She winks at me. "Open it."

I pull off the wrapping paper. Inside is a small white box. The same kind my Christmas PJs came in last year. I lift off the lid, and my jaw drops. A few seconds later, the box gets a little blurry, and there's a lot of pressure building in my eyes. Mom got me my own apron. And it says, 'I'm the Big Sister.'

She's smiling at me. It's her worried smile. The one she uses when she's not sure about something. "I started to give you this earlier, but then I thought I should wait until after the baby comes. I've decided now's a better time. Do you like it?"

"I love it!" I pull out the apron and hold it up. It's gonna be the perfect size for me. "Thank you."

I tell her how excited I am to try it out. That's when she tells me she wants me to start helping with menu planning. I'm like gobsmacked! Mom keeps total control over the menu. But I get it. My role is gonna change. She's gonna let me do more 'cause she trusts me. The whole thing feels awesome.

"Mom, can I ask you a question?"

"Of course, Sweetie. Does this have something to do with your investigation?"

I shake my head. "It's totally different."

"Oh. Well then, hop in bed, and let's talk."

When I slip under the covers, she sits on the edge of the bed next to me. I remember the first time she did this. I never thought I was gonna have a mom who loved me or would talk to me about girl stuff until we moved here. That's when our lives totally changed. "I'm so happy to have you as my mom."

She leans over and kisses my forehead. "I feel exactly the same. And that's not going to change once this baby comes."

I shake my head. "I'm sorry I got kinda weird about it. I'm actually looking forward to having a baby brother."

"So, what did you want to ask me?"

"Are Mr. and Mrs. Grayson getting a divorce?"

She laughs and shakes her head. "It's amazing how the rumor mill in this town can be so fast and so wrong all at the same time. You've heard about all their trips out of town?"

I nod. "Yeah. People are saying they're going to counseling. And Maxie won't talk about it, so it's gotta be true. Right?"

"People, Alex? Are you referring to Lydia?"

My face gets all hot. Oh, man, I never wanted to get Lydia in trouble. "She was just telling me stuff other people told her."

"Alex, do you know why I don't repeat things other people tell me?"

This is super embarrassing. We've had this talk before. "Because people don't always get things right."

"And because gossip can hurt people. Think about poor Maxie for a minute. If she's at school and her friends are talking behind her back about her parents splitting up, how do you think that makes her feel?"

My shoulders slump, and the room gets even hotter. "Kinda like I did when stupid Billy Thornton told me you and Daddy weren't gonna love me as much."

"Exactly. I know you can be good at keeping secrets when you want to."

"I guess so."

"And you want your articles for the *Cove Talkers Newsletter* to be accurate, don't you?"

Uh oh. "So I shouldn't talk about it until I can confirm the truth?"

"Actually, I'd suggest regarding gossip as a secret that should be kept, not spread."

"Lydia knew about it, so it's not really a secret."

"It's also not correct."

"Everything kinda fits, though. Lydia has to be right."

"Sweetie, I know for a fact that Lydia is wrong on this." She makes a face like she has to make a hard decision. "Abby asked me to keep this quiet. However, I can assure you they are not having problems. Since Ken told your dad, and you and Maxie are friends, I don't think Abby will mind if I tell you what's really going on. There's one stipulation, though. You have to promise me that you won't repeat this to anyone." She holds up her hand with her pinky extended.

Whoa. Mom doesn't pinky swear unless it's super important. I put my little finger around hers. "I swear."

"Ken and Abby are in the same situation as us."

I scrunch up my face and look at her. Then, all of a sudden, it hits me. "They're having a baby?"

"You can't tell anyone. You promised."

"For sure. Can I tell Maxie that I know?"

"Only if you do it privately. You have to be certain there's nobody else around. And I mean nobody. You can't even tell

Sasha or Robbie. You heard what Traci said tonight. Mr. Silvan assumed she wasn't listening, and now she's passed along the information he wanted to be kept quiet. The Graysons will tell everyone when it's time. Until then, we need to help keep a secret they've entrusted to us."

That makes sense. It's also confusing. "Okay. I kinda get it, but I still don't understand why they don't want anyone to know. This is good news, right?"

"That part I can't tell you. I wish I could. Now, are you ready to get some sleep?" She fusses with the covers, smoothing them out the same way she always does. She leans over, kisses me again, and whispers, "Do you want to know another secret?"

I suck in a little breath and whisper back. "Sure. What?"

"Close your eyes and listen."

I do what she says. The only sound is the wind hitting the outside wall. My dad says since the house is over a hundred years old, it's entitled to a few groans now and then. "All I hear is the house making noise. It creaks and groans a lot."

"When I was a little girl, Captain Jack told me that this old house had a spirit of its own and that all those creaks and groans were the house singing a lullaby. The house is singing you a song. It's telling you everything it's seen over more than a hundred years."

I close my eyes and listen again. This time, the sounds are different. "I hear it," I whisper.

When I look at Mom, her eyes glisten. She wipes her lower eyelid with one finger and smiles. "Now, go to sleep."

She kisses me on the forehead and stands. On her way out, she turns off the light. My eyelids droop closed. The lullaby is there. Making me sleepy. Comforting me.

I get a picture of Maxie in my head. She looks kinda sad and lonely. I get that. It's how I felt a lot of the time before we moved to Seaside Cove. I'll see Maxie at school on Monday, and that's when I wanna talk to her alone. I bet she's been sad 'cause she's hearing the rumors about her parents splitting up, and she can't say anything. Mom's right. All this gossip can hurt people. I don't wanna hurt Maxie. She's my friend.

On Monday, I'm gonna try to cheer her up.

37

RICK

RICK STOOD IN THE CORNER of the dining room while he surveyed the smattering of guests who had come down for breakfast. This Sunday morning, like most others, was off to a slow start. Brid Ochoa, Liz Ravel, and their significant others had shown up. Carson Coulson was conspicuously absent. In addition to the four members of the Band of Six, the Dixons had made it along with one other couple. It seemed most guests drew the line at keeping the same schedule on a Sunday morning as they did during the week.

Even the help was taking it slower, Rick thought. Lydia needed the day off, and Alex was working on a school project. Even though it was just him and Marquetta, the pace had been manageable so far. He had his fingers crossed that things wouldn't go haywire.

When Liz Ravel glanced at Rick and raised her mug, he gave her a nod and grabbed the carafes for both the regular and decaf coffees. He approached the table, his attention being somehow drawn to both Barnaby Pauley and Guy Silvan. He thought the two men would be happy their partners had realized they were siblings. Instead, Pauley was in a foul mood, and Silvan was acting more like an attention-starved child than a boyfriend.

While pouring coffee into Liz's mug, Rick asked, "Have you heard from Mr. Coulson?" Only after having asked the question did he realize she'd just taken a bite of her toast. "Oops. Bad timing. Sorry."

Liz shook her head as she chewed and held up one finger. After swallowing, she said, "It's okay. That's how it always works in restaurants. Right? Anyway, none of us have heard from Carson. He doesn't always sleep well, so he probably had a bad night and is just sleeping in. I'll bet he shows up grumpy right before you shut down."

"It wouldn't be the first time," Brid added.

"That guy can be a total jerk when he wants to," Silvan grumbled. When Brid shot him a nasty look, he winced. "Sorry. That's just the way I feel. He's always got that I'm-better-than-anyone attitude."

Pauley snickered to himself, then looked across the table at Silvan. "Hey, maybe we got lucky, and somebody bumped him off, too."

The two women both gasped, but Silvan seemed to enjoy the comment, hiding a smirk behind his mug as he sipped. Rick moved on to his next table, saying a silent thank you that he had more guests to attend to. He was happy to do anything to avoid another conversation with Pauley and Silvan and kept busy filling coffee mugs and chatting at the other tables.

When the new guests who had checked into the Captain's Quarters the day before showed up, he took their orders and talked to them about things to do until Carson Coulson walked in. "I guess I'd better see if I need to take another order," Rick said to the new guests. He wove his way through the tables to where Coulson was not looking any too happy.

Liz wore a concerned smile, one that seemed entirely genuine. "Carson. We were beginning to wonder about you. Are you feeling okay?"

"Chipper as can be," Coulson said sarcastically. "Mind if I join you?"

Guy Silvan chugged down the last of his coffee and stood. "Here. You can have my spot. I was just leaving." He looked down at Brid. "Coming, babe?"

"No. I think I'll stay here. Liz and I have some more catching up to do."

"Right. Sister stuff," he sneered.

Pauley stood without even a glance at his wife. "I'll join you."

The two men pushed past Coulson and strode out of the dining room without looking back.

After Rick removed Silvan's place setting, Coulson sat in the vacated chair. He had a quizzical look on his face. "What's his problem? Today. And what's this about sister stuff? Have I missed something?"

"Before we get into that, don't you want to order?" Liz raised her eyebrows and gazed at Coulson.

He sighed. "I suppose. Tea and toast."

"What kind of tea, Mr. Coulson?" Rick was about to list the teas when Coulson cut him off.

"Earl Grey, since you don't have Darjeeling."

"Of course. Are you sure you don't want something more?" Rick asked.

"Positive," Coulson snapped, then his tone softened. "I've a bit of a queasy stomach this morning. Didn't sleep well." He rolled his eyes. "The beds in this establishment are atrocious."

"What?" Brid turned sideways in her chair and stared at Coulson. "Are you kidding? Mine's extremely comfortable. And you slept fine the night before. Didn't you?"

Coulson ignored the question, rubbed his palms together, and asked, "So what did I miss?"

Rick stepped away from the table. He knew exactly where this was headed. The children were about to argue again. As he was walking by the table for the Dixons, the wife flagged him down. "Yes, Mrs. Dixon?"

"Don't pay any mind to him, Rick." Filomena Dixon winked. "I saw plenty of his type in my time as a nurse. They're never happy and always have to blame their troubles on someone else. The rooms here are exquisitely comfortable."

"Thank you. That's very kind of you to say." Rick lowered his voice and winked at her. "I'd better get that order of tea and toast before his highness has something else to complain about."

Walking away from the Dixon's table, Rick winced at what he'd said. He knew better than to make snide comments about the guests. The problem was the Band of Six had pushed all of his buttons multiple times, along with Marquetta's. It was only yesterday that Coulson had sent his breakfast back because it was seasoned incorrectly. While Marquetta had taken the comment in stride, he knew it had bothered her. He'd had about as much as he could take.

"Mr. Coulson would like tea and toast."

Marquetta rolled her eyes and huffed. "Good. Maybe I can make the toast to his liking."

"I know. I just made a snide comment to Mrs. Dixon about him. I shouldn't have. It just sort of popped out of my mouth." Rick kissed Marquetta, then smiled. "You know what? I'm not even sorry. Guy Silvan had it right. Coulson is a complete jerk. He doesn't even have to try."

"Let's not go down that path, Rick. Tempting as it is, it can only cause problems."

"You're right." Rick hooked his thumbs into the tie of his apron. "It's time for this nonsense to stop. If Carson Coulson wants to send his toast back, I will defend my woman."

Marquetta chuckled as she popped two slices of bread into the toaster. "My knight in shining armor. Go get the man some tea."

"Right." Rick added loose-leaf tea to one of the infusers, then placed it in a mug of hot water. He set the timer and leaned against the counter while he waited. "By the way, I didn't get to ask you last night how your talk with Alex went."

"She gets it. Intellectually, she knows gossip is bad. And she knows it can hurt people. I encouraged her to resist the pull by making it more personal. Hopefully, she'll do better."

"Maybe one of us should talk to Lydia, too?" Rick asked.

"I can do that. I'll explain to her how impressionable Alex is and how we're trying to keep her from becoming a gossipmonger. Lydia will understand. She's got some friends who like to dish about everyone and everything."

Rick shrugged. "We certainly can't tell her what to do in her off time, but we can try to make sure she doesn't repeat it here."

"Exactly. Okay, here's that toast." Marquetta handed Rick a plate and motioned with her hand for him to leave. "Go before this cools off. We don't need to have Mr. Coulson complaining again."

As he rushed out the door, Rick took a deep breath, preparing himself to be on his best behavior when he delivered the order. His preparations felt wasted when he walked into the dining room and saw only an empty table where Brid, Liz, and Coulson had sat minutes before. "Really?" Rick muttered to himself.

"Rick?" Mrs. Dixon said.

He took a deep breath and looked at her. "Yes, Mrs. Dixon?"

"I've always had a fondness for Earl Grey tea. Perhaps I might trouble you for a cup."

Her husband, a man of substantial girth who'd claimed he was trying to lose weight, winked. "And we can take the toast off of your hands, too. This marmalade looks delightful."

This was the kind of couple that made running a B&B a pleasure. They were easy-going, pleasant, and always upbeat. He set down the mug of tea and the toast. "Absolutely. Thank you both. And Mr. Dixon, if you'd like a little more coffee, I'd be happy to get that for you."

"Wonderful. And perhaps I could get a little of that blackberry jam. For the other slice."

His wife snickered. "Oh, Thomas. You and your sweet tooth."

"Mr. Dixon, you and my daughter would get along very well."

For once, the man actually flushed pink, and he suppressed a smile. "She's the one who told me to try it. She said it's locally made." He gave Rick a sly smile and added, "I'm a big believer in sampling the local fare."

From the looks of him, Mr. Dixon did a lot of sampling. He was the kind of tourist Seaside Cove loved. "As a matter of fact, the blackberry jam is locally made. If you like it, I'll tell you which shop in town carries it. Mention us when you go in, and they'll give you a discount. Be right back with a little of that jam."

Rick left the dining room and almost ran into Guy Silvan, who was pacing near the butler door to the kitchen, a cell phone pressed to his ear.

"I'm telling you I can't come to see you right now, honey. I'm out of town, and I won't be—call me back in a couple of minutes." The color in Silvan's cheeks drained. He glanced at the butler door. "Rick. I hope you don't mind me being in this area. It's not off limits, is it?"

"Only on the other side of that door, Mr. Silvan. I'm afraid I have to switch hats here for a moment. Who were you talking to?"

Silvan straightened, the line of his jaw tightening. "I don't see how that's any of your business."

"Not my personal business, but as a consultant to the police...." He let the threat hang in the air. Even though the threat carried almost no weight at all, it was worth a try. And it seemed to have the desired effect.

"Sure. Whatever. My wife left me right after my dad died. It was a tough time, and the stress of leaving a life of seclusion made things too difficult for both of us. It got to the point where we couldn't reconcile, so she filed for divorce. If you must know, I've been talking to my daughter. I haven't seen her in a long time, and I contacted her recently."

Thank goodness. Now they'd never have to reveal what Traci had told them. "And you don't want the others to know about your divorce?"

"Right."

"If I could make an observation on a personal level, you should tell Brid. The fact that you're hiding part of your past from her will put a tremendous strain on your current relationship."

Silvan shrugged. "That relationship's not going anywhere anyway. Brid was only with me because we were doing all these fun things on Snappy's dime. Now that the money's dried up, I expect her to dump me."

"Really? Was your relationship that fragile?"

"Are you kidding?" Silvan snorted and looked away. "Brid had her sights set on Snappy next. I was just a stepping stone. I think she was planning to make a move on him during this trip."

"Are you sure about that? I thought she didn't like the man."

Silvan snorted again. "Heck, she doesn't really like me, either. For all I know, she made her move, and he rejected her. Maybe that's why he's dead." His phone rang again, and Silvan looked at the screen. "My daughter again. I gotta take this." He walked away without another word.

38

RICK

RICK DUCKED INTO THE KITCHEN to grab the blackberry jam for Mr. Dixon. The moment the butler door swished closed, his heart went to his throat. Marquetta wasn't there. He swallowed hard, then called out her name.

"Back here."

He found her at the large table in the back of the kitchen, the same one they'd sat around last night. Rick started to ask what she was doing, then realized how tired she looked. "Are you okay?"

"I just got lightheaded all of a sudden. I'll be fine."

He rushed to the table and sat next to her. Taking her hand, he gazed into her eyes. He saw an unusual weariness. "You're exhausted, aren't you?"

Marquetta gave him a weak smile. "I thought I could still handle things."

The doctor had warned them about trying to do too much. There was no question that they'd reached Marquetta's limit. "That's it. I'm talking to Lydia about taking on more hours. Mary Ellen Herbert volunteered to help out, too. I think we need to give you more time to rest."

"Rick...."

"No. You've resisted long enough. We've got you and a baby to consider, and if we need to take on more help, that's just the way it is."

Marquetta rubbed her forehead with her fingertips and nodded. "Okay. You're probably right. It's gotten harder these last couple of days. I'm not sleeping as well, and it's taking its toll." She let out a heavy sigh and gazed back at the stove and sink. "There's a lot of cleaning up that needs to be done. I'll help you with that."

"Absolutely not. You are going upstairs to take a nap. I'll get Alex to come down and help me. Come on. Let's get you upstairs."

Once again, Marquetta seemed to accept his demands and let him help her stand. It wasn't until they were passing the dining room that Rick remembered Mr. Dixon's jam. "Oh, shoot. Why don't you sit in the living room for a minute? I've got to grab some of that blackberry jam for Mr. Dixon."

"I'll be fine, Rick. Really. I'm doing much better now." She gave him a kiss on the cheek, then said, "Now, go. Take care of the guests. I promise I'll go upstairs and rest."

Reluctantly, Rick released her elbow and dashed back to the kitchen, where he put a small amount of the jam in a serving bowl. He delivered it, explained the delay, then went in search of Marquetta. He made it to the top of the stairs just as she entered their bedroom. Feeling confident that she would be fine on her own, he knocked on Alex's door and told her he needed help downstairs.

Alex bit her lower lip and sucked in a breath. "Is Mom okay?"

"She just needs rest, kiddo. I think she didn't realize how hard it was going to be to keep up her regular pace while she was pregnant. Anyway, I really do need some help if I'm going to get out of here to help Adam."

"I'm coming." Alex put away her laptop. When she closed her door, she looked in the direction of the master bedroom, the worry clearly showing on her face and in her voice. "Should we check on her?"

Rick put a hand on Alex's shoulder. He massaged it gently while reassuring her Marquetta would be fine on her own. They were walking through the living room when Alex asked what progress he'd made on the case.

"I'll tell you in a minute." In a whisper, he added, "I think the walls have ears."

He and Alex spent the next thirty minutes cleaning up the kitchen and dining room. As they worked, he told her about Guy Silvan and his suspicions about Brid Ochoa. Alex, who was stacking the dishwasher, rolled her eyes. "No way. She was only involved in their group so she could spend time with Liz."

Rick mentally debated the options. That Brid would not be after Welles seemed like it made sense. After all, the man wasn't exactly catch-of-a-lifetime material. On the other hand, love did appear to be blind. It could also be that she was into men with lots of money and power. "Are you sure about Brid?"

"Totally. Daddy, I talked to both her and Liz for a long time when they connected."

She'd talked to them both for a long time? Of course, she had. She'd discovered the sister connection. Then why did she still have a look of guilt on her face? What had she done? This time. "Have you been spying again, kiddo? Tell me the truth."

Alex scrunched up her face and looked down. "I got a look at the notes she was keeping about her search for Liz. She knows I read them, and she's totally fine with it."

"Alex, you know we're not supposed to invade our guests' privacy."

"I told her what happened. She wasn't mad. I promise."

"Are you telling me everything, Alex?"

"Totally. Daddy, I got her to talk to Liz. She was afraid she might ruin things between them. I told her she should try. So in the end, she was happy that I did what I did."

That was probably an exaggeration. More likely, Brid was accepting Alex's interference because things had turned out well. If they hadn't, she might have felt differently. "Consider this a warning. You cannot violate our guests' privacy. Do you understand?"

Alex stuck out her lower lip. This time, it was no put-on act. She really was contrite. At least for now. He'd come to realize his daughter had little impulse control, so when she wanted to do something, she put the plan into action before thinking it through.

"I get it," Alex said. "What I did was wrong. Daddy. I promise I'll do better."

Rather than belabor the point, which, who knows how many times he'd been over with her before, he decided to move on. "Fair enough. Let's get the last of this mess cleaned up while you tell me all about these two sisters and how they came together."

By the time the clean-up was finished, so was Alex's story about Brid and Liz. At that point, Alex said, "Do you think Mr. Silvan is the killer?"

Rick thought about it for a few seconds. Deep down, he was sure that wasn't the case. "No. I don't. But I do think what he knows could help us find the killer. Even though his past doesn't seem relevant to this murder, I have a feeling that it is. That means I have to somehow get him to talk."

"Did you check his social media page?" Alex asked.

"He doesn't post much."

"What about his friend list? Maybe his daughter is on it."

Rick closed his eyes and tilted his head back. Of course. Leave it to the tween investigator to come up with a possible solution. "I'll check that." Rick's cell phone rang. He could tell from the ringtone that it was Adam. "Hey, buddy. You missing me?"

"We need to go see Dennis Malone. He may have witnessed our murder."

The tone in Adam's voice, combined with the fact that there had been no preamble, clearly indicated that this was urgent. "Okay. When do you want to do that?"

"Can you break away now? You know how Dennis is. Here one minute, gone the next."

Rick did know. And Adam wasn't talking about physical presence. Dennis had done a few too many drugs in his younger days. It was a lifestyle that was just now catching up to him. "I have some things to check out on Guy Silvan that I can do later."

"I can do it!" Alex chirped. She had a smile on her face, and she practically beamed up at Rick.

He had never been able to resist those blue eyes. That was just like any other parent, he supposed. The internal debate began—let her help; no, it's dangerous; don't be silly, it's only online research. And when Alex raised her right hand and told him she'd report directly to him and only do the research in her room, he caved. "I'll meet you at Ocean Surf in ten minutes, Adam. See you then." After disconnecting, he said, "I am absolutely insane for doing this, but okay, as long as you stick to the rules. You're only researching online. There's no in-person investigating. Are we clear?"

"Crystal!" Alex snapped to attention and saluted. A moment later, she nearly doubled over when she burst into laughter.

Rick wrapped his arm around her shoulders. "You know what, kiddo? I do love you."

Alex melted into his embrace, and at that moment, Rick said a silent prayer that the child he was about to have with Marquetta would be equally lovable.

39

ALEX

THIS IS SUPER AWESOME! I get to do some real research on the murder case without getting in trouble! I'm gonna do the best job ever on this so Chief Cunningham and my dad will see how valuable I can be. I get out a notepad to start. I know that's, like, so old school. But, hey, my dad and the chief aren't exactly tech whizzes, so I'm gonna do this the old-fashioned way and give them my notes.

I write the word 'SUBJECT' in all caps. That's perfect. I add Guy Silvan's name right after it and underline it. Awesome. Below that, I write the name of the social media network I'm checking. When his profile comes up, it's kind of a disappointment. My dad was right. He doesn't post much at all. He also hasn't hidden his friend list from the public. There's Brid's name. According to his status, he's single. So does that mean he hasn't updated it because they haven't been going out long? Or maybe he thinks it's not gonna last. Or maybe he just doesn't know how to update it.

His friend list includes all of the Band of Six and thirteen others. The others include eight men and five women. His daughter has to be one of those five. I hope.

The first female friend I check is super popular. She's young and pretty and is wearing a sexy negligee. Oh, whoa! She's got like a thousand friends, and most of them are men. And her posts all have links to her website. I click the link and suck in a huge breath. My face gets super hot, and I can't stop staring. She's not wearing.... "Oh. She's that kind of friend."

I close the page. My whole head and neck are burning with embarrassment. I've never seen that kind of photo before. Swallowing hard, I go back to Mr. Silvan's profile. One thing I know for sure, I'm not following any more links!

The next female friend is a lot older. She looks like she could be someone's grandmother, and she lives in Connecticut. She's totally not his daughter. The next couple of friends are younger. One of them works for the same company as Mr. Silvan. She lists her occupation as a driver, just like him. She's thirty-five years old, so they're probably coworkers. The next one is named Holly. She looks like she's about my age.

I bite my lower lip and click the link to her profile. Holly goes to middle school in Hartford, CT. Why does that sound familiar? The grandma! I start checking Holly's list of friends. Whoa! There's grandma. And there's even a photo of the two of them together. Holly lives with her, and she's got a birthday coming up soon.

Sitting there, staring at the page, I think about what my dad said. Online research. That's all I can do. I bite my lower lip again. Holly's in Connecticut. And because she's just a kid, I don't think she's gonna hurt me. I could send her a friend request. What would be the harm? That's online research, right? I hover the cursor over the send button. This is so not a good idea.

"You're gonna get in trouble for doing this, Alex," I whisper to myself. But I was supposed to find Mr. Silvan's daughter. And if I don't tell her who I really am—I shouldn't do this. I should tell my dad. So he'd do what? Have the local cops bust down

Holly's door? No way. She looks nice. I don't wanna do that to her.

My finger clicks the trackpad. The friend request is gone.

"I am so dead." My dad is gonna kill me. It gets worse about ten seconds later when I get a message, "*Do I know you?*"

Now what? I can't tell her the truth. If she thinks I'm trying to get her dad in trouble, she'll shut me down for sure.

—My name is Alex. I live in Seaside Cove in a B&B and I think your dad is one of our guests. Is his name Guy Silvan?
—That's what he calls himself now. Why?

Maybe that should be a hard question, but it's not. My mind is already spinning with ways to answer it. And one of those ways is almost guaranteed to bust through her defenses.

40

RICK

OCEAN SURF, LOCATED ON THE opposite side of the roundabout from the B&B, was barely a ten-minute walk. On the way, Rick passed Marina Park. He smiled to himself as he gazed at the bench where he'd met with Brid, Liz, and Alex.

Once he passed the park, Dennis Malone's t-shirt shop was easily visible. Like most of the downtown, the store had been built when Seaside Cove was nothing more than a small fishing village. In its heyday, it had been a general store. It had also gone through iterations as a small market, a real estate office when developers first concocted big plans for the town, and eventually, a series of small retail stores. With its dark green and bright white color scheme and flat roof, it resembled a gawky cousin in a village of Craftsman and Victorian elegance.

Though the shop was still closed, Adam's 4x4 was parked in front, and the double entry doors were ajar. Rick pushed one of the doors open, poked his head inside, and called out. "Adam? Dennis?"

"Back here." Adam waved from where he stood about midway back in the store.

As Rick weaved his way between the racks of clothing, a bright purple sweatshirt with Seaside Cove emblazoned across the front caught his attention. It was exactly the color Alex would love. It was perfect for her. And he was tempted to combine a little pleasure with his official reason for being here.

"Hey," Dennis said in his typical laid-back baritone. "Pretty awesome, huh? Your daughter would love one of those."

Dennis was, as usual, wearing shorts and flip-flops. Whether it was his years in the ocean as a surfer and diver or just that he had no personal thermostat, Dennis was one of those people who never seemed to feel the cold. His only accommodation to the chilly morning was the Save the Planet sweatshirt he'd donned, and Rick doubted he'd have that on for long.

"You know my daughter too well, Dennis," Rick said. "How much are those purple sweatshirts?"

Dennis ran his fingers through his sandy blond hair and nodded enthusiastically. "With your local discount, it'd be twenty-five. Best of all, that line is all environmentally sustainable."

In fact, Rick had noticed the sign as he'd walked by the rack. He'd also seen a couple of posters on the wall advertising a complete line of eco-friendly clothing. Once Alex heard about this, he knew what she'd want. "I'll take one."

"Just wait until you've got another one to buy for," Adam snickered. "You might have to open another B&B."

"Or have the town start paying me to help you," Rick shot back.

"Touché. Tell you what. You can shop til your heart's content after we get done with our business." Adam turned to Dennis. "You said you saw two men fighting on the street on Friday night."

Dennis's gray eyes blinked a couple of times, then he nodded. "Right. Gotcha. I got off work late and was on my way home when I heard loud voices."

"And you're sure it was two men who were arguing?" Rick asked.

"Two dudes. Totally sure. They were, like, really going at it. It sounded like they were arguing over some book or something."

A book? Oh no, this wasn't another of Dennis's delusions, was it? Dennis made no secret of his past, and Rick often wondered if, or how much, the drugs he'd used in his younger years still affected him. How close to reality was Dennis standing today? "Did you catch names? See faces?" Rick asked as he snuck a peek at Adam, who was flipping through his notepad.

"No, man. No names. Just some seriously bad name-calling. The one dude was, like, maybe this tall." Dennis held up a hand to indicate someone who would have been just under six-foot tall. "He had like this scruffy beard and was kinda scrawny."

Rick shot another glance at Adam. He was getting the same look in return. That description sounded very familiar. Maybe there was hope for this case, yet. And maybe Dennis was a better witness than he'd expected. "Do you have the photos, Adam?"

"Sure do," Adam said as he pulled out his phone. He turned the screen so Dennis could see it.

"That's him! That's one of the dudes. Yeah, man. They started arguing, then he shoved the other dude and grabbed this book thing out of his hands."

Adam tapped the screen on his phone and showed Dennis another photo, this one of Snappy Welles. "Was this the other man?"

"For sure." Dennis's head and shoulders bobbed in what was close to a full-body motion. "Yeah, Chief. That's the other one. He's the dead guy, right?"

"Right. His name is Snappy Welles," Rick said.

"Snappy, huh?" Dennis grinned. "Cool name. Who's the other dude?"

"Guy Silvan," Adam said. "He's not necessarily a suspect, but he seems to have something to do with this case. We've heard about this argument from another witness."

In a way, Rick was surprised that Adam had revealed Guy's name. Then again, maybe it did make sense. "Adam, are you concerned that Silvan might come in here before he leaves town?"

"I am. Dennis, if you see him, you can't say anything about this conversation. I don't want you getting involved in this case or putting yourself in danger."

"No worries, Chief. What conversation?" Dennis grinned at Adam.

The expression on Dennis's face was so innocent that Rick wondered for a moment if perhaps he had already forgotten what they'd talked about. But when Dennis winked, Rick's opinion of Dennis's mental status rose just a smidge. The guy wasn't quite as 'out there' as the rumors said he was. "Perfect, Dennis. Now, what else did you hear? Can you give us any specifics?"

Dennis finger-combed his hair as he pursed his lips and blew out a breath. He sounded like a kid who was playing motorboat. His eyes darted away for a second, and Rick's confidence plummeted. That hadn't lasted long. It looked like their great witness was falling apart already.

As quickly as his attention had wandered, Dennis seemed lucid again. "Yeah, man. I remember. That Guy dude was yelling about being tired of being spied on. He said he was gonna get even once and for all and take away what your victim loved most."

"Did he say what that was?"

"No, man, those were his exact words. Yeah, that was it. Next thing I know, he grabs this book, so I figured that's what he was talking about."

"What did this book look like?" Rick asked.

"There wasn't enough light to really see it. I guess it was like so." Dennis formed a rectangle with his hands that was six inches by nine inches, or maybe five-by-seven, or larger because he kept moving his hands into different positions.

Rick's pulse quickened, and he looked at Adam. "I think we've found the missing notebook."

Adam nodded, then turned his attention back to Dennis. "So Guy Silvan met up with our victim, argued with him, made a threat, then grabbed some book. Is that what you saw, Dennis?"

"Yeah, Chief. That was it. That's all I saw."

While Adam made a note, Rick asked, "Did you see Mary Ellen Herbert?"

Dennis frowned and shook his head. "No, man. Was she supposed to be there?"

"She was on a break and standing near the back door of the Crooked Mast."

"Dude, you can't see that door from where I was. And I wasn't really stopping to watch. I was on my way home."

"Did you see what happened after Guy Silvan grabbed the book?" Adam asked.

"No, Chief. Guess I should've stopped and said something. Huh?"

Adam reached out and put a hand on Dennis's shoulder. He shook his head. "No. I think you were right to do what you did. There's no telling what might have happened if you had intervened. However, you could have called us. We might have been able to defuse the situation."

From what Rick had seen of the Band of Six, being able to defuse anything was a stretch. They'd found so many things to argue about, and if the incident hadn't happened when Dennis saw it, it could have been five minutes later. Even an hour or a day wouldn't have made a difference.

"Dennis, think carefully," Rick said. "Was there anybody else nearby? Maybe someone else standing around? Maybe someone in a car?"

"Nope. Nobody else."

Rick sighed. So Dennis hadn't seen the car. Maybe Mary Ellen had given them all they were going to get as far as a description of the vehicle. They still couldn't prove that Pauley was guilty of a hit-and-run, maybe even murder.

After quizzing Dennis for several more minutes, Rick and Adam agreed that they'd gotten everything they were going to get from him. The acknowledgment worried Rick. They'd been able to reconstruct part of the evening, but there were still critical gaps. Would another talk with Guy Silvan provide more insight? Maybe. Especially if they put pressure on him to stop hiding what he'd done that night.

41

ALEX

I HESITATE JUST A SEC before I click the reply button. Holly. She's about my age. Am I really gonna lie to her? I don't wanna hurt her. Just get information for my story. And maybe solve a murder. That's what this is about. The reason my dad helps Chief Cunningham—it's for the greater good. I gotta do it.

—*Hey, Holly. Thanks for getting back to me so fast. You and me are kinda alike. I grew up not being able to see my mom. Parents just don't get how hard it is on us kids when they have problems. Right?*

—*Totally. They can be so oblivious to what we need. Do you ever see your mom now?*

—*No. She stayed in New York when my parents got divorced. My dad's married again.*

How much do I tell her? We're talking more about me than I wanted, but it feels good. It might even let her know there's hope. And then, when Holly's message comes through, I smile.

—*Do you like her? Your new mom?*

—*She's awesome. She totally understands me. Have you met your dad's girlfriend?*

—*No. He said she can't know about me.*

—Why?
—I dunno. He's been weird ever since the accident.

My hand goes to my heart. It's pounding super fast now. What accident? Did it involve Holly? Is that why she's not with her dad? What about her mom? Is she okay?

—Is that why you can't see your dad now? Because of the accident?
—That's what he says. I dunno. He like won't talk about it 'cause it ruined his life. It makes me super mad. Like he's the only one who got affected by it.
—I get it. Totally. Was anybody hurt?
—One of the kids on the bus. Even though it wasn't my dad's fault, he got blamed. He got fired, and then he started drinking. My mom couldn't deal with it, so she divorced him, then she moved us here with my grandma.

What? A kid on a school bus died? When? How? My stomach churns. I know a bunch of kids at school who ride the bus. If that happened to one of them.... I squeeze my eyes shut tight to force out the thought. It helps, but I can't get away from the feeling of darkness closing in. The anger Holly must feel all the time. The hurt.

—Your whole situation must be super hard.
—Yeah. It sucks. My grandma says I should talk about it, but nobody here understands my side. All they see is their own.

I don't know why I feel like I can talk to Holly. Maybe it's 'cause what I said in the beginning is more true than I realized. So I tell her about my real mom. Our time in New York and how we had to leave. She asks questions, and we talk. When I tell her about moving here, she kinda perks up.

—*Really? That's awesome. It's like you got a total redo. I wish I could get that.*
—*I was lucky. Your dad seems like he's still in a super dark place. You know?*
—*Totally. I don't think he's ever coming out.*
—*Wow. That sucks. Is that why he changed his name?*
—*Yeah. He says he's trying to start a new life. He totally doesn't act like it. He acts more like he wants to get back at the guy who caused the accident.*
—*How old were you when it happened?*
—*It was a week before my fourth birthday. It totally ruined everything.*
—*That's about when my mom got super weird, too. My birthday's right after Christmas and I was super sad for the whole holiday. When's your birthday?*
—*November 15. I'll be 14.*
—*Me, too. How awesome, we're the same age.*
—*Yeah. Hey, Alex, I gotta go. I gotta help my grandma with lunch. Can we talk again?*

I shouldn't. I know that. The thing is, we get each other. I just hope she never tells her dad about me. If she does, I could be in super big trouble. What if he's the killer? I hope he's not 'cause I like Holly. And it sounds like she needs a friend. I grit my teeth, type my reply, and send it. Yeah. We'll totally talk again.

42

RICK

GUY SILVAN LOOKED LIKE A man about to be sent to the gallows. His cheeks, drained of color, were splotchy, and his eyes, which had seemed fearful on his previous visit to the police department, flitted around the interrogation room like a butterfly in flight.

Rick felt sorry for the man. He obviously had some deep, dark secrets. Those secrets might include his stated fear of guns. Or was that another lie told simply to hide his past from the police? Being kind, Rick could reason out how the man had 'forgotten' to mention his encounter with Snappy Welles on the night of the murder. That type of thinking wasn't going to solve the case. Doing his job as a consultant to the Seaside Cove Police Department could damage his reputation as the owner of the town's premier bed-and-breakfast. On the other hand, that would only be with the Band of Six. After all the lies they'd told, he no longer cared what they thought.

"How hard do you want to be on him?" Rick asked.

"Look, if you want me to handle this, I can do it on my own." Adam pulled in a long breath as he gazed through the glass observation window at Silvan. "I just thought you'd want to be there. That's all."

"We work better as a team," Rick admitted. "I hope it doesn't complicate his stay at the B&B."

"By complicate, I assume you mean make him want to take revenge or something of that nature."

Rick grimaced, then reminded himself that justice was more important than a good review. "Let's do this before I change my mind."

He strode purposefully into the room right behind Adam, and they sat side-by-side. "Guy, I'm sorry that Chief Cunningham dragged you in here like this, but we've received information we felt warranted immediate follow-up."

With a furrowed brow, Silvan shook his head. He rubbed his hands over his arms and looked everywhere but at Rick. "I don't understand. Why are you doing this to me?"

Adam put a hand on Rick's forearm, and Rick got the message—he didn't need to take the brunt of Silvan's outrage. "Mr. Silvan, we've found a witness that puts you in direct contact with Mr. Welles at approximately the time of death. We're giving you this opportunity to amend your previous statement."

Silvan's grip on his arms tightened. "No. I told you everything."

Adam wrote a single word on his yellow notepad in all capital letters. *PERJURY*. His voice hardened. "Then let me refresh your memory and also remind you that there are penalties for lying to law enforcement. You were seen having an altercation with Mr. Welles. During that altercation, you pushed him and grabbed a book he was carrying." Adam rested his elbows on the tabletop and leaned forward. His eyes were laser-focused on Silvan. "Sound familiar?"

"Okay. What of it? Yeah, I got into it with Snappy." He turned to Rick and smiled. "You've seen how he was. Nobody got along with that man. Right, Rick?"

"I agree that he was difficult." Rick licked his lips. "Why don't you just tell us what really happened? The whole story."

Silvan craned his neck back and gazed at the ceiling. Tears welled in his eyes when he looked back at Rick, then Adam. "I didn't kill him. I swear. The man was selfish and arrogant. You want the truth? I loathed him. Yeah, I admit it. Everything he did was centered on him. He didn't care who he hurt. It's why he was so interested in Brid. He didn't care about her. All he wanted to do was make Liz jealous. If he took Brid away from me in the process, that was just icing on the cake."

Rick's phone vibrated with an incoming message alert. He ignored it and watched Silvan with one eyebrow raised. "I thought you said Brid was the one who had her sights set on Welles."

"Yes. Maybe. I don't know. There was something going on."

"Look, Guy, I understand how you felt about Mr. Welles. That doesn't change anything. We just need to know what happened in your argument with him. We also need to know what happened to the notebook. It may contain information we need to find his killer."

Silvan huffed, then ran his fingers down his throat. "Okay. Snappy left dinner. He was all smug because he'd caused so much commotion. He headed downtown like he was going to go for a walk or something. I followed him until we got to the alley. That's when I yelled at him. I think, for once in his life, he was afraid. He ran away, and I chased after him. I guess he wanted a weapon because he tried to reach down and grab a little branch that had fallen off of a tree. That's when his notebook fell out of his pocket. I caught up to him while he was picking it up. I shoved him and grabbed his precious notebook. He stumbled backward and almost fell down. Then he held up this little stick like he was going to hit me with it or something. The guy looked so pathetic standing there gripping that thing like it was some kind of sword."

Rick remembered the area where they'd found the body. There had been a few downed branches, none of them of any significant size. They were the kind of thing that could have broken off during a good stiff breeze. "And what did you do?"

"That was when I realized just how impotent the man was. The only way he could get what he wanted was to buy it or bully someone into doing what he wanted. So I laughed at him. That made him angrier. I told him he'd lost his power over me, and I didn't care anymore about what he'd done to me in the past. I walked off and took the notebook with me."

"And where did you go?"

Silvan shrugged. "I didn't want anybody to know where I was, so I walked back to the B&B."

Rick's phone buzzed with another message. "Sorry, this might be about my wife." He checked the screen and saw that he had two messages from Alex.

—*Silvan lost his job as a bus driver after an accident 10 years ago.*

—*Drunk driver hit his bus*

Rick sent Alex a return message with a thumbs-up emoji. "False alarm," he said. It seemed everything about the Band of Six revolved around what had happened in the past. "So what did he do to you in the past, Guy?"

"He ruined my life."

"How?"

Silvan licked his lips and stared back at Rick. He whispered, "Please, don't make me talk about this. It's too much."

As much as Rick wanted to be sympathetic, he knew it couldn't happen. "I'm sorry, Guy. We need to know what happened. Tell me about the accident."

Guy Silvan's lower lip quivered as the last vestiges of any color drained from his cheeks. "You know about that?"

Rick nodded. "We'd like your version."

"I lied to you before," Silvan croaked. "My name hasn't always been Guy Silvan. I changed it about ten years ago after I was in an auto accident that was caused by Snappy Welles."

Thank you, Alex, Rick thought. He pursed his lips as he gazed across the table. None of this made sense. Lots of people were in auto accidents. That didn't mean they went and changed their identities. There had to be more. "Why don't you just tell us the whole story?"

"I was a school bus driver. I had a wife, a daughter, and a good life. It was my job to take a group of our kids to a football game out of town. All it took was one careless moment to destroy all that."

"You haven't answered Rick's question," Adam insisted.

Silvan snorted. "Do you know what kind of stigma there is when you're responsible for the death of a child, Chief? Even though the accident wasn't my fault, I was the one driving. That poor kid who died was under my care. Sure, people blamed Welles because he was drunk, but he hired attorneys and a private investigator. They planted all kinds of stories. The bus driver had been drinking, too. He'd been out partying the night before. He was high. All that stuff. My life turned into a disaster. My wife left me. My daughter lost her friends. Finally, it got to be too much, so I just disappeared."

"What was your name before you changed your identity?" Adam asked.

"Harry Giles. Date of birth, July 14, 1977. Harry Giles doesn't matter anymore. As far as the world is concerned, he's dead."

"Mr. Silvan, or is it Giles?"

"Silvan."

"Very well. You do realize I'll be checking out your story. Don't you?"

"Go ahead. It's all there."

As Adam made a note with Silvan's date of birth, he asked, "Are you still legally married?"

"No. I told you. My wife divorced me. She took back her maiden name and moved my daughter to Connecticut. They both live with her mother now."

"I'll be back in a few minutes," Adam said. "Rick, I'm sure you have questions for Mr. Silvan."

Did he ever. So many. "Why don't you leave the notepad with me?"

When Adam closed the door behind him, Rick sighed and gazed across the table at Silvan. "You could be in a heck of a lot of trouble, Guy."

"I know. But I didn't kill Snappy."

"Why should I believe you? You hated him. You've misrepresented who you are. I could go on. Please, I want to believe you. What I need is for you to give me a reason. You have to level with me about the argument with Welles."

"What I told you about following Snappy is the truth. I followed him, confronted him about the way he treated all of us, but then I left."

"And you took the notebook with you? Why was that so important to him? And why did you take it?"

"Snappy kept tabs on everyone. It was how he kept control. He was probably going to be making notes about the dinner. All the buttons he'd pressed, the reactions he got, and that sort of thing."

Rick raised his eyebrows and inched closer. "So it was something like a diary?"

"Not exactly. No. It was more about other people. It was all about the ways he could put pressure on people in the future. If you made a mistake, he made a note so he could bring it up later. He had notes about everybody. How Carson did in his competitions. Brid's interest in California history. He had a checklist of things he'd done to bring her into the group. That was why he bought that stupid pocket watch."

Narrowing his gaze at Guy Silvan, Rick eased himself back in his seat. "Levi's Folly? The one he was showing off at dinner?"

"That's right. That's the one."

"This is all in his notebook?"

"I think so. I didn't stop to read it, obviously. I drove up to that lighthouse parking lot figuring it would be empty. That's when I started flipping through pages. One of his recent entries was about the auction for the watch. Snappy bid on it to impress Brid. Barnaby did it so he could prove to Liz that he was better than Snappy. Talk about a couple of roosters in the barnyard."

Rick's pulse sped up. If there were details concerning the auction, that might help with the investigation. They needed to see this notebook, but first, he wanted to know what Silvan had read. "What kind of details did Mr. Welles include in there about the auction?"

"It looked pretty extensive. Look, I was drained. I just glazed over it. He was bragging at dinner about how he outsmarted the other people who wanted that stupid thing. Even the ones who joined up against him. He wanted to make sure Brid knew he was the one who owned it. That's why he was showing it off. I'm just positive he was going to make his move on her."

"Guy, we need to see this notebook. Where is it?" Rick held his breath as he waited for the answer.

"Back in the room. I put it in my overnight bag. I was going to destroy it."

For the first time since they'd started working on this case, Rick felt like there was a ray of hope. Maybe, just maybe, they were getting a break.

43

ALEX

AFTER TALKING TO HOLLY, I'M totally sure I'm getting close to knowing who killed Mr. Welles. And once I know that, this is gonna make an epic news story. I need to dig deeper. This is so not gonna make my dad happy—but at least I told him part of what I know. And he didn't tell me to stop.

Awesome. I'm gonna talk to Brid next. I've already talked to her, so I can't get in trouble for doing something I've already done once before. Right?

I go to the Mainsail Room and knock on the door. There's no answer.

Down the hall, I hear the vacuum. It's Lydia. She must be cleaning the Port Room 'cause the Dixons are leaving today. Bummer. I like them. They're nice people.

Maybe Lydia's seen Brid. When I go into the room, Lydia's just wrapping up the cord for the vacuum. "Alex, hey, did you hear about Mary Ellen Herbert? She and that no-good husband of hers are having problems again. I heard that she's thinking of divorcing him. This would be the second time!"

Tempting as it is to find out more, I think about what my mom told me. And what if Lydia is wrong? "Lydia, how do you know this?"

"When I was at the market, I ran into one of the girls who works with Mary Ellen."

This sounds a lot like Lydia's last bit of gossip. I get it now. It's what Mom was trying to tell me. "Nuh-uh. I don't believe it. Whether it's just a rumor or it's true, spreading rumors like this could get back to Mary Ellen and hurt her. How would you like it if people talked about you that way?"

Lydia plants her hands on the handle of the vacuum and looks at me. For a minute, I think maybe she's gonna get mad, then she straightens up and smiles. "I'm sorry, Alex. I shouldn't have said that. Old habits die hard. You are growing up. Just a week ago, you thrived on this kind of stuff. Now, look at you. Thinking about other people. Your mom and dad should be proud."

My face feels warm. I rest my hand on one of the bedposts while I study the intricate pattern of the rug that nearly fills the room. The wood on the bedpost is smooth and polished. The rug is a classic Victorian with deep burgundy and green colors. I guess I'm trying to avoid the fact that I'm embarrassed by Lydia's compliment. I don't know why. Maybe her approval means more to me than I thought. "Thanks, Lydia." I reach out and give her a hug.

She squeezes me back. "You know, Mija. You and your parents have become very dear to me." She kisses the top of my head, then pushes me back, looks at me, and sniffles. "You're quite the special young lady. It makes me wish I had a daughter of my own, but God cursed me with three rambunctious boys." She laughs, and I laugh with her because I know how much she loves those boys.

"Thanks, Lydia. And you know what? I'm super sorry about what happened in the Mainsail Room. I never wanna get you in trouble."

"Don't worry, Mija. Everything's fine, but I need to get back to work now." She hugs me again.

"Do you know where Brid is?"

Lydia leans back. Her eyes get super wide. "You're not going to be snooping again, are you?"

As much as I love Lydia, I can't be sure she won't repeat what I tell her, so I'm gonna keep my reasons to myself. "I just wanted to talk to her. She's pretty cool."

"I have no idea where she is. When I knocked, there was no answer. I figured I'd get the room tidied up while they were both out." She arches her eyebrows. "What do you want to ask her?"

"Nothing special. I can find her whenever. I'll talk to you later. Okay?"

As I walk out the door, Lydia is humming to herself. She sounds happy. She really has fit into the B&B like she's part of the family. I wish she didn't tempt me so much with all her gossip. Then again, my dad always says that if it wasn't for the rumor mill in this town, there would be nothing to talk about.

Going down the stairs, I hear voices. One of them is my dad's. The other belongs to Mr. Silvan. They sound serious. I hurry down the stairs to find out what's going on.

44

RICK

GUY SILVAN CLENCHED HIS HANDS into fists several times as he stood just inside the entrance to the B&B. The whites of his eyes were wide, his anger flaring and obvious. "I don't understand why I can't just go up to my room, get that stupid notebook, and hand it over to you. I feel like a criminal."

"I'm sorry, Mr. Silvan," Adam said. "This is not Rick's fault. We need to establish a clear chain of custody in case this notebook becomes evidence at a trial. And don't forget. You did forcibly take it from Mr. Welles. Now, let's get on with this."

Rick stopped at the base of the stairs and watched Alex take the last few steps. "Hey, kiddo, what are you doing?"

"I heard voices. I wanted to see what was going on. Are you trying to find Mr. Welles's notebook?"

"I'm sorry, Alex, but we need to get to Mr. Silvan's room. Step aside, please." Rick tried not to sound gruff despite the fact that he could almost feel Silvan's anger boring a hole in his back.

Alex's gaze went past Rick. "Mr. Silvan, are you okay? You look mad."

Even though the question was innocent and filled with concern, Rick fully expected Silvan to lash out. He turned, ready to cut off any outburst, but the outburst never came.

"No, kid. I'm not. I've done something stupid. I was angry with your dad and the chief, but this mess is my own fault." He looked up at Rick and smiled weakly. "My daughter's about the same age as yours. I miss her so much. Let's just get this done."

"Sure." Rick turned to Alex and winked at her. "I'll talk to you later, kiddo. Okay?"

Alex nodded, stepped to one side, and headed out the front door. Rick watched her, and it occurred to him that she seemed to be in a hurry, as though she had to deal with an issue of her own. Why hadn't she asked more questions? She'd cooperated far too easily.

They turned left at the top of the stairs and went to the second door on the right. Silvan used his key to open the door, and they followed him in. He started toward the small closet, but Adam stopped him.

"I'll get it, Mr. Silvan."

Once again, Rick felt terrible for his guest. An apology was not in order, however, because Adam's caution was in everyone's best interest. Guy Silvan could have anything in that bag. Even a weapon. He rested a hand on Silvan's shoulder. "It's okay. He's just following procedures."

Silvan's eyes widened, then he nodded. "I get it." He stood to one side, arms crossed over his chest. "Wow. The things you never think of."

Adam pulled a black nylon overnight case from the closet. "Is this yours?"

"Yes. That's it."

After putting the case on the bed, Adam unzipped the top. His eyebrows went up, and he turned the bag sideways so they could see inside. "It's empty."

Silvan's mouth dropped open, and he sputtered an almost incomprehensible, "What?" He took two steps forward, jerked the bag out of Adam's hands, and stared inside. "It was right here. I swear."

There was only one other person who had access to this room. No, two. Maybe even three. Rick's stomach felt heavy. Alex. Had she been here already? Hoping he was wrong, he asked, "Did you tell Brid about the notebook?"

"No, no. I haven't told anyone," Silvan stammered. "Especially Brid. She'd go ballistic if she knew about it. She'd have returned it to Snappy. I'm sure of it."

At that moment, Rick believed he had more faith in Brid than Silvan. Faith or not, he still felt like he had a lump of clay in his stomach. If Silvan hadn't taken the notebook, and Brid didn't know about it, the only other people with keys to this room were the staff. Lydia would never think of stealing a guest's personal belongings. What about Alex, though? Rick replayed the interaction on the steps. She'd been in a hurry— maybe. Had he misread the situation? He wanted to trust her, but there was a good chance she'd just pulled off one of her capers.

"Adam, I need to check on something. Do you want to stay here with Mr. Silvan for a few minutes?"

"I have some questions, too, Rick." Adam cocked an eyebrow, a move Rick thought might indicate that he, too, suspected who might be behind the missing notebook.

"I'll get answers." Rick rushed out the door. Just to be sure, he went to Alex's room first. He got no answer when he knocked, then used his key to look inside. Empty. He closed the door and went downstairs. Standing in the lobby, he looked first at the front door, then toward the kitchen. If she had been leaving, he wouldn't find her. Maybe she'd doubled back and gone to the kitchen.

On his way, he noted that Carson Coulson sat in the living room, scrolling through his phone. He had a definite scowl on his face. It did not look like a good time to interrupt him, so Rick continued on. As he'd expected, the dining room was empty.

Rick pushed through the butler door and found Alex and Marquetta sitting at the kitchen island chatting. Marquetta's face lit up when she saw him. She gave him a little wave and nudged Alex's elbow. "Hey, we were just talking about what to do for lunch. Is Adam with you?"

"Daddy! Did you catch the killer?"

Rick's gaze went to Alex's face. Her eyes were wide with curiosity, and as he searched for any sign of guilt, he saw none. There was no sign that she might be hiding something, either. Otherwise, why would she have asked about the killer? There was no time for subtleties. He had to come out and ask the question.

"Alex? Have you been in the Mainsail Room at any time since Mr. Welles was killed?"

She shook her head. Her infectious smile was suddenly gone, replaced by a frown. "No. Why? Is something missing?"

The heaviness and that small lump in Rick's stomach grew in size and weight. How would she have known something was missing unless she'd taken it? "Alex, I'm serious. This is no time for games. Don't lie to me. Were you in Mr. Silvan's room? Did you take something from there?"

The creases in Alex's brow deepened and her eyes misted over. "Daddy...I didn't...."

"Rick? What's going on here? Why are you treating her that way?"

There was an edge to Marquetta's voice that Rick seldom heard. This whole thing was going in the wrong direction. He took a deep breath to steady his voice. "The notebook Mr. Welles kept was a diary of sorts. Guy Silvan stole it from Welles right after the dinner at the Crooked Mast. Just before the murder, in fact. It could be a critical piece of information. There may be clues to who killed him in that book."

"And it's missing?" Marquetta asked. She turned to look at Alex and placed her hands on Alex's shoulders. Looking straight into her eyes, she said, "I want you to tell me the truth, Sweetie. Whatever you tell me, I will believe you. What I'm asking is that you not break our trust. Did you take that notebook?"

Alex swiped away a tear and shook her head. "No," she croaked. "Why won't anyone believe me?"

A longing to trust his daughter was telling the truth suddenly went to war with her past behavior. She'd stretched the truth too many times to count in the past. On the other hand, he desperately wanted to believe in her sincerity.

Marquetta nodded and scooted closer to Alex. Slipping her arm around Alex's shoulders, she pulled her closer and kissed her forehead. "I believe you." Marquetta turned her gaze to Rick. "She didn't do it. Someone else had to take that notebook. It's hard for me to even think that Lydia would do that. What about Brid? She's got access to the room."

Rick involuntarily groaned. His shoulders slumped as resignation set in. "She didn't know about it. Silvan never told her." Rick's throat felt tight as he regarded Alex. "I'm sorry, kiddo. I shouldn't have doubted you."

Swiping again at her cheek, Alex said, "I don't like being a suspect. I didn't do anything."

"I know." Rick went around the island, wrapped his arms around her, and pulled her close. "I'm sorry. Really. I am."

After a few seconds, she nodded. "It's okay. I don't think Lydia took it, either."

Rick eased Alex back and sat on the stool next to her. "Why's that?"

"Because she was cleaning the Port Room. The Dixons checked out this morning."

"That's right. I forgot. Once again, it feels like Adam and I are chasing our tails." Rick gazed at the ceiling and sighed. "So if it wasn't you, and it wasn't Lydia, it had to be Brid."

"Or one of the others in that group," Marquetta said. "Could someone else have known Mr. Silvan had this notebook?"

"Silvan swears he didn't tell anyone about it. The only way they'd know is if they saw him take it from Welles."

Alex cocked her head to one side. With her brow furrowed, she gazed off into space, looking as though she were working through the possibilities.

"What are you thinking, kiddo?" Rick asked.

"Where was the notebook stolen?"

"In the alley at the back of the Crooked Mast."

"Daddy, they all went in separate directions after the dinner. Any of them could have seen it."

"Maybe so, but only one of them could have entered that room. Which means Brid had to know about it. Adam and I need to talk to her. Do you know where we can find her?"

45

RICK

OUT OF A COMBINATION OF habit and caution, Rick knocked lightly on the door to the Mainsail Room before he used his key to enter. Guy Silvan sat on the edge of the bed with his shoulders slumped in defeat. He stared at the oversized tub in the corner of the room as though it might contain a solution to his problems.

Adam stood nearby; the muscles in his jaw were tense, his face, stern. Rick felt sorry for Silvan. Being questioned by the police—especially when it had anything to do with murder—was as serious as it got. The man was right. He'd brought on his own troubles. Just as nobody else could take ownership of his remorse, he alone would have to deal with the consequences of his actions. Rick passed on what he'd learned from Alex, then said, "We're going to need to look for Brid. Do you know where she might be?"

"She's been hanging out a lot with Liz. They've taken a liking to that muffin shop. It has that funny name. Crusty Buns?"

Guy Silvan looked up at Adam, who was now standing near the pedestal sink and gazing at the shelf above. He pulled a piece of Seaside Cove B&B stationery from beneath the small basket that was used for incidentals. After reading the note, he handed it to Silvan.

"This looks like it's for you. For what it's worth, I'm sorry."

Silvan took the note from Adam and laid it on the dark blue runner at the foot of the bed. "I already know what it says. 'Guy, we're never going to work. I'll be staying with Liz for the rest of the trip.'"

Rick shot a glance at the closet. He hadn't realized it before, but Silvan's bag had been the only one there. Brid's dark green roller bag was nowhere to be seen. "How did you know what the note said?"

"It was on the bed when I came back from breakfast. She must have been preparing to make a quick getaway." His jaw worked from side to side as he rubbed his scraggly beard. "I told you she was done with me. She just wanted to be with Snappy. Now that he's dead, she doesn't need me anymore. Are we done here?"

"Yes," Adam said. "For now. Mr. Silvan, we may have more questions. When were you planning on leaving town?"

"Tomorrow." He looked at Rick. "That's our checkout date. Right?"

Rick nodded. "It is. Adam, we've got other guests coming in, too."

"Then let's hope we wrap this up today. Let's go find Ms. Ochoa."

They took Adam's 4x4 and parked behind Crusty Buns. The store was, as usual, bustling with activity. Everywhere Rick looked, customers sat around white-topped tables eating from small plates and drinking from Crusty Buns' mugs. In the middle of it all, Mary O'Donnell flitted about like a hummingbird in a garden filled with brightly colored flowers. She looked like the quintessential happy grandmother as she chatted with customers, refilled coffee, and cleaned up after those who had finished.

Rick was relieved to see that she and Angus had taken on a helper, a young woman who'd recently moved to town with her husband and family. When Mary spotted Rick and Adam, she raised her coffee pot and weaved her way in their direction.

"Gentlemen, are you here for a little pre-lunch snack?" Mary's Irish brogue made the words sound like a song. "I could find you a table if you'd like."

"Mary, why are you doing all the hard work while your employee is standing behind the cash register?" Rick asked.

"Ah, because this is the part of the job I love." She laughed and leaned in close. "I figure if she can handle the money, make the customers happy, and not mess up, I've got a winner. I've been keeping an eye on her. Now, about that table. I've got a nice blueberry muffin with your name on it, Rick. And for you, Chief, we've got those pecan swirl muffins today."

Adam rolled his eyes and sighed. "I wish we had time, Mary. Actually, we're looking for one of Rick's guests. Brid Ochoa. She's about five-foot-six, light brunette, glasses."

"I know what she looks like, Chief."

"I think you know everyone in town by name," Rick said. "Even all the tourists."

Turning to Rick, Adam smirked. "You're right. And she probably knows more about Ms. Ochoa than you and I put together."

"Wouldn't surprise me."

"Oh, Chief Cunningham, you flatter me," Mary tittered. "All I know about her is that she and her friend Liz came in here yesterday jabbering like a pair of chipmunks. I was working the register while they were here and didn't get to talk to them at their table."

And there it was, thought Rick. The thing that kept Mary O'Donnell young. She might be well into her golden years, but her interest in her customers, both local and tourists, was a high-octane fuel that drove her forward each day. That's why she was out here instead of behind the counter. Mary thrived on talking to people.

"You're amazing, Mary," Rick said. "Since they haven't been here, do you have any idea where we might find them?"

"Sorry. I don't know. Now, how about if I wrap up one of those muffins for each of you? You boys look like you won't be getting much lunch."

Adam smiled and nodded his head. "You do know how to make a sale, Mary."

They followed her to the register, where Mary placed their order. As they waited, Rick noticed that Howie Dockham was sitting at a nearby table talking to Marquetta's mother. "Be right back, Adam."

Immediately after Rick, Howie, and Madeline exchanged greetings, Madeline began peppering Rick with questions about the B&B.

"Give the man a break, Madeline," Howie said. "He's probably busy working. Am I right, Rick?"

"You are, Howie. We're looking for one of my guests, Brid Ochoa."

Madeline's eyes widened, and her lips rounded. "Oh, the Band of Six. That must mean you're working that murder case?"

As usual, Madeline had done nothing to hide her disapproval. Rick knew well that she thought police business was for the police, not civilians. Prior to coming to Seaside Cove, he'd have agreed.

Rick cocked his head over his shoulder at Adam. "Maybe you can help us out, Howie. Did you think of anything else about that pocket watch?"

"Levi's Folly? I did a little checking. Apparently, there were only a limited number of bidders at the auction."

"Oh, don't be modest. You did quite a bit of detective work to get that information."

Madeline beamed at Howie. Rick was shocked at the double standard. It was okay for her new love to do some 'detective work,' but heaven forbid anyone else should help out. Well, he wasn't going to turn down information, no matter how Madeline felt about civilians helping the police. He glanced back toward where Adam stood and motioned for him to join them. The fact that Howie had been able to discover anything relating to the auctioning of the watch was definitely something Adam would want to know about, too.

"How many bidders were there, Howie?"

"Six, altogether."

"Six what?" Adam asked as he approached.

"Bidders. On Levi's Folly."

Adam's eyebrows knitted together as he inched closer.

Rick said, "Yeah, I thought you'd want to hear this, too."

"Do you know who these bidders were?" Rick asked.

Howie leaned to one side in his wheelchair and nodded. He gazed at Madeline, then took her hand. "Madeline's the one who gave me the idea. Not that she intended to."

After waving her hand dismissively, Madeline made a little poo-pooing sound. "I merely said that I was surprised you weren't 'following the money,' as you law-enforcement types like to say."

"And I said...."

"Howie," Adam interrupted. "The watch?"

"Oh, right. Sorry, Adam. As I told Rick, there were six bidders. The successful one was, of course, your victim. Rick, two more of your guests bid on it, also."

"Two?" Rick shook his head. "Which ones?"

"Barnaby Pauley and Brid Ochoa. Of course, she only bid early on. Once they got into some serious money, she dropped out. Your Mr. Pauley hung in there with Bidder #12 until near the end."

So Silvan had been correct? Pauley had bid on the watch, even though he had no money. Rick stared at Howie. "Are you sure about Pauley? From what I understand, he's broke."

Howie stuck his hand into the pocket of his khaki slacks. He pulled out a piece of paper and handed it to Rick. "There it is. My friend got me the final bid for each person. As you can see, Pauley bid fifty thousand before he dropped out."

Rick handed the bidder list to Adam. "Do you suppose all these events are related?"

Adam shook his head. "Beats me. I'm still not convinced this is relevant to the murder."

"Passions can run high when people are bidding on one-of-a-kind items, Adam." Howie shifted again in his chair. He flicked a crumb from the chest of his tan sweater. "I think it's quite possible your murder is related to this watch."

"That seems like a big stretch, Howie." Adam fingered the paper, then held it up. "Can I keep this?"

"Of course. That's a copy I made for you."

"Can I see that again?" Rick took the note when Adam handed it to him. He'd never have expected Brid to have bid on the watch. And Pauley? Where had he gotten the money? There were two other names he didn't recognize, and a third identified only as Bidder #12. "Howie might be onto something, Adam. I'm not so sure we should dismiss this. Brid was fascinated by road agents. Alex saw a book on them in her room when she was cleaning. And Brid even told me one of the reasons she wanted to come to Seaside Cove was because of the legend of Gentleman

George and Levi's Folly. Guy said something about Welles beating out even the bidders who joined up against him. Do you suppose that was Brid and Barnaby?"

Adam's look of skepticism faded. He rubbed the back of his neck, apparently torn on what action to take next. "I hate to go chasing after some rich man's bauble when we've got a murder to solve."

"Adam, the watch is missing and the notebook was stolen. Bidder #12 lost the watch to Welles by just a few thousand dollars. What if all of this stuff and the murder are interrelated? Maybe this Bidder #12 is our killer."

"Then we've got an even bigger problem on our hands. We don't have a name."

"No, but we have resources. We might even have some leverage."

46

ALEX

AFTER ME AND MOM TELL my dad he might find Brid at Crusty Buns, he leaves, and that gives me another idea. She might be at Marina Park. Since Chief Cunningham would drive right by there, they'd see her if she was there. I'm curious, so I tell Mom I've got stuff to do. She's cool with me leaving, so I head out to the park.

The park is empty when I get there. Now what? Brid's got to have the notebook. Other than me and Lydia and my mom and dad, nobody else had a key to the room.

I walk across the grass to where I can look out over the marina. That's when I see someone sitting on the edge of the dock with their feet hanging over the edge. It looks like Brid. She's kinda far away to be sure, but if I go back and grab my bike, I can get down there super fast.

Nobody sees me when I take the path along the side of the house to the shed where I keep my bike. I kinda speed walk back to the street 'cause I really wanna get to the marina before Brid leaves. When the wind blows, it makes me wish I'd gone up and grabbed a heavier jacket, but that would've taken too much time.

Brid is still sitting in the same place when I get to the marina and lock up my bike. I bite my upper lip as I walk. I'm still not sure what I'm gonna say to her.

It's almost totally deserted out here today. No tourists wanna come down on days like this. It's way too cold. And it's too late for the fishermen. It feels kinda lonely. Maybe that's why Brid is here—because she wants to be alone and think. I look up at the B&B. My dad says it looks like a sentry watching over the harbor. I can almost imagine what it would have been like over a hundred years ago when the house was built.

When I'm almost to the end of the dock, Brid turns, waves, and then looks out at the ocean again. My heart is pounding in my chest. I'm totally winging this. What questions do I want her to answer? I wish I knew. It would sound awful to just say, "Where's the notebook?"

"Alex! What a nice surprise. I didn't expect to see anyone down here."

I smile. Wave back. Butterflies flutter around my stomach. "Hey, Brid. I was up at the park and saw you sitting down here."

Brid twists around so she can see. She gets a funny look on her face. "You recognized me from up there?"

Thank goodness she didn't get suspicious and ask me why I was at the park on a day like this. "Kinda. I recognized your jacket." It's not a hundred percent a lie. I did sort of recognize her. Rather than asking permission, I sit down and dangle my feet over the edge just like she's doing.

We sit quietly for a minute, the water lapping against the pilings. It reminds me of the first time my dad brought me down here. "I did this with my dad when we first got here. It was in the summer. It was a lot warmer, and we sat here for almost an hour just watching the boats come and go."

Brid laughs quietly and shivers just a little. "You're right. It's cold, but I wanted some time to think."

"About Mr. Welles?"

She leans away, scrunches up her face, and shakes her head. "Why would you think that?"

"He was your friend. And he did just die."

"Well, yes. I guess I was thinking about him a little. Actually, I was thinking more about Guy. I left him a note this morning telling him that we're through."

"Wow. He's having a super bad day."

Brid does that thing with her face again and asks, "What's that mean?"

"My dad and Chief Cunningham were looking for something in his room. Well, your room." I'm tempted to tell her what else her boyfriend said about having done something stupid, and maybe even about him having a daughter, but my dad always says you gotta keep people focused on one subject at a time. "Why are you leaving him?"

"It's a long story." She looks away. Her eyes get kinda misty, and I can tell something's bothering her.

"What's wrong, Brid?"

"Guy is not who I thought he was." She pauses, looks down at the water, then mutters to herself. "How did I become so blind?"

Oh. That must mean she knows about his past. Maybe she thinks I don't, and she's trying to keep it a secret. If I tell her that I know about Holly, maybe that will help. "Did you know he's got a daughter?"

Brid slaps her palms down on the wood. Her face opens up in shock. "How did you find that out?"

My insides cringe. I just wanna throw up. Is that how Maxie's gonna react when I tell her I know about the baby? I hope that's gonna be different. Maybe telling Brid about Holly was stupid, and it's too late to take it back. "He told me in the hallway just outside your room. He said she was about my age. You didn't know about her?"

"This is the first I've heard of it. In all the time we've been dating, he's never said a word about her. I knew he had secrets because that's what Snappy did. He cobbled together this group of misfits. All of us had something in our past that he could make use of."

"Do you have secrets, too?"

She looks away from me, stares down at the water, and mutters, "They wouldn't be a secret if I told you. Would they?"

We just sit for a couple minutes, not saying anything until she starts making another face like she's having a big argument in her head. Is she gonna tell me?

"What's wrong?" I ask.

"I guess if the police are involved, it won't be long before it all comes out. Guy stole a notebook from Snappy. When Guy came into the room after the dinner at the Crooked Mast, I could tell he was hiding something under his jacket. I didn't see what it was. All I knew was that I heard him rummaging around the closet. The following morning, his bag had been moved, and it was zipped closed."

"So you opened it?"

"While he was in the shower, I looked inside and found Snappy's notebook. I didn't know what it was at first, but all I had to do was read a couple of pages to know it was some kind of diary. It included a lot of dirt on other people. A lot of boasting by Snappy about his conquests. There was a lot about Liz and how he planned to win her back from Barnaby. He was obsessed with her. The sick part is that his plan was less about winning her love than forcing her to come back. It was terrible stuff." She wraps her arms over her chest and shivers. "It gives me the creeps just thinking about it."

Me, too. Mr. Welles was way worse than I thought. And with all that stuff in there, whoever read it could have had a motive for murder. And that includes Liz. Oh man, I hate that thought. I don't want it to be her. I can't stop now. There's only one way to find out—keep going. "You must be a super-fast reader."

Brid smiles at me and shrugs. I feel so lame. What a stupid thing to say after she told me all that stuff.

"I am pretty fast," she says. "I'm a librarian and do a lot of research. I learned to speed read a long time ago." She nudges me with her elbow. "One of the best things you can do if you're going to college is to learn to speed read. It will make everything easier."

"So you read the whole journal in, like, what? Five minutes?"

Her face flushes a little. She looks away. When she looks back, she wrinkles her nose. "Actually, I had more time. When Guy got out of the shower, I confronted him about where he'd gone after dinner. He told me he'd been alone. I knew it was a lie because of what I'd found. I thought maybe he was the killer."

"You didn't tell him that, did you?"

"No. I just knew I had to get away from him and walked out. I left him standing there. He never knew I had the notebook in my bag."

It's awesome that she's sharing all these details with me. Her being nice makes me feel guilty about not being completely honest. "Brid, I'm working on a story about Mr. Welles's murder for our local newsletter. I should've told you before I started asking questions."

She stares at me for a few seconds. "You're right. You should have." She licks her lips, then says, "I guess I haven't told you anything you wouldn't find out otherwise. How did you become a writer for your local newsletter? Aren't you kind of young for that?"

"I'm the youngest reporter the *Cove Talkers* has ever had. Actually, I'm the only other reporter we have. The newsletter's kind of a hobby of an old guy who's lived here like forever. My dad says I'm following in his footsteps. He was a reporter in New York. He worked the crime beat."

"Aha. Now I understand why he consults with the police. He must have been pretty good."

"He won some big awards." My face feels kinda warm. It feels good to brag about my dad. I guess that means I'm proud of him. "Are you okay if I ask more questions?"

"You're very inquisitive. I think I see why you're interested in journalism. I guess all of this is going to come out soon. Will you be fair? Or are you one of those journalists with an agenda?"

I'm not sure I totally get what she means, but I can promise her I won't make stuff up. "I'm not out to hurt anybody. I just wanna get to the truth."

"That's pretty grown up for someone your age. You know what? I think I trust you, Alex. What do you want to know?"

That's simple. I totally wanna see the proof. "Do you still have the notebook?"

"No. I gave it to Liz."

47

RICK

ADAM'S 4X4 PULLED INTO THE parking lot at the Seaside Cove Marina. The lot was deserted with the exception of two cars, both of which Adam said belonged to divers who'd been out at sea for nearly a week. There was also a bicycle that Rick recognized as Alex's.

"There they are." Rick pointed at two figures who sat out at the edge of the dock. "The other's got to be Brid."

"Once again, Nancy Drew is a step ahead of us." Adam chuckled as he parked the 4x4.

"Just once, I'd like to work a case without her interference," Rick grumbled. Despite his efforts to be irritated with Alex, he found himself smiling.

"Your daughter's got a nose for trouble. That's for sure." Adam snickered. "Why don't we just go out there and try to play a little catch-up?" He pushed open his door and got out.

A chilly gust blew in off the bay, and Rick's first thought was to wonder if Alex might be getting cold. He sighed. Even when he was mad at her, all he could do was be concerned for her welfare. He noticed that she'd locked her bike as they walked past. "At least my daughter does one thing I've told her to do."

"Seaside Cove doesn't get a lot of bicycle thefts, Rick."

"Until we got here, it didn't have a lot of murders, either."

"Touché. Tell you what. If we start getting a lot of bicycle thefts, I'll be sure to deputize the munchkin and let her find the culprits. Save you and me a lot of trouble."

Their footsteps seemed to drift away on the wind as they walked. The marina felt deserted with so little activity. While it was never big-city busy, there were usually boats coming and going. They were about thirty feet away when Alex waved, got up, and ran to them.

"Thanks for calling me, kiddo," Rick said. "You saved me from having to call Marquetta and have her dig out Brid's number."

Alex hugged herself when the next gust blew through. Rick unzipped his jacket and slipped it around her shoulders. Watching her snuggle down into the warmth, he felt a small stab of pain in his heart. He could remember how when she was younger, she'd practically gotten lost in the jacket when he'd loaned it to her. Now that she was nearly as tall as Marquetta, the jacket no longer seemed as gigantic as it once had.

"She doesn't have the notebook." Alex pulled the jacket closer and turned to look at Brid. "She said she gave it to Liz."

"Let Adam and me talk to her. We've got some other questions."

"Good work, munchkin." Adam quirked his cheek and clicked his tongue. "You did the right thing in calling your dad."

Alex's small fists clutched the pocket of warmth tightly about her neck and shoulders. She looked up at Rick with hope in her eyes. "Please don't make me go home, Daddy."

"I want her to stay," Brid said as she took the few steps from where she'd been sitting to join them. She put an arm around Alex's shoulders and hugged her. "She's kind of a friend."

"Very well. I don't have an objection." Adam turned a pointed gaze on Rick. "She's your daughter. I'll leave it up to you."

Rick took one look at Alex and knew he couldn't turn her away. Those dark blue eyes once again melted his heart. There was no real danger here, right? Rather than rationalizing further, he simply gave in. "Fine. You can stay."

"Now that we've got that out of the way." Adam extracted his notepad from his pocket and looked at Brid. "Ms. Ochoa, Alex says you don't have Mr. Welles's notebook. She said you gave it to Ms. Ravel. Is that correct?"

"Yes. Liz has it. Or had it. I gave it to her when I came down here." She hung her head and hugged herself. "I probably should have turned it over to you, but when I told Liz about it, she said it could ruin her if anyone ever saw it. She begged me not to turn it in. She's my sister—what could I say?"

That it was evidence in a murder investigation? Rick buried the thought; he hadn't always made the best decisions, either. "Did you read what was inside?"

"I did a quick read."

"Brid can speed read," Alex said proudly.

Rick made a mental note that Alex, at least for the moment, seemed impressed by the idea of speed-reading. Before that enthusiasm faded, he'd want her to learn how to do it herself. He also wanted to see if Brid would corroborate Guy Silvan's statement regarding the auction. "The Levi's Folly auction. Did Welles write about it?"

Brid's eyes widened. She sucked in a breath, and Rick was immediately on guard. What Guy had told them about Brid's fascination with the watch must be true. When Rick didn't get an immediate answer, he pressed again.

"Brid, we've heard that you have an interest in the watch. We also heard that you were one of the early bidders at the auction. Is that true?"

"I didn't have enough money. I was out before the serious bidding started." She laughed and looked down at the wooden planks. "The upside of my job is that it's very rewarding. The downside is I don't make much money."

"Okay. Thanks for clarifying that. Adam and I think the auction and Levi's Folly are key pieces of the puzzle. If we knew what Welles was thinking at the time, it could help. Did he talk about it in this diary of his?"

Her cheeks flushed as she ground out the words. "There was plenty. Snappy described me as a 'little fool' for even trying to bid. And he called Barnaby an idiot. He was so pleased with himself because he knew Barnaby couldn't outbid him."

"What about Bidder #12?"

Brid shook her head and shrugged. "Whoever that was, it infuriated Snappy. He thought it was fun to bid against Barnaby because he knew exactly how high Barnaby could go, but he didn't know this secret bidder. Snappy never did figure out who it was. The bids came in through an attorney."

Rick looked at Adam and grimaced. "Sounds like someone who wanted to protect their identity. I wonder why?"

"It could be that they knew who they were up against. Or maybe they wanted to maintain the advantage," Adam mused.

"Lot of good it did them. Welles still got the watch." Rick sighed and added, "Unless Bidder #12 found another way to get it."

Adam nodded. "Which makes him or her our killer."

"And that means the bidder's here in town. Or maybe I should say, was here."

"Let's hope he still is," Adam said. "If someone left abruptly, it would make them look suspicious."

"The only people who have checked out are the Dixons. I doubt that one of them was this Bidder #12. Besides, they left on their scheduled date." Rick stopped and glanced at Brid. "They even took all the commotion your group caused in stride."

"Sorry," Brid said. "Believe me. I understand how much of a pain we've been. I'm truly sorry for all the trouble we caused."

"Thanks, I appreciate that." Rick's insides cringed as he said the words. Brid's apology and his acceptance had both seemed more ritualistic than heartfelt. He wondered how sincere she really was but saw no point in pushing his luck. They might as well simply move on. "Do you know where Liz is now?"

"No. After I gave her the notebook, she said she had some things to do and left."

She couldn't have gone far, thought Rick. "Which direction did she go?"

"Toward the B&B. We'd walked to the park so we'd be away from the rest of the group. I told her about the notebook, gave it to her, and that's when I came down here. I felt awful. Chief Cunningham, there was a lot of information in there. I hate the idea of it coming out, but Liz shouldn't destroy it, either."

Rick looked up at Marina Park, then eyed Brid. "You're sure she walked back toward the B&B?"

"Totally. She said she wanted time to think."

"Would you mind calling her and asking her where she is? We want to talk to her."

"I wish I could. On the way to the park, she made a comment about having rushed out so fast that she forgot to grab her phone." She shrugged. "Maybe she went back and got it."

Rick urged Brid to try. She pulled out her phone, dialed, then disconnected after only a few rings.

"Voicemail. I guess she didn't go back for it."

Rick glanced at Adam. If Liz hadn't gone back to the B&B, there was one other place in that direction she might have gone —the lighthouse. A half mile beyond the B&B, it was a place of solitude where none of the others were likely to disturb her. It was also a place where she could dispose of the notebook and ensure it was never seen again.

48

RICK

ON THE DRIVE TO THE lighthouse, Rick figured that if Liz walked, it would take her about twenty minutes. Logically, he knew they couldn't be that far behind her. They might even catch up. Still, deep in one corner of his mind, there was a niggling doubt and a vision of them arriving just in time to find Liz looking out over the craggy cliffs, the notebook still in her hands. If she threw it, that evidence would be lost forever in the crashing surf below.

Rick's pulse quickened when he spotted a lone figure sitting on a bench facing out toward the ocean. Even from the back, Rick could tell that the person was shivering. It was just one more example of how quickly a decent day could turn cold and windy on the coast. Today was a perfect example of a swing season in action. Gusts of wind whipped through the trees, moaning a mournful song.

"Can I talk to her first?" Rick asked. "If she still has the notebook, maybe I can get her to turn it over voluntarily."

"Go for it. I'll be right here if you need help."

Rick walked quickly toward the bench. The closer he got, the more features he recognized. The curly hair. Her jacket. And when she shivered again, he recognized the slightness of her build. He circled to Liz's left, fully aware that this could turn into a tense situation in a heartbeat. It was when she looked up that Rick's caution turned to concern. Her cheeks were smeared with black mascara and tears. Apparently, he'd arrived in the middle of an emotional meltdown.

"Liz? What's wrong?" Under other circumstances, Rick might have wanted to kick himself. The question sounded, as Alex might describe it, so lame. There were plenty of things that could be wrong, up to and including the fact that she might know who killed Snappy Welles.

"It's all in here," she croaked. "Every last, dirty little detail."

Rick pointed at the small notebook she clutched in one hand. "That's the one that belonged to Mr. Welles?"

Like her fingertips, the blue faux leather of the cover was now smeared with black stains. The little book measured about five inches wide by seven inches tall. An elastic strap to secure it dangled from the back.

She nodded, then held it out. "Here, take it. I want nothing to do with it."

Thank goodness, Rick thought as he took it from her. In a way, he felt guilty for taking possession of what he suspected were so many secrets. "I take it you've read it?"

Liz made a face. "Parts. Brid is the speed reader. I flipped through some of the pages. Saw my name a bunch of times. Read a little bit. Snappy was disgusting. And to think I once thought we might have a life together."

"Love can be blind," Rick muttered. It was true. He'd felt the same way after breaking up with Giselle. At least he'd gotten Alex out of the deal. What had Liz gotten? "Mind if I sit?"

She glanced down at the spot next to her. "Go ahead. You probably have a million questions. Not that I have any answers. I thought I knew Snappy, but apparently, I didn't. Did you know he was supposed to be on medication for manic depression?" She paused, shook her head, and barked out a laugh. "No, there's no way you could have known. All you knew was that he was a jerk who brought all these misfits into your life."

As much as Rick wanted to deny it, she was right. "We certainly got more angst than we planned on when we booked your group."

She laughed again, this time more quietly. "That's being kind."

"You said he was supposed to be on medication? Are you saying he wasn't taking it?"

"No. He wasn't. Not according to that." She gestured at the notebook. "In there, Snappy claims he wanted to change and be a nicer person. That was right about the time I was threatening to leave him. He did get serious for a little while. He even started an addiction program. In there, he talked about how he was progressing. That's a lie. The truth is I wasn't seeing any real change. I realized it was all superficial. That's when I gave up and left. I never realized he only got partway through the program and quit. The really sick part is he blamed everyone else for him not finishing."

"Did that include you?"

"Of course. I was so stupid."

Liz wiped her lower eyelid with her fingertip, and Rick wished he had a tissue he could give her.

"Did you talk to him about it?"

"Are you kidding?" Liz croaked. "Snappy didn't do conversations. And I was too afraid of making him mad, so I avoided it."

"I see. What about Levi's Folly? Do you know anything about it?"

"I know Barnaby wanted it. I'm pretty sure Snappy wanted it more because of Barnaby than because it was a piece of history." Liz rolled her eyes and shook her head. "Once again, it was a competition between those two. Barnaby couldn't seem to figure out he could never win against Snappy."

Rick looked back to where Adam stood, watching patiently, his hands buried in the pockets of his heavy jacket while Rick handled the situation. He was thankful that he and Adam worked so well together. If they were like the Band of Six, they probably would get nothing accomplished. No wonder the group was so dysfunctional. Everything was always a competition. There was no camaraderie. And, except for Brid and Liz, no real friendship. "I think I understand why your group is...." Rick stopped short, the heat rising in his chest at the thought of what he'd almost said.

"So screwed up?" Liz laughed. "Don't worry about it. We are the epitome of bad behavior. To be fair, it's not all Snappy's fault. Every one of us has let ourselves get sucked in."

"The competition between your husband and Welles—is that why Barnaby wanted to marry you?"

Liz sniffled once and then sat straighter. "I think so. I doubt that Barnaby would admit it, but we've never been that good together. I suppose that if I'm being really honest, the reason I married him is that I was hurt and confused and wanted to get back at Snappy." Liz gave Rick a small smile, then sighed. "I told you we're all screwed up."

"Are you planning on staying with Barnaby?"

"No. Not really."

Not quite sure what to say, Rick touched the base of his neck and gazed at Liz. Deciding on divorce had been gut-wrenching for him, yet Liz sounded like she was trying to decide between two tomatoes in a grocery store. "Do you think Barnaby knows how you feel?"

"Probably not. Maybe. Who knows?"

It certainly didn't appear as though Liz did.

"I know," Liz said. "You're thinking that if Barnaby found out I was leaving him for Snappy, he might have had a motive to kill him. Honestly, Rick, I don't think Barnaby's that invested in our marriage. Besides, if it was one of us, my money would be on Carson or Guy. They both had plenty of motive."

Okay, they'd ruled out Guy Silvan, thought Rick. What about Carson Coulson? "Did Snappy write anything about Carson?"

"I don't even need to look to answer that. There was no love lost between Snappy and Carson. That was another marriage of convenience. Carson needed a sponsor, and Snappy wanted to be visible in professional sports. One thing about Snappy, he did know his limitations. He didn't have enough money for something like a football team, but he could afford an individual sponsorship."

"He did that even though they didn't get along?"

"Yes." Liz pulled in a quick breath. "There was something I saw in there. Here, I'll show you."

Rick paused for only a moment before he handed the notebook to her.

"Don't worry. I won't try to get rid of it." She thumbed through the pages. It only took a moment for her to find what she was looking for. "Here it is. Listen to this. 'Struck gold today on that loser Coulson. I always knew there was something wrong with him. Bribed the maid at the hotel where he was staying. She let me in while he was at breakfast. Pretty good move on my part because I found out Coulson is on beta blockers for angina. My lawyer says that's an illegal drug according to the World Anti-Doping Code, and because Coulson never got an exemption, I could get him thrown out at any time. Easy out on my contract. He's so screwed.'"

"Do you think Welles wanted to Carson?"

"At first, I didn't think so. Snappy liked to know that he had things on people. He liked knowing that he could blackmail them if and when he wanted something. But then I found this. Look at his last entry. It was made just a couple of hours before dinner. She read as she pointed at the entry. 'It's time to deal with Coulson. Tonight, I'm cutting him loose. He's the biggest loser of them all."

Rick stared at the words on the page. That could have been Coulson's motive had he known what was coming. The question was, had Welles told him? Threatened him? "I need to talk to Adam. I think we're going to need another conversation with Mr. Coulson."

49

RICK

AFTER RICK TURNED OVER WELLES'S notebook and briefed Adam on what he had learned, they agreed that any conversations with Carson Coulson and Barnaby Pauley should happen as soon as possible. They put Liz Ravel in the back of the 4x4 and drove to the B&B.

As they entered the foyer, Liz checked her watch. She glanced toward the back of the house and crooked her neck in the direction of the dining room. "Carson is a creature of habit. He likes to stop for tea around three-thirty. I'll bet that's where you'll find him."

"Adam, I have a suggestion. Why don't I go to the dining room and check the supplies? If Coulson's there, it's a perfect excuse for me to strike up a conversation with him." Rick smiled at both Adam and Liz. "It wouldn't do to have us run out of tea."

Liz rolled her neck in a circle. Her cheeks, normally smooth, were puffy and still stained with mascara. "If you don't mind, Chief, I'd like to go up to my room. This has been a stressful afternoon. Would you mind accompanying me? Just in case Barnaby's there?"

"No problem, Ms. Ravel. Rick, why don't you check on your supplies while I escort Ms. Ravel upstairs? If her husband is there, I'll let you know."

"Sounds like a plan." On his way to the dining room, Rick passed a couple of the new guests who were seated by the fire in the living room. They smiled and murmured compliments about the 'lovely ambiance.' He thanked them, then excused himself, once again wishing that the Band of Six had been as easygoing. Upon entering the dining room, he found both Carson Coulson and Barnaby Pauley. They were seated at one of the window tables and were leaning into each other. It was obvious from how they stopped whispering when he walked in that neither wanted to be overheard.

"Gentlemen, Chief Cunningham and I would like to speak with each of you. I'll let him know you're here."

Pauley pushed his chair back and started to stand. "I have things to do."

"It's not really a request, Mr. Pauley," Rick commanded. "This is part of the police investigation into Mr. Welles's death. Make yourself comfortable while we wait."

"Why are you badgering me like this?" Pauley barked. "What did I do to you?"

The urge to shoot back a comment about how the man had done nothing but cause trouble and lie since his arrival was tempting. Rick focused instead on the investigation. What did they have other than circumstantial evidence? How did he say that Pauley was acting guilty enough to make it seem like he'd done something? This wouldn't be the first time he'd had to bluff his way through a difficult situation. Although, he had to admit that working with Adam made this easy. They had the power of the law.

Rick spoke absently as he texted Adam. "Well, actually, this is about the both of you." When his phone whooshed to indicate the message had been sent, he skewered the two men with an irritated stare. "It's taken some time, but we've discovered that neither of you has been completely honest with us. You've lied during a police investigation."

Carson Coulson grimaced and placed his hand on his chest. "Me? I never saw Snappy after dinner."

Pauley, on the other hand, blanched. Beads of sweat formed on his forehead. Rather than giving the man time to fabricate something, Rick stepped into his personal space, forcing him to lower himself into his chair. "You saw him. Didn't you, Mr. Pauley?"

"It was an accident!" Pauley blurted.

"What was?" Rick demanded. "Were you the one who was driving the car that hit Welles? You were, weren't you?"

"I didn't mean to! He was just so—he was like a maniac. Like he'd gone off the deep end or something. He was ranting about Guy being a thief and how he was going to destroy him and everyone else. He said he'd decided to take everything I had." Pauley's shoulders slumped. He let out a defeated groan. "Then he flashed that stupid pocket watch and said it was proof he could do anything he wanted."

Pauley stared down at the table. He jerked his hands up and down as if punctuating each word. "He was talking crazy talk. He said the game was over, and he was going to take Liz back. I couldn't listen to another word, so I got in the car and backed up. I didn't look where I was going. I just hit the gas. There was this thump, and I saw Snappy there on the ground. He was shaking his fist at me and yelling. I don't even remember what I did. I guess I panicked and drove away."

Tempting as it was to slip into parent mode and scold Pauley for leaving the scene of an accident, Rick knew the law would take on that duty. All he needed to do was find out what happened afterward. "Where did you go after the accident?"

"The marina at first. Then Liz came down and tied into me. I couldn't take it, so I just started driving. Somehow, I ended up on that road that goes out by the Silver Gulch mine and went all the way to the end before I had to turn around. By the time I got back, it was after eight."

It had been a long time since Rick had been all the way to the end of the road. In its entirety, the washboard dirt surface snaked along the coast for just over a mile. He could see how someone unfamiliar with the drive would take it slowly, especially if they were in the dark. Even then, it would take no more than twenty minutes out and another twenty back. That still left almost an hour unaccounted for.

Did that hour really matter? Mary Ellen Herbert heard Welles yelling after the accident. As Rick thought about the timing, he realized there was no way Pauley could have come back, parked, and committed murder. None of that necessarily let Carson Coulson off the hook, however. Tired of the group and their lies, Rick turned an icy stare on Coulson.

"What about you, Mr. Coulson? Can you prove you didn't see Mr. Welles after dinner?"

"I went back to my room."

"Which means you were alone. Did anyone see you on your way upstairs?"

Coulson looked down and stared at the floor. "Yes! That older couple. They were in the living room when I came in. I'm afraid I wasn't very nice to them."

"Can you tell me their names? Or at least describe them?"

Of course, Coulson didn't know the names of the people he'd seen, but as he laid out his description, it sounded a lot like the Dixons. "Have you seen this couple since that night?"

"I think they checked out."

"That would be Mr. and Mrs. Dixon. Why don't we see what they have to say? I have a phone number for them. Give me a minute, and I'll call them."

Rick told the two men to stay put, stepped away and dialed the number for Thomas Dixon. After a short explanation of why he was calling, Rick listened as Mr. Dixon held the phone away and asked his wife if she recalled the incident.

"Rick? This is Filomena. I do remember him. A very disagreeable man. He's the archer. Right?"

"That's correct, Mrs. Dixon." He thanked her for her help, said goodbye, then went back to the table. "This is your lucky day, Mr. Coulson. Mrs. Dixon does remember you. She called you very disagreeable."

Coulson's nostrils flared, and his chin rose. The intensity of his stare convinced Rick that he was about to be on the receiving end of another Band of Six tantrum. In the few days that the group had been staying at the B&B, those tantrums had become the talk of the house. Filomena Dixon had merely voiced what the other guests had been whispering about.

Instead of throwing a tantrum, Coulson glanced away, his eyes defocused, and his shoulders slumped as though someone had forced all the air from his lungs. "Is that what they say about us?"

Rick hesitated. Coulson looked as though he might be feeling at least a smidgeon of guilt. Was he? Was this real? Another act? "Do you really want to know?"

"Yes."

Pauley sat with his arms crossed. Right now, it appeared that guilt and worry had become his two best friends. He looked withdrawn, and there was probably no better time than now to level with him. "Around the B&B, your group is known as the Band of Six. Several guests have commented about your squabbles. Your group's stay has quite probably hurt our reputation because the other guests are not enjoying themselves when you're around. As a description, disagreeable is being kind. Would you like me to go on?"

"No," Coulson whispered. "I think I've got the picture. Being around Snappy has changed me."

"It changed all of us," Pauley grumbled.

"You're right, Barnaby. We used to be such a fun-loving group." Coulson looked up. He gave Rick one of those grimace-type smiles that people use to express regret, then continued. "There was always some needling that went with our friendship, but it was the friendly sort. Somehow, Snappy tapped into that and amplified it. Gradually, it grated on each of us until we couldn't stand each other—or him. And yet, we stayed. Yoked together by chains of money."

"If you both truly regret your actions, it's a good time to make a change. Perhaps all of you can take this time to start the healing process." Although Rick said the words and meant them, the sentiment came with a huge caveat. Someone had killed Welles. Which meant one of them would be facing justice, not a chance for redemption.

Rick looked directly at Coulson. Narrowed his gaze. Inched closer. "Mr. Coulson? Are you Bidder #12?"

Coulson's eyes widened, and he sat back in his chair. "What the devil are you talking about? Bidder for what?"

"Levi's Folly. The miniature pocket watch that caused so much commotion at the Crooked Mast."

"What would I want with a pocket watch? I have no need for anything of that sort."

"Good. Then you won't mind if Chief Cunningham and I search your room."

50

ALEX

Hey Journal,

I just heard my dad downstairs talking to Creepy Coulson and Mr. Pauley. It sounded super intense. It sounds like the two Band of Six guys are sorry for all the trouble they've caused. I don't think any of them are really bad people. It seems like they all got pushed into doing bad things by Mr. Welles. It's kinda like Billy Thornton at school. I wonder if maybe he acts like a bully 'cause other people let him. The next time he tries to push me around, I really am gonna punch him in the nose. I bet he won't ever bother me again!

Do you think the pocket watch is what's behind the murder? Mr. Boyd told us the watch was cursed. Maybe he could tell me more about how the curse works.

Uh oh. Mom just texted me. 9-1-1? Dinner emergency? Gotta go!

Xoxo

Alex

I put my journal back in the desk drawer and lock my room on my way out. There's nobody around as I rush down the stairs. All the guests are either in their rooms or are out doing stuff. A lot of the ones that are here will be leaving soon for dinner, so this is a super quiet time of the day. When I push through the butler door, Mom's got a lot of stuff from the refrigerator pulled out on the counter.

"Is something wrong? What's a 9-1-1 dinner emergency?" I ask.

"I've just spent the last ten minutes trying to find the eggs. Didn't you go to the store this afternoon?"

My face gets super hot. I promised her I would. "I forgot. I got so wrapped up with the investigation and then had to find Brid so I could track down Mr. Welles's notebook."

Mom holds up a hand. "Okay. Stop. Sweetie, I know you're trying to balance your investigation with helping me, but if you promise me you'll do something, I really need you to actually do it. I could have made time to go to the store if I'd known you weren't going to follow through."

Omigod. That makes me feel so awful. "But you were tired and needed to rest."

"I know, but the problem is now we don't have the eggs I ordered for dinner or for tomorrow's breakfast. I can certainly make something other than a frittata for dinner. What are we going to do about tomorrow morning? We can't very well tell our guests there's no breakfast tomorrow. Right?"

Oh, yeah. I could just see that one, especially with someone like Mr. Coulson. "I'm super sorry, Mom. It will only take me a couple minutes to get there on my bike. I can be back in like fifteen minutes."

Mom looks at the clock, then out the window. "The market's still open. It'll be light for another couple of hours." She looks at the clock again. "I hate to have you go out this late in the day, but your dad just left with Adam. Maybe I should go right now."

"It's okay. It was my job to do it, and I didn't. I'll go."

She makes a face, then says, "Okay. I want you to be careful. Right to the market and right back. No detours. No investigating. Do you understand?"

"Got it!" I say goodbye, rush upstairs to grab my coat, then hurry back down. After getting my bike out of the shed, I ride straight to the market and lock it to the lamppost out front.

The market is kinda deserted. Jessica is standing near her register and waves to me when she sees me. "Hey, Alex. It's late for you to be coming in. Isn't it?"

"I was supposed to pick up our order for the morning and didn't do it."

"Oh." Jessica winks at me and locks her register. "I'm sure it's still back in the fridge. I'll go grab it. Be right back."

While Jessica's gone, I check out the headlines on the covers of the tabloids. "Ewww," I whisper when I read the one about who my favorite singer is dating. "Not him."

It's taking Jessica longer than I thought it would, so I start to walk around. Down one aisle, I see Traci Peterson. She must have stopped for a few things on her way home. On the frozen food aisle is Mr. Boyd. He's reading the label on the back of a package. I wonder if he'd answer my question about the curse on the watch.

Jessica's still not back, so I walk down the aisle. "Hey, Mr. Boyd."

He cocks his head and looks at me kinda funny as he puts the package back in the freezer. "Do I know you?" Before I can answer, he raises his left hand and points at me. "Oh, I remember. You were with the group from the school. I never forget a face, but I'm terrible with names."

"I'm Alex Atwood. My dad was one of the chaperones."

He wags his right finger in the air. "That's right. You're the one who got into it with that troublemaker, and your dad was talking while I was going through the Silver Gulch mine's history."

Oh. I didn't think he'd remember all of that. "I'm sorry about Billy Thornton. He's just a big bully."

Mr. Boyd nods. "Got that impression. This sure is a friendly little town. Back in Phoenix, nobody talks."

"New York was the same way. You'll like Seaside Cove. Can I ask you a question?"

"Guess so."

My phone rings with a text from my mom. *Don't dawdle.* It's followed by a string of hearts. The message makes me smile. She totally knows me.

"You kids. You're never away from your phones, are you?"

"I have it with me all the time."

Mr. Boyd grunts. "Mine makes a better paperweight than it does a phone. Doesn't work out at the mine, and when I need it, it's always dead. Waste of money for me. It's my turn to ask you a question. You're the one who writes for the town newsletter. Would you be willing to write up a nice story about the mine?"

"For sure."

"All right, then. Guess we got ourselves an arrangement. What did you want to know?"

"Is it true that there was a curse on the watch?"

Mr. Boyd leans forward and plants his elbows on his cart. He gets a big smile on his face. "That's not directly related to the mine, but it's a good story. It's true that as Levi Clark lay dying, he cursed the watch. You see, Levi's father was a wealthy businessman, and his mother was a gypsy who'd cast a spell on her husband when she wanted him to fall in love with her. She taught Levi all of her secrets. Yes, indeed, Levi was well-versed in the dark arts."

That sounds like an awesome story. And totally bogus. At least Mr. Boyd looks like he's having a good time telling it.

From behind me, I hear Jessica's voice. "Hey, Alex, I've got your order."

"Thanks, Jessica." I take the bag from her and look back at Mr. Boyd. "That's a totally awesome story. Did you know that Levi's Folly was recently sold at an auction?"

Mr. Boyd does a double take, then he shrugs. "I guess you have done your homework. Please don't tell the other kids that. You'll ruin the whole story."

Looks like my dad was right about Mr. Boyd. He is just a big showman. "I better get going, Mr. Boyd. Otherwise, I'm gonna be late for dinner. Nice talking to you."

He opens the freezer door again, takes out the package he just put back, and says, "Right. I need to get back out to the Silver Gulch, have dinner, and then get ready for a trip to LA."

"Are you gonna be gone long?"

"Not long. Just have a little business to take care of."

"Wait. Do you live out there? At the mine?"

"That little trailer you saw out there is my home. Thanks to the miracle of satellite communications, I even have the Internet. You sure are an inquisitive one." He looks at his watch. "Sorry. I have to go."

As I start peddling home, I keep thinking about the watch and Mr. Boyd's story. I guess he's right. An auction isn't nearly as much fun as a hundred-year search and a gypsy curse.

51

RICK

THE SCOWL ON CARSON COULSON'S face hadn't let up since Rick had told him what Filomena Dixon had called him. The good news was that Coulson had consented to the search, just as Barnaby Pauley had. So here they stood, just inside his room, with Coulson making grumpy faces.

"I really don't see how this is going to be of any help," Coulson grumbled.

Adam, who'd been bent over the dresser, straightened up and faced him. "We're in the process of ruling out suspects, Mr. Coulson. If we find nothing incriminating here, you'll be one step closer to being in the clear."

Coulson threw one hand in the air and muttered dramatically, "Couple of Nosey Parkers. Search on, Chief. Let's get this done."

Returning to the search, Adam worked his way through the bottom drawer of the dresser.

Having finished with Coulson's overnight bag, Rick returned it to the closet where he'd found it. "Nothing, Adam. I think we can rule out Mr. Coulson with some confidence."

Adam closed the last drawer, faced Coulson, and nodded. "I agree. Mr. Coulson, thank you for letting us do this search. Rick, let's go check Mr. Pauley's room. Why don't you go get him while I let Ms. Ravel know what we're doing?"

"Will do."

Adam was knocking on the door to the Jib Room when Rick started downstairs to retrieve Barnaby Pauley. He found him in the dining room, still sitting at the table where he'd been instructed to wait. "We're ready for you now."

Pauley grunted and followed Rick upstairs. Adam gave Rick a thumbs-up as they approached. Pauley seemed to miss the signal and remained sullen as he opened the door.

"This should only take a couple of minutes," Rick said.

The Jib Room was decorated in a white-and-gray theme with gray-blue accents. A chandelier hung above the four-poster bed, the focal point of the room. With its four black pillars, the bed seemed to compete with the chandelier in a contest to dominate the room. The first time he'd seen it, Rick thought the entire design to be just another of Captain Jack's unnecessary extravagances. He'd learned how wrong he was after almost two years of feedback. Most of the guests who stayed in this room seemed to love it.

Even the white dresser and nightstands, which Marquetta said Captain Jack had gotten for next to nothing at an estate sale, were now considered *tres chic* antiques. He opened the top drawer of the dresser.

"That's Liz's stuff," Pauley said.

Obviously. Wrong-gender underwear. Rick nodded to Pauley, then moved on to the other drawers. When he finished, he said, "I'll check the suitcases."

Rick pulled a teal carry-on from the closet. Once again, this was Liz's, not Pauley's. The bag contained a few articles of clothing along with an envelope that had been ripped open. It reminded Rick of someone using their finger as a letter opener because they were in a hurry. He held up the envelope. "Barnaby, do you know what's in this envelope?"

"Not a clue. Snappy gave it to Liz the day he died. He told her he'd made some decisions. I don't get into her business. She doesn't get into mine."

Rick opened the envelope and stared at the heading. "Adam, I think you're going to want to see this."

"What is it?"

"The last will and testament of Mr. Welles. A full power-of-attorney in the event of his death."

"What?" Pauley exploded. "Why would he give that to her? Wait, is she the executor? I don't believe this. What did he do? Leave everything to her?"

Pauley stepped forward as if he might rip the documents from Rick's hands, but Adam moved in front of him. "Back off, sir. You are here as a courtesy because you voluntarily agreed to let us search your room."

"It's just—don't tell me she gets it all!" Pauley's voice rose to a high-pitched whine. His eyes searched Rick's for an answer, and when he got none, he shuffled back and slouched against the wall. "I can't believe it," he muttered. "Now I know why she wants to divorce me."

Rick handed the will to Adam, who read it with raised eyebrows while Pauley continued to mutter to himself.

"I'll lose everything. Snappy screws me over again."

Watching as Adam scanned the documents, Rick tried to make sense of what was happening. The timing of the delivery of the envelope, Liz Ravel's pronouncement that she wanted a divorce, and even the death of Snappy Welles, were all way too coincidental. There had to be more. "Mr. Pauley—Barnaby, you said Welles gave this envelope to your wife the day he died. What time was that?"

"A couple of hours before dinner. She was all hush-hush about it." Pauley sat on the edge of the bed with his eyes misting over and his shoulders slumping forward. He buried his face in his hands. "I let him do it to me again," he whimpered. "Snappy always wins. I should've known."

Suddenly, Pauley stood and went to the closet. He pulled out his bag, set it on the bed, then went to the dresser.

"What are you doing?" Rick asked.

"Packing. I know what's coming next. She'll move Brid in here. Liz and I are through. I'm done fighting it."

Rick motioned toward the door. He and Adam left Pauley alone, and when the door was closed, Rick said, "Poor guy."

Adam quirked his cheek. "Yeah. But let's not lose sight of why we're here."

"I know. We've still got a killer to find."

"I agree. There are too many things happening all at once. And we both know there's no such thing as coincidence."

Rick smiled at the memory of their first few cases together. At the number of times he'd drilled that very message into Adam's brain.

"What's so funny?" Adam asked.

"Just thinking of where you learned that." Rick winked, then looked back at the documents. "So what do you want to do about this?"

"I think we need another talk with Ms. Ravel." He returned the will to the envelope and handed it to Rick. "Can we use your office?"

Though he wasn't fond of the idea of bringing a guest into his office, at least it was a quiet place where there were no prying eyes. That's something there would be plenty of once word of this got out. "Sure. I'll see if I can find her. Why don't you wait for us there?"

Rick's search didn't take long. He found Liz Ravel sitting on one of the couches next to Brid Ochoa. Liz had a mug of hot tea cradled in her hands and had taken the seat closest to the fire. She didn't seem to notice Rick's approach as she stared straight into the flames. Brid sat with her arm around Liz's shoulders. She was speaking in a voice barely above a whisper. Brid saw Rick and nudged her sister.

"Rick," Liz said with a grimace. Her eyes focused on the envelope in Rick's hand. "I figured you'd be looking for me. You found the will."

"We need to talk." Rick held up the envelope. "I'm sure there's an explanation."

Liz shrugged and gave him a small laugh. "It's pretty simple. Snappy left me everything. I am now a very rich woman with a husband I don't love and friends who are going to hate me."

Brid hugged her sister and leaned her head against Liz's shoulder. "I don't hate you."

Reaching up, Liz placed her hand on Brid's. "Thank goodness. At least I'll have you left."

"Chief Cunningham is waiting for us in my office," Rick said. "We'd like to see how this fits into our investigation."

"What you really want to know is if I killed Snappy. Well, I certainly had a motive, didn't I?"

"Please, let's just talk this through."

"Sure. Has Barnaby figured things out?"

"He's packing."

Liz nodded, took a sip from her mug, and handed it to Brid. "Would you mind?"

"No problem." Brid watched her sister with sympathetic eyes. "We just got here."

"I know," Liz said with a deep sigh. She gazed at Rick and forced a smile. "Lead the way."

In Rick's office, they found Adam already seated in one of the guest chairs on the opposite side of Rick's desk. He stood as

Liz entered and sat only after she'd taken the other guest chair. "Ms. Ravel, has Rick told you that we'd like to talk to you about Mr. Welles's will?"

"He has," she sighed. "And I know how it looks. I should have told you about this before, Chief. I just didn't think it was relevant." She paused, closed her eyes, and shook her head. "No, that's wrong. I didn't want it to be relevant. Deep down, I knew it was wrong to hide it. I also know this gives me motive. I'm sure everyone you talk to claims they didn't kill Snappy. Actually, to be honest, I don't even want his money. I saw what it did to him. It ate away at him until there was nothing left on the inside."

She stopped, craned her neck back, and gazed at the ceiling. "Why am I telling you all this? I don't know. I suppose maybe I'm trying to cleanse my soul. Maybe I'm feeling guilty for all the subterfuge." She turned her gaze back to Adam. "What do you want to know?"

"You originally told us you returned to the B&B after dinner. Did anyone see you?"

"Let me save you the trouble, Chief. I really don't have an alibi. I didn't see anyone until Barnaby returned."

Rick placed his elbows on the desktop and rested his chin on his knuckles. "Liz, I don't think either of us suspects you of killing Mr. Welles. Besides, you actually do have an alibi. You walked back to Marina Park with Brid and then went to see your husband at the harbor. That alone proves you didn't have time to go back and commit murder. The thing is, we think you might know something that can help us find the killer."

"I don't know what I could tell you that I haven't already."

"We believe the murder may have something to do with Levi's Folly."

Liz barked out a laugh. "What? Why? That was just a trinket for Snappy. He didn't really care about it. The only thing that mattered to him was beating out the other bidders. It was just another token to prove he was successful."

"For him," Rick said pointedly. "For the killer, it could have been much more. Do you know who the bidders were?"

"Not really."

"Your husband bid on it."

"I knew that. He told me."

"Did your sister tell you she put in some early bids?"

"Brid? Really?" Liz sat back and gazed at Rick with wide eyes. "I had no idea. Who else?"

Adam glanced down at his notebook, then back to Liz. "M.K. Aspen and Jody Wiffle. They're both curators of museums. One is from San Francisco, and the other lives in Sacramento. Neither of them has been to Seaside Cove. Ever. I had my deputy check."

"I've never heard either of those names," Liz said.

"Did Mr. Welles say anything about an anonymous bidder? Or maybe Bidder #12?"

"Quite a bit, actually. It made him crazy that he didn't know who it was. As much as Snappy liked to spring things on people, he hated it when he was the one who was surprised. He was frustrated beyond belief when he couldn't figure out who that bidder was. It drove him nuts."

Rick let out a heavy sigh. He knew the feeling.

52

ALEX

AFTER GETTING MY BIKE PUT back in the shed, I grab the bag from the market and rush to the kitchen. Mom is standing inside the French doors. When she sees me, she puts her hand over her heart. The look of worry on her face is replaced by a smile.

"What took you so long, Sweetie?"

"Sorry. Jessica had to go get the order, and then I saw Mr. Boyd."

"I'm guessing you had to ask him questions about something."

She's smiling at me like I'm totally predictable. I guess I am. "About the pocket watch. That whole story he told my class at the mine was made up."

"The whole story?"

"Well, parts of it, anyway."

Mom looks up, smiles, and says, "Hey."

I turn around to see who's there. It's my dad, and he's with Chief Cunningham. My dad asks, "What was made up?"

When I tell him how I think Mr. Boyd made up the story about the watch being lost for a hundred years, he laughs. "What's so funny?" I ask.

"It makes sense. Why would you bore a bunch of kids with the facts when you can keep them entertained?" He looks at Mom. "Is there any chance Adam can stay for dinner?"

"Of course. Adam, you're always welcome."

"What about Traci? I saw her at the market. Could she come, too?" I ask.

Mom shrugs. "Why not? If that's okay with you two." She looks at my dad and the chief.

"I'm always happy to have dinner with my fiancée."

"That settles it, Adam. I'll call Traci and come up with a menu. Alex, you need to go wash up so you can help me with some of the prep work. Now, scoot."

Less than an hour later, Traci joins us, and we work on a whole new menu while we sit around the table in the kitchen. Mom is gonna put together an enchilada casserole, and Traci has already brought a salad. The dessert is going to be ice cream and cookies. None of it's fancy, but everything we're having is on my top-ten favorites list.

All the way through dinner, I keep trying to ask what my dad and Chief Cunningham have done on the case. Each time I try, they just say we'll talk later. Ugh! When we get to the ice cream and cookies, my dad says it's time for him and Chief Cunningham to get down to business.

"Did you know that Levi's Folly has a curse on it?" I ask.

My dad is grinning at me when I finish. "I take it you've changed your mind about Roy Andrew Boyd's story?"

"I think the part about the curse is totally true."

"So you believe in this curse, but you don't think the watch was lost for a hundred years?"

"Totally. Curses are real!"

"Sorry, Alex. I don't think a curse caused this murder," Chief Cunningham says.

"Oh, Adam. How do you know?" Traci looks at him. "Not everything can be explained by logic."

"Says the girl who runs a candle shop for a living."

Traci glares at the chief. "Just for that, there'll be no more bubble baths for you, Adam Cunningham."

My dad buries his head in his hand and looks down at the table. "I don't even want to know. Please, this sounds like way too much information."

"Bubble baths?" Mom winks at the chief. "Why, Adam Cunningham, I had no idea you were so domesticated."

Traci giggles and then takes a sip of her wine. "I'm working on him."

"Good for you," Mom says. "Rick, I don't necessarily believe in curses. I'm not sure you can discount them either. Mr. Welles certainly didn't die from the curse, but maybe the person who killed him believed in it enough to think he deserved to die because he owned the watch."

My dad and Chief Cunningham are staring at Mom like she's lost it. I'm sure they don't believe a word about this curse, but I kinda think her logic's pretty awesome. We talk about her idea for a long time, and eventually, we end when my dad calls it a stalemate.

"Marquetta, we're just going to have to agree to disagree on this."

Mom nods her head and then smiles at my dad. "Should we make a small wager?"

My dad blinks. "On what?"

"On whether the curse is linked to the murder. After all, if you're so confident in your skepticism, why not make this interesting?"

"Awesome! I agree!"

Mom puts her hand on mine and squeezes it. "Don't get too cocky, Sweetie. Remember that if I'm wrong, so are you."

Oh. Well, yeah. I guess so. "That's okay. What are we betting?"

Daddy clears his throat, then says, "I don't know that we should be making bets on a police investigation."

"Dinner at the Crooked Mast," Chief Cunningham says. "Markie, if you three are right, I'm buying. If we're right, then it's up to the three of you to treat us."

Traci plants her hands on her hips. She looks defiant. "Adam Cunningham, you are on. It's the girls against the boys." She gives me and Mom a high five.

Wow. This is just like middle school.

53

RICK

RICK HUNG HIS HEAD, ONCE again reminding himself that it was never a good idea to engage in a conversation about an ongoing case with Alex. He knew better. Somehow, everything always seemed to go haywire. Case in point, now he and Adam were wagering dinner at the Crooked Mast on whether a curse had been responsible for Welles's death. Seriously? Without some sort of concrete proof, how was anyone going to prove that one way or the other?

With a sigh, Rick looked at Adam. "You do realize this will also give my daughter bragging rights if it turns out she's correct."

Looking across the table, Adam rubbed the back of his neck. "If it turns out she's correct, she should have them."

Rick suppressed the groan he felt deep inside. That was the last thing he needed, the Chief of Police validating Alex's wild theories. "So how do we go about proving we're right?"

"Oh, no. Proving we're right." Traci looked at Alex, and they exchanged another high-five.

Oh boy, it was starting already. "How about proving this one way or the other?" Rick said.

"You need to start by finding Levi's Folly," Marquetta said.

"Now that's something we can agree on. Adam, why don't we begin by having our own conversation with Mr. Roy Andrew

Boyd? He told Alex he knew about the auction. Let's see what else he knows."

"You better hurry," Alex said. "He was going home to have dinner and pack 'cause he's going on a trip tomorrow. He lives in the little trailer out at the mine."

Rick planted his elbows on the table and sighed. The image of the small travel trailer flashed into his thoughts. A trip to the Silver Gulch Mine was not what he'd had in mind for tonight.

Leaning back in her chair, Marquetta shifted position. "Alex? Are you sure? It looked pretty small based on that photo you showed me."

"That's what he said. He even has Internet," Alex said enthusiastically.

Rick raised his eyebrows and shrugged. "I guess modern life is everywhere. How bad do you want to talk to this guy, buddy?"

Adam tapped his fingers on the table, his gaze narrowing as the seconds ticked by. "Bad enough to make a field trip right now."

"That's not what I was hoping you'd say, but I want to get this over with, too."

Twenty minutes later, Adam pulled his 4x4 to a stop in the dirt parking lot at the Silver Gulch Mine. There was a truck parked directly in front of the trailer. Lights blazed inside.

"Well, looks like he's home. Man, it gets dark out here fast," Rick said.

"No kidding," Adam said as he exited the vehicle.

Standing in the dirt parking lot, Rick felt a small tingle crawling down his spine. Even though Boyd had invested in a power hookup for the trailer, he wasn't wasting money on area lighting. Other than the beacons of illumination peeking out from the trailer's two windows, the area was almost completely dark, saved only by the pale light of the moon and stars.

"Eerie place," Rick muttered. "It's like it's desolated and soothing all at the same time."

"It's pretty quiet out here. That's for sure."

"Maybe we should have called first?"

"This guy doesn't have a landline, and there's no cell service out here. Besides, why ruin the surprise?"

"One thing I learned in New York is that surprises can go both ways."

"I know. That's why I called Kama as a backup while you were getting your jacket. She should be here any minute. Let's go see what Mr. Boyd has to say for himself."

A pair of headlights from a vehicle stopped at the entrance to the parking lot, flooding the tiny road with light. "Right on cue," Rick said.

"I'm having her wait out at the entrance because I don't see a reason for a show of force unless we have a problem."

The speaker squawked with a voice Rick recognized. "Chief? I'm in position, and I confirmed the results of the background check you requested on Boyd. You were right. He's got a prior for felony aggravated assault."

"What?" Rick blurted.

Adam grimaced. "Did he serve time?"

"Four years. Apparently, he was dissatisfied with his legal defense and attempted to strangle his lawyer."

Looking at Rick, Adam sighed. "Sorry to bring you out here on this. You can wait in my vehicle if you want while Kama and I check this out. Come on in, Deputy."

The headlights on the road arced into the parking lot, forcing Rick to shield his eyes against the glare. The move was futile. He still felt blinded. "No way. We're in this together. Amy can be our backup."

Standing in the middle of the dirt parking lot with Adam and Amy, Rick noticed the sudden rise in his anxiety level. His breathing was more shallow. His heart beat faster. Even his hearing felt like it had kicked into overdrive. From their footsteps crunching on the bone-dry dirt to the wind blowing in his ear, everything seemed to put him further on edge.

Finally, Rick asked the question he was sure they were all contemplating. "Do you think Boyd's our killer?"

"I don't know. I just don't want to take any chances."

"Chief, maybe you and I should assess the situation first?"

"Good idea. Rick, I'd feel better if you stayed in my vehicle while Deputy Kama and I made sure this is a safe situation."

"You do think he's the killer."

"We're just being cautious."

"The chief's right, Rick. This is part of our job, not yours."

Rick noticed that they both kept their hands near their holsters. It should give him comfort that they were armed. Not so. It only served to raise his anxiety level further. "Be careful."

Halfway back to Adam's 4x4, Rick spotted a light moving up one of the hills a few hundred yards away. "Adam? I just saw something. I think Boyd has given us the slip."

Adam went to the door of the trailer, knocked, then knocked again. He swore, then said, "What did you see?"

"There was a light going up the hill over there." Rick pointed at a spot near a hilltop to his right.

"Boyd's got to be trying to make his escape into the hills."

"He's got survival training, Chief. He might be crazy enough to give it a try."

"Tough way out. You sure about that, Deputy?"

"The survival training? Absolutely."

"I guess I completely misjudged Roy Andrew Boyd." Rick let out a long breath. He looked around. The silhouette of mountains against the moonlit sky surrounded them. There were only two ways out—over those mountains or out the front entrance. Suddenly, the valley and hills gave up any sense of peacefulness. Instead, the entire scene felt cold and threatening.

"Sorry, Rick. I don't like the idea of leaving you here alone while Kama and I try to follow Boyd. He could easily double back. I think you'll be safer if you come with us."

Rick wanted to laugh. This was exactly the kind of adventure that Alex would love and that he'd cautioned her about. And here he was, smack dab in the middle of an impromptu manhunt in the dark. "Maybe we should get the sheriff involved."

"It'll take them at least an hour to get here. And we don't have anything concrete. And, by the time they arrive, Boyd could be anywhere. I think we need to try. If we don't find him, I'll have the sheriff out in the morning. We'll stick together. It should be safe."

In New York, Rick had gone on a couple of police operations. This was completely different. There was no SWAT support, no army of officers—not even a canine unit. What they had were two local cops and an amateur with some investigative experience. It didn't bode well for the outcome.

"Okay, Adam, let's fan out and find this guy."

"Rick, you're not trained."

"None of us are trained for this kind of thing. Come on. We're wasting time."

Once Rick had a flashlight and a radio, they set off on a trail that led them in the direction of the light Rick had seen. Adam and Deputy Kama were the only two with guns. Rick wasn't sure if that worked to his advantage or not. He just hoped Boyd wouldn't shoot an unarmed man.

As they trudged off into the darkness, their torches tracing patterns across the landscape, he had a sick feeling that this night would not end well for someone.

Adam took the ridge top while Rick and Deputy Kama took the lower sections. They kept Rick in the middle so that they were each no more than a hundred feet apart. Rick took some comfort with the arrangement. At least he had armed support to his right and his left.

The terrain began feeling familiar as Rick made his way across the hill. And as his eyes adjusted, he began to notice more details. At one point, he stopped and turned to look down the valley. To his left, he recognized the rock outcropping as the one where Alex's team had fallen apart. This was difficult territory in the daylight. At night it seemed nothing less than treacherous.

Rick's heart jumped at the crack of a twig to his right. His pulse pounded in his ears as he stared at nothing. After swinging his light over the area, he decided it was just his nerves getting the better of him.

It was the next sound, a metallic clicking, that sent a chill down his spine. "Easy to let your mind run wild out here, isn't it?"

The voice belonged to Roy Andrew Boyd, and he had what looked like an old revolver trained on Rick.

"Turn off the torch. It's time to finish this," Boyd commanded.

Rick flicked the switch to extinguish the flashlight. He just hoped it wasn't the last thing he'd ever do.

54

RICK

"You know you'll never get away. Don't you, Boyd?" The words sounded almost pathetic in the face of the situation.

Brush rustling was the only response Rick got. He cursed his dependence on the flashlight. Slowly, his eyes adjusted, and a shadowy figure took shape. It was a man who moved with confidence through the darkness.

"It was never my intention to hurt anyone. Things with Welles just spiraled out of control. Man was too stubborn for his own good."

"Kind of like Levi Clark?"

In the half-light, Rick focused intently on Boyd's face. Dark eyes. Hard jaw. An amused grin. "I see where that kid of yours gets her spunk."

Rick stiffened and inched closer to Boyd. "Leave my family out of this."

"Don't worry, Mr. Atwood. I have no interest in hurting you or your family. Just saying I like that little girl of yours. She's got spunk. Now, let's get going. With luck, you'll be home in time for breakfast."

"Where are you taking me?" Rick demanded.

"No need to worry about that yet. Now, real slow, hand over that torch."

Rick held out the flashlight. Boyd took it and nodded appreciatively. He jammed it into a small pack that lay at his feet and threw the pack on his back. He held out his hand again. "Now the radio."

A knot of regret formed in Rick's stomach as he did what he'd been told. "What do you need that for?"

"I don't." Boyd tossed the device over his shoulder into the brush. "Let's go. Down the hill. We're taking a little trip. And don't get any ideas about calling out to your friends. That will only end badly for all of you."

Boyd pointed the way to a path that took them behind Deputy Kama and further away from Adam. As the flashlights fell further behind, Rick's thoughts turned from rescue to escape. After several minutes of silence, he said, "Tell me something. How are you any different from those road agents you told the kids about?"

"I didn't confront Welles with the intention of stealing the watch. I wanted to buy it. He wouldn't sell. When I asked him why, he said he just wanted it and laughed."

"I've heard a lot of things about Snappy Welles, and one thing I've learned is that he was not a sympathetic man. From what I've heard, just the act of asking him to sell you that watch was probably enough to make him dig in his heels."

"That's about what I saw."

"You do realize there's only one road out of town. Don't you?"

"We're not driving. We're walking. Don't worry. I know exactly where I'm going."

Walking? Was the man insane? "Where exactly are we going?"

"I told you. No need to worry about that yet."

Rick's gaze darted around the darkness, settling on a rocky outcropping that stuck out of the hillside like bandits waiting for a stagecoach. "This isn't the Wild West, Boyd. Give yourself up."

"Mr. Atwood, I don't have a single thing to gain by doing that. And you have nothing to gain by talking. Now, please, be quiet. And walk." Boyd poked Rick in the back with the barrel of the gun. "Your daughter shouldn't have to grow up without her daddy just because he got too obnoxious."

Rick did an abrupt about-face, saw the gun pointed at his chest, and grumbled, "Fine."

In the distance, he saw what he'd hoped for—Adam's flashlight raking the side of the hill. His voice, distant but clear, called for Rick to identify his position. Rick pushed the temptation to call for help out of his thoughts and focused on finding a way to get his captor to lower his guard.

"Take a right," Boyd said.

Moonlight bathed what appeared to be an offshoot from the main valley. They seemed to be climbing steadily now. Adam's and Amy's voices faded into distant, barely audible background noise. He and Boyd had probably climbed a hundred feet already. If Boyd was taking him over the mountain, they had what? A few thousand feet to go? There had to be a way out of this that did not include calling for help. Rick was sure that even if he called out now, he wouldn't be heard.

"Alex said she met you at the market."

"Inquisitive little girl you got there, Mr. Atwood. I congratulate you on raising her well. I hope you'll do just as good a job on the next one. Now, scramble up those rocks. And don't try anything funny if you want to see your family again."

Rick climbed through the crevice Boyd pointed out, noticing how his breathing became increasingly labored because of the exertion. Boyd, however, appeared to be having no difficulties.

"I'm guessing you hike these hills a lot."

"Nearly every day. If you've got enough supplies, there's a trail that will take you all the way to Sacramento. Take the right fork."

"Have you ever made that trip?" Rick asked as he reached for a handhold at shoulder height.

"Nope. Plant your foot on the small boulder just to your left."

The trek continued, weaving first right, then left. Up one outcropping, down another. After what felt like hours, Boyd commanded Rick to stop. "Welcome to the Silver Gulch Mine, Mr. Atwood. This is the end of the line for you."

The chill Rick had felt at the sound of Boyd's gun being cocked returned. You could hide a body inside one of these old boarded-up mineshafts, and it might never be found. "You don't need to kill me. I'm unarmed and lost. I get the sense you could just disappear, and no one would ever find you."

"You are correct on all points, Mr. Atwood. Don't worry. I'm not going to kill you. What happened with Welles was a mistake. I let my emotions get the better of me."

"And you've got control of them now?" Rick asked skeptically. Actually, Boyd seemed remarkably confident and calm, given that he would face kidnapping and murder charges when this was over. "Look, if you turn yourself in, I'm sure things will go better for you."

Boyd laughed, then pointed at the twisted trunk of an old oak tree. "Stand with your back against that tree." He pulled out a coil of rope from the pack he'd been carrying. "They should find you by morning. These valleys are tricky, but it shouldn't take a search and rescue team more than a few hours to get here. You'll be fine. I'll be long gone by morning. Far enough away that they'll never find me."

Rick looked toward the sky. Stars twinkled against a coal-black backdrop that was occasionally dotted by scattered silvery clouds. The moon hung low on the horizon, its light just enough to add texture to the landscape. It was getting very cold. While a search team might find him in a few hours, what if they didn't? What would Marquetta think during the time he was missing? How would the stress of his disappearance affect the pregnancy? Rick's pulse pounded in his ears. There had to be a way out of this. He just needed time to find it.

"You wanted that pocket watch enough to kill. Why?"

Boyd stopped uncoiling the rope and held Rick's gaze. Even in the moonlight, it wasn't hard to see the hard line of his jaw tighten. "You, of all people, should understand."

"I'm afraid I don't. What are you talking about?"

"That B&B of yours. You wouldn't give it up for anything. Would you?"

Rick shook his head. Of course not. What did that have to do with a pocket watch? "You've lost me."

"If someone tried to take away your B&B, you'd fight them. Am I right?"

"Of course. It's become more than a big old house. It's our home."

"And who did you inherit it from?"

"Captain Jack. My grandfather."

"Right. And you didn't know the man at all. Did you?"

Rick's breath caught in his throat. He had plenty of words he wanted to say, but they all seemed to be trapped by an invisible cloak of fear. How had Boyd known about Captain Jack? Or that Rick had barely known him?

Boyd chuckled. "Yeah. Kind of scary what other people can learn about you on the Internet. Isn't it? I'm not a stalker Mr. Atwood. I'm just a man with an interest in the past. And, since you've come this far with me, you might as well know the truth. Levi Clark was the brother of my third great-grandfather. You might say that watch has sentimental value to me. Just like that big old house does to you."

"The reason we came to Seaside Cove was Alex, not the inheritance. You didn't inherit that watch. It was...." Rick stopped in mid-sentence and stared at Boyd. "It was you. You were Bidder No. 12."

"Very good," Boyd nodded his head. "I've read some of your old news stories and thought they were very insightful. You always did your research. I guess you've finally figured out the connection. Tell you what, Mr. Atwood. We made good time getting up here. You did better than I thought you would. Consequently, I have a few minutes before I have to leave. Who knows? Maybe you'll write my story."

Rick had seen it so many times before. Part of the secret to his success as a reporter had been a knack for finding the source who wanted to talk. Or maybe he'd just made it easy for people to do it. Right now, his every sense told him Boyd was that source. The man who was eager to tell his story. Maybe not to the law, but to someone who could retell it. "Okay, Mr. Boyd. Maybe I will. You said Levi Clark was the brother of your third-great-grandfather?"

"That's right. Levi's Folly has been part of my family history for about a hundred and fifty years. My father, Roy Andrew Boyd II, was born in 1948. By his twenty-first birthday, he was a wealthy businessman with substantial resources. He put some of those resources to work in hopes of finding and buying the watch he'd heard about his entire life. Even after he was able to find it, the owner refused to sell. He never gave up on recovering that watch until the day he died. On his deathbed, I swore to him that I'd find a way to get it back into the family."

A coyote's call in the distance filled the silence. Another returned the call. Were they hunting for food? Would they find it? Boyd, too, seemed to contemplate the sounds.

To break the silence, Rick said, "When the watch went up for auction, you saw your chance."

"Yessir. I figured it would go for about fifty thousand on the high end. I was prepared to spend that to fulfill the promise to my father and restore a piece of my family's history."

"And then along came Snappy Welles. A man who didn't even care about the watch. He only wanted the win."

Boyd dropped the hand holding the rope to his side and gazed down the valley. He muttered a quiet, "Exactly." A moment later, he took a deep breath and turned an intense stare on Rick. "What I didn't realize was how narcissistic the man was. He just kept bidding. Wouldn't stop."

"Did you know then that you were going to kill him to get the watch back?"

"No. I just assumed I'd lost."

"You must have been angry with him."

"Of course I was."

Something didn't make sense. It seemed unlikely that Boyd would have resigned himself to losing so easily. What if he had? Then why was Welles dead? "I don't think you'd just give up like that."

A wry smile formed on Boyd's lips. "I did, at first. Then I found another way. Problem was that I made a deal with a man I should never have trusted."

The coyote yips continued, and the meaning of Boyd's claim sunk in. "You had a deal with Barnaby Pauley?" Rick asked.

Boyd's gaze turned cold as steel. He gritted his teeth, then muttered, "How stupid could I be? You weren't here because of him. Were you?"

"No. We came out here to talk to you about the curse on the watch. You told Alex you were leaving tomorrow, so the Chief and I wanted to talk to you before you left."

For the next few seconds, Boyd stared off into space. When he looked at Rick, he sighed. "Looks like what we have here is a night of misunderstandings. It's done now. The truth is that Mr. Pauley had a plan. According to him, it was foolproof. We were going to pool our resources. We agreed to put in $50,000 each. He said he had a way of getting some notebook with all the man's secrets. Once he had that, he could force Welles to deal with us. I was going to get Levi's Folly, and he'd be able to save his business."

"How did he expect to pull that off? Welles would never have given up that notebook willingly."

"That's where the dinner came in. Pauley wanted it to turn into a free-for-all. He figured after they got thrown out, the two of us could corner Welles and relieve him of the notebook."

"You can't be serious. That's extortion."

"Pauley convinced me it was the only way. The only thing Welles would understand. There was information in that notebook that could ruin Welles. He would have been forced to sell me the watch and leave Pauley's business alone, but the whole plan fell apart at the last minute."

Rick had a mental image of Guy Silvan describing how he'd followed Welles and confronted him. He could only imagine how livid Welles must have been at the thought of losing his leverage. "Because Guy Silvan stole the notebook first."

"That's right. I should've walked away right then and there. Should have realized I was dealing with vermin. But I didn't."

55

RICK

THE COYOTE YIPS IN THE distance came faster, building in urgency and intensity until they reached a crescendo.

"The hunt," Roy Andrew Boyd mused. "It's nature's way. There's no shame in killing, Mr. Atwood. Not when it's for the right reasons."

Is that how Boyd justified the murder? He'd done it for the right reasons? "How did you know where to meet up with Pauley?"

"Got your curiosity up, huh? Fair enough. I was there."

"Where? At the place where you killed Welles?"

"No. In the bar."

A final, mournful howl pierced the night.

Boyd chuckled. "That's right. You had no idea, did you? Pauley told me they were going there for dinner. I heard the whole dinner argument. All I had to do was wait for them to leave. Pauley didn't count on getting into that argument with his wife, though. He also didn't count on that other one following Welles. So I just followed him. Looked like something was going to happen, so I hung back."

"You're talking about Guy Silvan? You followed him while he went after Welles?"

"That's right. I saw the whole thing. Right down to the fight. Pretty pathetic, actually. In my experience, that's how fights are when you don't know what you're doing. Once I saw Silvan take off with the notebook, I figured Pauley might start having second thoughts."

"If that's the case, why didn't you deal with Welles right then? Why wait?"

"There was some guy there. You probably know him—a carryover from a bad 60s surfing movie."

Dennis. But Rick wasn't about to give Boyd a name. "So you waited until Pauley showed up? Did you see him back into Welles?"

"Yep. Once he heard the notebook was gone, he jumped in his car and took off. Found him out here when I got home. He wanted to cancel our deal."

The missing time on Pauley's drive now made sense. He'd come here and had to wait for Boyd to show up. "What did you tell him?"

Boyd snorted, then shook his head. "Anything I hate, it's someone you can't trust. I told him that. Also told him Welles was dead. All he had to do was keep his mouth shut, and he'd get everything he wanted."

"And if he didn't?"

"I made it clear he didn't have a choice. Neither did I after Pauley hit Welles with his car and I tried to help the man. When I approached him, he started going on about having Pauley and me arrested for conspiracy to commit murder."

"You thought you'd go back to prison if Welles made trouble for you."

"I'm a man with a record, Mr. Atwood. At that point, I had nothing to lose. In my opinion, the world's a better place without vermin like Snappy Welles in it. Well, I need to be moving on. I hope you'll write that story. Do some research on my family. It's quite interesting."

"I'm not sure I can do that. Not unless you turn yourself in."

Boyd tensed all over. Standing ramrod straight, his breaths came quicker. Darkness clouded his face. "You lied to me? You're not even interested in my family's story?"

The change put Rick on alert. *There's no shame in killing.* Did that mean there was no reason Boyd couldn't commit one last murder? Or that he should get away with the ones he'd committed? Rick looked down at the pack at Boyd's feet. It wasn't substantial, and there was no sleeping bag, no tent, no food or water. How could the man survive a journey over a mountain range that climbed as high as five-thousand feet? He wasn't dressed for the elements or a climb. Which meant he either didn't intend on surviving. Or didn't intend on making the trip.

What were Boyd's real intentions? He seemed overly taken with Alex, a fact that scared Rick more than death. He had to take this man down. With one glance down at the pack, he reached out and shoved. Boyd's boot caught. He fell back and landed with a heavy thud. Rick turned and scrambled back down the way they'd come, bracing himself against the rough surface of a boulder the size of a house.

Behind him, he heard Boyd groaning, then cursing. "You shouldn't have done that, Atwood. I was going to let you live! I'm coming for you now."

The trail was nothing more than a narrow gap between two giant rocks. Thankfully, Rick's memory of their path to get here was still vivid. When Rick reached what looked like a small mountain of rock that had been sheared in half, he turned right rather than taking a left to return from where they'd come. Behind him, boots crunched on loose rocks and gravel. The footsteps sounded deliberate and filled with purpose.

Then, the sound stopped, and Boyd yelled, "You'll get lost out here, Atwood. This place is a rabbit's warren with dead ends and trails that lead to nowhere."

Rick moved with as much stealth as he could muster to pick his way along an ever-narrowing fissure between two rock walls. He stopped when another of those walls loomed directly in front of him. Just as Boyd had predicted, he'd found a dead end. A sliver of sky shone overhead, twinkling stars against a black sky. The granite walls loomed skyward on both sides and in front of him. There was no way out. And if Boyd followed along this path, Rick didn't want to think about the consequences. The only option was to throw Boyd off his trail. Rick pressed his back into another small crevice on one of the walls and waited.

Listening to the night's silence, Rick began to count his breaths. He braced himself against a chill as the cold granite seemed to suck the warmth from his body. At the count of forty-two, he again heard Boyd's voice. This time, it was further away.

"You can't get away, Atwood. The longer this goes on, the worse it's going to be for you."

Rick crossed his fingers and pushed away from the granite, glad to exchange a cold rock wall for the night air. He took a deep breath and whispered to himself, "Okay, Rick. Use your wits. You can get out of this."

What he needed to do was navigate back to the parking lot without the use of the GPS on his phone. In this darkness, the light of a cell phone's screen would be like a beacon for Boyd to see. No, he had to go old school. He retraced his steps to the main trail and looked up to search the sky for the Big Dipper. He found it and ran an imaginary line through the outer edge of the bowl. Even though the North Star was hidden by another towering wall, the star's absence gave him a general idea of which way he didn't want to go. It was impossible to recall every turn they'd made. There had been far too many. And even if he could recall the turns, so many of these rock formations looked alike.

Standing still, Rick closed his eyes and took a deep breath. He listened. Tried to slow his breathing, then listened again. He could almost hear the breeze drifting in off the coast. Looking up, he saw wisps of fog creep across the sky. "Not tonight," he whispered. "I need to be able to see the stars."

Further down in the valley, the beam from a flashlight winked, then was gone. That was probably Adam or Amy. He had a sudden image of Boyd stalking them to stage an ambush. He took a step, wincing at the sound it made. If only he could be perfectly silent. Then again, Boyd was at the same disadvantage. As long as he was moving, he would also be making noise. Rick took a step in the direction of the flashlight beacon and what he felt sure was trouble.

He counted steps as he made his way back. Every hundred steps or so, he recalibrated by getting his bearings from the stars and listening. At one point, he thought he heard Boyd calling to him. This time, telling him that he'd had a change of heart and would let him live. Somehow, the words sounded hollow. If Rick were on his old job and writing up the story, he'd add a few tidbits about Roy Andrew Boyd. One of those would be that the man was someone who did not take kindly to being bested. Much like the man he'd killed.

Right. Left. Each turn felt like an opportunity to become lost and wander off into the wilderness. Rick pushed the urge to panic down each time it came. When he discovered an offshoot that went up toward the top of another large boulder, he took it. His fingers felt raw by the time he reached the top, but his perch gave him an overview of the valley. He could now make out two flashlight beams in the distance.

From up here, he could also feel and hear the breeze. He relished the cool air after what felt like a near-vertical climb. Still no sign of Boyd. The man was smart; Rick had to give him that. Rick clenched his jaw. Adam and Amy were probably walking into a trap, thinking they were looking for a friend. Instead, they'd probably never know what hit them.

To Rick's right, another narrow trail led back down to the main path. By taking that, he'd be able to make up some of the time he'd lost coming up here. Halfway down, Rick's foot slipped, and a tiny avalanche of rocks cascaded down the trail. Steadying himself against the nearest boulder, Rick waited for his pulse to settle while he also listened for Boyd. That little rock shower had felt like the equivalent of a small thunderclap. He waited to a count of fifty. When there were no nearby sounds, he decided that if Boyd had heard the noise, he wasn't coming back this way. At least, not yet.

Rick stepped up his pace. His friends were in trouble. He couldn't dawdle. Soon, he could make out voices. There was Adam's, calling Rick's name. Then Amy Kama's. Too bad he couldn't return their calls. If he did, it would surely alert Boyd to his location. For all Rick knew, Boyd was already lying in wait for his next victim.

Rick scanned the craggy landscape. If Boyd was going to stage an ambush, he'd want the high ground. A place with an escape route if he needed it. He'd also need to be close enough to use his handgun. Or to simply create his own avalanche and let nature do the work.

And there it was. The perfect overlook. High above the trail. Plenty of cover from return fire. Rick watched the spot intently for a few seconds, trying to make out every detail. It was possible that there was someone crouching in the rocks on top. If only he could be sure. It was an all-or-nothing gamble.

Stepping with as much stealth as possible, Rick threaded his way along the narrow trails to the outcropping. There had to be a half dozen ways up. If Boyd was waiting there, he'd probably taken the main path. That route would give the man three easy targets. There had to be a better way. Maybe a trail with some cover that was less direct? And then he found it. A windy path he hoped would give him the advantage of surprise. Rick made his decision and stepped off the main trail.

56

RICK

RICK'S LUNGS SCREAMED FOR AIR as he studied a small opening between two large boulders blocking his path. This was the last obstacle before he'd have to confront Boyd. He had little energy left. Unwilling to give away his position, he fought the urge to breathe deeply and instead took slow, measured breaths, mimicking what he'd seen Marquetta do during her yoga sessions.

After letting his pulse settle, he peered through the opening. The top of the overlook was right on the other side of this crevice. It was where he felt sure he'd find Boyd. He had to get to him before he could ambush Adam and Amy.

The trail up here had gotten progressively more treacherous. Each foot of elevation had been a little tougher, each obstacle a little harder to overcome. Standing here just feet from the top, he couldn't stop. His back and legs ached. This was it, the final push. Looking down, he realized how much easier it would be to take this trail in the daylight. With only the moon's light to navigate, shadows concealed every drop-off and obstacle. And in this final section, he'd had to straddle the stone walls on either side of the trail to avoid setting off another of those rock avalanches.

Rick turned back to the sliver of an opening. Was his plan solid? Rick had no idea. What he did know was that success depended not only on him, but also on Adam and Amy. Before slipping between the two massive boulders, he pulled his phone from his back pocket, turned on the flashlight, and laid it on a waist-high boulder. The flashlight shined like a beacon aimed at the sky. It reminded him of the old-time searchlights he'd seen in New York. There was no way anyone could miss it. That included Roy Andrew Boyd.

Taking a final, deep breath, Rick squeezed through the narrow opening. As he'd expected, Boyd stood before him, his handgun again leveled at Rick's chest.

"You surprise me, Mr. Atwood. I didn't expect you to find your way back." Boyd's voice was cool and determined. His eyes glinted in the moonlight, then flicked toward Rick's makeshift beacon. "Glad I didn't take that thing away from you. You've helped me create a better trap than I could have hoped for."

Rick shot an involuntary glance over his shoulder at the beacon. Why hadn't he foreseen that possibility? He raised his hands in surrender and stepped forward. "You can't win, Boyd. You have to know that."

"I do." The man motioned with the gun for Rick to move to his right.

Rick complied, being sure to stay clear of the cliff just a few feet away. Despite his heart hammering in his chest, Rick kept his voice level. "If you shoot me, they'll know you've got a gun and that this is an ambush. You'll also add another murder charge to your legacy. Is that really what you want?"

"None of this is what I wanted, Mr. Atwood. All I wanted was to get back what belonged to my family."

"And all I want is to get back to my wife and daughter. As far as I'm concerned, you can walk off into the wilderness and disappear. I think you know the law won't let you do that. They will find you no matter what happens here."

Boyd's lips twisted into a grim smile. The intensity Rick had seen moments ago faded into resignation. "I can't go back to prison."

"Then make your case. Get yourself an attorney and fight this legally. The days of road agents escaping the law are long gone, Mr. Boyd."

"I'm a realist, Mr. Atwood. I know that if I go to court, I'll lose. Out here, though? Out here, I have a fighting chance."

No more so than the prey they'd heard those coyotes hunting down, thought Rick. Boyd would surely disagree, so why go there? "Is your alternative to kill me? And the two officers who are down there?"

"Maybe."

"I could yell. Warn them."

"And I could shoot you right now."

"But you haven't. Why?"

Boyd licked his lips. His shoulders, normally held back and erect, slumped ever so slightly. "I told you. I never intended to kill Welles. Even though he was nothing more than vermin."

"To be completely accurate, you're not the one who killed him. He died of a heart attack. By attempting to strangle him, however, you triggered it."

"Really?"

Though Boyd's heavy load seemed to lighten, Rick knew that whether the charges were murder or manslaughter, Boyd was destined to do time. Right now, reminding him of that reality didn't seem like a very good negotiating tactic. "That's the truth. And with a good attorney? Who knows?"

Boyd chuckled. "Please, don't patronize me, Mr. Atwood. I know my situation."

"Then put down the gun."

"I can't."

"You mean, won't. What do you want? One of those cops to shoot you?"

"Considered it."

"I have a wife and daughter at home and a new baby on the way. I don't think you want my wife to become a widow and my kids to grow up without a dad. Do you?"

"No, sir, I don't. The problem, as I see it, is that the outcome here isn't entirely up to me."

It was impossible to calculate how long it had been since Rick had set up his signal to Adam. Two minutes? It felt like hours. "You don't have any kids, do you?"

"So now we're going to chat like a pair of old pals, are we? If you think this is the part where you talk me down off the ledge and walk away a hero, you're in for a letdown. Not happening, Mr. Atwood. Not happening. I guess I'm still hoping you'll write my story. That's why you're still alive. You know, I never felt like I'd found home until I got here." He blew out a quick breath. "For a time, I even reconciled myself to never getting back Levi's Folly. Nearly killed me to break that promise to my father."

It was the second time Boyd had mentioned the man. "You said he was Roy Andrew Boyd II?"

"That's right."

Could he keep Boyd talking until Adam showed up? "And you said you made a promise just before he died that you'd get the watch back?"

Boyd snickered. "You're not very good at stalling. Are you, Mr. Atwood?"

"I'm not used to staring down the barrel of a gun."

"That's a fair point. As much as I've enjoyed your company, I should just end this."

Difficult as it was to make out all of Boyd's features in the darkness, the meaning in the man's tone was crystal clear. Was this how he would die? He hadn't ensured Alex's safety. Or Adam's. Or Amy's.

Boyd bent down, picked up a small rock, and palmed it. He tossed it up and down as if it were a baseball. "Are you a betting man, Mr. Atwood?"

"You mean, do I like to gamble? Not particularly."

"And yet you took chances quite a few times to get your story when you were a reporter. So let's see what happens with this." He tossed the rock into the air again. "If I hit a rock when I throw this, I answer your question. If it just lands in the brush, you'll never know. How's that sound?"

"I'd rather you just answer. Who knows, I may change my mind about that story."

"You shouldn't have said that. Now I know you won't do it. What else are we going to do while we wait for the cavalry?"

With that, Boyd threw the rock off into the darkness. A few seconds later, they heard a distant crack.

"Guess it's your lucky night, Mr. Atwood." Boyd stroked his chin as he eyed Rick. "Despite all my father's resources and the years he spent tracking down Levi's Folly, he was never able to convince the owner to sell. The only reason I got a crack at it is that the owner died, and his son inherited it. That was more than twenty years ago."

"Let me guess," Rick said. "The son died, and his family wanted the money."

"I suspect you considered doing the same thing when you inherited the B&B."

The back of Rick's neck prickled with suspicion. Boyd was right. The man certainly had done his homework. "It was too far in debt. My inheritance would have bankrupted me. So you consider Levi's Folly to be your family legacy?"

"I always figured that watch would be my undoing. At least I'm ready to fulfill my promise. Now, it's time for the watch to return to where it belongs. Levi Clark's grave."

This time, Rick couldn't stop the laugh from escaping. "You have got to be kidding me. Do you intend to hike all the way there?"

"Yessir. After I retrieve it."

"You'll never make it over the mountains."

"I may never make it past those two cops. If it hadn't been for Welles rubbing my nose in his victory, I wouldn't be here."

And there it was. The blame game. "I've heard that excuse so many times. It's not my fault I killed someone. It was the victim's fault."

"It's true!" Boyd snapped.

"I probably shouldn't say this, but have you considered how much like Snappy Welles you are?"

"I'm nothing like him!"

"You both wanted to win at all costs. He was willing to use his money as a weapon to destroy people. You used your fists. Is there really that much difference?"

For the longest moment, Boyd stared at Rick, his eyes glistening in the moonlight. He started at the sound of Adam calling his name.

"Roy Andrew Boyd! I've radioed for the sheriff. There's a helicopter and backup on the way. Give yourself up."

"Game's over, Mr. Boyd," Rick said. "You need to make a decision. You must realize that since Adam notified the sheriff, the entire state will be looking for you soon. You'll be just like Gentleman George. You won't be able to go anywhere, and sooner or later, you'll be caught. Besides, Welles died of a heart attack. Remember?"

Boyd lowered the weapon. "Are you saying you think they won't charge me with murder?"

Rick wanted to laugh. How was he supposed to know? On the other hand, it might be the only way to bring Boyd in safely. Wasn't it better to give him hope, even if it was temporary, than to have him try and go out in a blaze of glory? "If it were up to me, I'd consider the circumstances."

"From what I know of your past, Mr. Atwood, you're an honest man. If you tell me I've got hope, I'll trust you." He held out the gun with the barrel facing the ground.

Rick stared at the gun for a moment, then called out to Adam to let him know Boyd had surrendered. "Shall we go down to meet them?" Rick asked as he reached for the gun.

Boyd nodded, then charged Rick and shoved him. Rick staggered toward the cliff. He caught his balance just feet before the edge. He bent over, sucking in deep breaths as Boyd squeezed through the opening Rick had used earlier. Within seconds, the sounds of another rock avalanche, followed by screams of pain, pierced the night.

Cautiously, Rick squeezed between the boulders and stood on the edge of the drop-off. He retrieved his phone, which was still shining toward the sky, and aimed it down the trail. At the bottom, Boyd lay with his foot wedged into a crevice and twisted at an unnatural angle.

"I'll get help," Rick said, then spun around at the sound of Adam's voice.

"No need. Sorry it took me so long to get up here. When we saw your signal, we figured it was an ambush. These trails are treacherous in the dark if you're not familiar with them."

Rick grinned as he cast a sideways glance at his friend. "And when did you become such an expert?"

Adam shrugged. "When I was a kid, my friends and I must have scoured every inch of this area looking for the lost mine. We never did find it, but we sure had a lot of fun."

"Get me out of here!" Boyd yelled, then groaned. "My leg's broken."

"I'm sorry, Mr. Boyd. We can't move you until the sheriff arrives. There's no way we can get you down safely without support." Adam quirked his cheek and looked at Rick. "It's going to be a late night. I'll get the sheriff to call Marquetta and tell her you're okay. I'll leave you and Kama with him. I've got a blanket in the back of my vehicle. The least we can do is make him comfortable before they take him away."

57
ALEX

Hey Journal,

I have all kinds of news! We're in the final countdown for Operation Baby Brother. Mom says she's gonna pop any day now. It's super awesome that I'm gonna have a baby brother in just a couple days. I wish he'd hurry up and get here! Mom does, too, but she says he'll show up when he's ready.

Liz and Brid came back today. They're staying for a few days and then going on a girl's road trip for a month. I guess now that Liz has all of Mr. Welles's money, she's decided they should have some fun. Liz has filed for divorce, and Brid left her boyfriend. There's even bigger news, though! It's about Mr. Boyd.

We heard a few days ago from Chief Cunningham that Mr. Boyd escaped when he was at the courthouse. The deputy took him to the restroom. Since Mr. Boyd was in a cast, the deputy wasn't worried and turned his back on him. Mr. Boyd whacked him over the head with his cane and walked out of the courthouse. Can you believe he actually got away?

Even better than that, I got an email from him yesterday! He wants me to write up his story! He said my dad refused, so he's asking me! That's like awesome!

I wrote him back and asked what he was gonna do. He said he had a lot of time to think while he was waiting for the sheriff's helicopter after his fall and while he was in jail. He said that once his leg heals up, he's gonna come back here and get Levi's Folly from where he hid it. He also asked me if I could get the photo of his great-great-great-grandfather that the cops found in his trailer.

When I asked my dad about the photo, he said Chief Cunningham had sent it to San Ladron along with a bunch of other evidence. They never did find the pocketwatch. My dad says Mr. Boyd never told him where he hid it. I wish he'd have hidden the photo, too, 'cause I don't think he's ever gonna see it again. That's kind of a bummer since it is a family photo. Anyway, he's gonna disappear. He says that before he goes, he wants people to know the real story behind Levi's Folly. Mr. Boyd said my dad felt like he had a conflict of interest, so he couldn't write about it. I guess that's true since he was working with the cops and all. Mr. Boyd wants me to do it because I think outside the box. He says that makes me the perfect person to do this. I'm super stoked that he trusts me.

I totally want to help him 'cause Mr. Boyd's kinda cool. He said he'd send me a whole bunch of stuff about his family. I told Mom and Dad about the email. When I did, my dad said the sheriff's got a super big manhunt going on. He thinks I should turn over whatever Mr. Boyd sends me, but I told him I need to protect my source. He almost had a total meltdown. That's okay. He'll get over it. He always does. Just to be safe, I've password-protected everything.

This is gonna be epic! You know what, Journal? I think Mr. Boyd is smart enough to fool them all and disappear forever. He's like a real-life Wild West bandit! I'm totally ready to write his story!

Xoxo
Alex

THANK YOU FOR READING

It's been my pleasure to bring you *Dead Men Need No Reservations*. I hope you enjoyed reading as much as I enjoyed writing the book.

You've probably heard it a thousand times, but marketing a book is tough. So if you enjoyed *Dead Men Need No Reservations*, I'd be very grateful if you would help others find it, too. There are many ways to do this: write a short review, talk about it on social media, or simply go 'old school' and tell a friend about it. Whatever you do, have fun!

To learn more about me and my writing, visit me on the web at terryambrose.com or visit my Amazon author page at www.amazon.com/Terry-Ambrose/e/B008NR7QZ4.

www.ingramcontent.com/pod-product-compliance
Lightning Source LLC
Chambersburg PA
CBHW051335250626
47155CB00007B/2612